Tai reached for the handle of her reserve parachute and pulled it. Nothing.

Three malfunctions in a row. Tai had run through all the emergency procedures correctly and she was still plummeting toward Earth at almost terminal velocity, the only thing slowing her down was her own body spread as wide as she could make it. She was going to die. At this speed, hitting the water would be like hitting concrete.

She faintly heard Vaughn's voice in her earpiece. "What are you doing? Over."

"Reserve malfunction!" she screamed.

Reserves weren't supposed to malfunction, Vaughn thought as he glanced down. She was at least four hundred feet below him and the gap was growing wider every second. There was only one option. It was stupid, it was insane, but Vaughn didn't hesitate.

He reached up, grabbed the metal covers over his cut-aways, flipped them open, put his thumbs in the loops, and pulled. The pins popped and his main parachute separated from his harness.

He was now in free fall.

ROBERT DOHERTY

SECTION 8

HarperTorch
An Imprint of HarperCollins*Publishers*

HARPERTORCH
An Imprint of HarperCollins*Publishers*
10 East 53rd Street
New York, New York 10022-5299

Copyright © 2005 by Robert Mayer
ISBN-13: 978-0-06-073583-8
ISBN-10: 0-06-073583-X

First HarperTorch paperback printing: October 2005

HarperCollins®, HarperTorch™, and ❦ ™ are trademarks of HarperCollins Publishers Inc.

Printed in the United States of America

Visit HarperTorch on the World Wide Web at www.harpercollins.com

10 9 8 7 6 5 4 3 2 1

SECTION 8

PROLOGUE

The world's greatest cathedral was in its 161st year of construction and still not complete, according to the original architect's grand vision. This morning, something that was not part of the architect's plan marred the promenade in front of the church: a man tied to a wooden stake surrounded by bushels of reeds soaked with flammable liquid. Before him, a crowd had gathered.

The cathedral was not the first place of worship to be built on the island in the Seine River. To make room for the massive cathedral, the ancient church of St. Etienne had been torn down in 1163, after standing there since 528 AD. Before that, there had been a Christian basilica on the spot, preceded by a Roman temple to Jupiter, when that empire from the south had held sway over the land. And before the Romans, there had been older forms of worship conducted on the spit of land in the middle of the river. It was consecrated ground, and today it was going to be blessed with blood and human ash.

Construction on Notre Dame had begun in 1163, based on the vision of Maurice De Sully, Bishop of Paris. He had dedicated it to the Virgin Mary, and instructed the architects to design the exterior to impress and the interior to retell stories of the Bible for his largely illiterate constituency via portals, paintings, and stained glass. De Sully was a wise man and knew how people's minds—and hearts—worked. Impress them, and then indoctrinate them.

The cathedral's choir was completed in 1182, after only nineteen years; though that was the life span of many at the time. The nave was completed twenty-six years later, and the imposing front towers that would dominate the skyline of Paris for centuries were finished between 1225 and 1250. Still, there was work to be done to complete the grand vision of the long-dead bishop and original architects. It was a project larger than the lives of any who worked on it, in an age when such things were considered by some to be the best way to worship and pay homage to their god.

Now, inside the church, on a platform near the top of one of the two tall towers that flanked the entrance, three men stood in the shadows, the distance each one kept from the others indicating mutual dislike and distrust. From their commanding position they looked out into the early morning gray light, eyes fixed on the man tied to the stake. The procession leading the condemned to his place of death had occurred just before dawn, and now all was ready for the final act.

The man in the center nodded. "It is time."

The finely garbed figure to his left, his royal status indicated by the ring with an embedded crest on his finger and the small crown on his head, seemed reluctant for a moment, then stepped up to the opening in the stone wall. He glanced once to his right, past the man who had just spoken, to the third figure, who also had an ornate ring, which indicated power of another sort, in his case, that of the Roman Catholic Church. The Pope barely twitched his head, indicating approval, albeit not an enthusiastic one. Even though they were in a church, it was obvious from the way the three interacted that the Pope was not the one with the ultimate power here.

King Philip called out in a voice used to giving commands: "Serve the sentence."

The voice of the executioner echoed against the stone walls of the cathedral in reply, carrying over the watching crowd. "For crimes against the state and the Church, the accused, Jacques De Molay, is sentenced, this day, the eighteenth of March, in the year our Lord 1314, to death by flame."

The succinct announcement was punctuated by the executioner putting his torch to the bundles of reeds arrayed around the condemned man. De Molay's once fine robe was now tattered and blood-spattered from both his arrest and a night of torture. He was looking toward the cathedral at the three who watched him from the shadows, in the same place he had stood with them, watching others suffer the same fate. He appeared not to notice the fire that was igniting around him.

The bundles were arranged at such a distance from the accused that he would not die quickly. Instead, heat and smoke would cause great suffering for a consider-

able period of time before overcoming him. The executioner knew his craft well and had assumed that
since the king himself was here to see the deed, he
would give his master a good show. There was an art
to everything. And because there had been little notice
of this event, and the condemned apparently did not
generate great sympathy from those who had gathered,
there were none who had brought their own reeds
among the crowd. Sometimes, a prisoner with friends
among the crowd would get a quick departure when
they would rush the stake and throw their own com-
bustibles against his or her body. It was the twisted
mercy of a quick death.

De Molay lifted his chin and drew in a deep breath,
one that was just beginning to be affected by the
smoke. He was a warrior, a man who had issued orders
to men in combat, sending them to their deaths. He
was also the Grand Master of the Knights Templar,
which until this morning had been the most powerful
and richest organization in Europe.

"Upon your heads be it," De Molay cried out in a
deep voice. "Philip, puppet of the Church and pretend
king. And Clement the great pretender from Rome.
You will join me and be judged before the Court of
God within the year. With my dying breaths I place this
curse upon your heads."

In the tower, the two men he had just named glanced
at each other once more. King Philip IV and Pope
Clement V had orchestrated De Molay's arrest along
with that of all the Knights Templar across France the
previous day. The two believed in God, but they also
lived in an age of superstition, and De Molay's curse
shook them. There was power in De Molay's words,
and the circumstances, which made them even more

ominous. The words of the dying were believed to have power.

De Molay coughed from the smoke beginning to swirl about his head, then shouted out once more. "And the one who pulls your strings. Who was also my puppet master. I name you—"

But before he could finish, a figure stepped out from the encircling crowd and heaved a small clay pot full of liquid. The Grand Master screamed as the flammable liquid splattered on his skin, caught the fire, and immediately immolated him, whatever he'd been about to reveal lost in his agonized screams.

De Molay's body arched and then contracted, almost ripping free of the ropes that bound him, as every muscle in his body spasmed, trying to avoid the pain as flame seared through his skin. But the external flame is not what killed him. It was the seering fire that poured into his mouth, down his throat, and into his lungs as he desperately tried to breathe. So great was De Molay's will, though, that he managed to live long enough to break free of his now burning ropes and stagger forward a few steps through the fire. He raised a hand toward Notre Dame, the fingers blackened and twisted, his mouth now moving wordlessly, his dead lungs unable to function anymore. Then he collapsed, body tightening into the fetal position, as those taken by the flame always did, before he finally died.

Inside the stone tower, Philip and Clement turned to the third man. He wore no rings or crown. He was dressed simply in a long black robe with a brooch on the upper right chest. It consisted of an iron cross with a silver circle laid upon it.

"You betrayed De Molay," Philip said. "He just said he worked for you. This was never brought up."

"I am the High Counsel," the man said. "I answer to no one and explain myself to no one."

"How do we know you will not betray us?" Philip demanded.

The High Counsel was staring at De Molay's burning body. "You do not. The Knights Templar needed to be cut down like a dangerous weed. You now have their money to fill your treasury. That was the agreement. This is the best course of action for the three of us and the organizations we represent."

"They fought for the Church," Clement said. "They were steadfast in their faith."

"They were steadfast in the profits they made from usury," the High Counsel replied. "Which, if my teaching serves me right, is against Church canon. They fought for the Church when it fit their needs or I told them to." He shifted his gaze to the Pope. "You had no choice, and have no choice. You will do as I order."

With that, the High Counsel turned and made for the stairs, leaving king and Pope behind him.

As soon as he was out of sight, Clement V made the sign of the cross and evoked his own curse: *"May God take His own vengeance on you and those you rule."*

Philip nodded his assent, but still fearful that the man might overhear them, he did not say anything.

The High Counsel slowly descended and was met halfway down the seventy-meter high tower by the man who had thrown the flammable liquid onto De Molay and silenced him. Like the High Counsel, he used no name other than his title: the Curator.

"The reports from across the continent are coming in," the Curator informed the High Counsel, and fell into step beside his superior, who retraced his route down the tower. "The knights are finished. A few managed to escape, but most are in custody. Their base of power is gone."

The High Counsel nodded but made no comment. They exited the tower and made their way through the silent cathedral, the early-morning sun casting long shadows through the stained-glass windows, which depicted various biblical scenes. Neither man paused to appreciate the displays. They exited at the rear, where a coach, surrounded by a dozen of the Curator's men armed with swords and crossbows, awaited them. The two entered the coach, the guards mounted their horses, and the entourage moved out.

Inside the coach, they sat across from each other. The curtains were drawn and the interior dark. Despite the lack of light and dialogue, the High Counsel could sense the mood of his chief of security.

"You are upset about disbanding the Templars?"

The Curator had worked for the High Counsel all his life. He'd been at the side of the High Counsel as his bodyguard and responsible for overall security of the organization for over twenty years. He knew better than to deny his true feelings.

"Yes."

"They were becoming too powerful, and coming out of the shadows much too far," the High Counsel said. "Worse, once De Molay became aware of our existence and that we were using his knights for our own means via the Church, the Templars became dangerous. Our best security is ignorance of our existence and surrounding ourselves with many rings of protection and secrecy."

"I understand," the Curator said. "But who will we use for our force in the world now? For our outer ring of protection? We need that buffer of ignorant protection to keep our secrecy."

"We will always be able to find and manipulate shadow warriors to unknowingly protect us. There are many ways to manipulate men's hearts and minds to do what we bid without them knowing that we bid it."

"And the Pope and king?"

"Ah, the real cause for your concern," the High Counsel said. "Let us make De Molay's dying curse come true. Make sure both are dead within the year."

The Curator nodded in agreement. "For the greater good."

"For the greater good," the High Counsel echoed.

CHAPTER 1

Jungle surrounded the Philippine army firebase, a dark wall of menacing sounds and shadows in the grayness of evening. The sounds of men preparing for battle—the clank of metal on metal, the grunts of rucksacks being lifted, the murmur of quiet talk between comrades—was muted compared to the noise of the jungle.

"Too close."

Major Jim Vaughn turned to the man at his side, his top noncommissioned officer and his brother-in-law, Sergeant Major Frank Jenkins. "What?"

Jenkins nodded at the wall of trees. "Field of fire is too short. You could get RPGs right there and blast the crap out of this place."

Vaughn had noted the same thing as soon as they landed. "Let's be glad this is our last time here."

"Damn civilians," Jenkins muttered.

" 'Ours is not to question why—' " Vaughn began.

" 'Ours is but to do and die,' " Jenkins finished. "Not the most cheery saying in the world, Jim."

Vaughn shrugged. "Okay. But this beats taking tolls on the Jersey Turnpike."

"Not by much," Jenkins said. "And maybe I'll be one of those toll takers next month. I'm so short—"

Vaughn held up a hand while he laughed. "Not another 'I'm so short' joke, Frank. Please. My sister knows how short you are."

Jenkins frowned. He reached into one of his pockets and retrieved a worn photograph of a young woman, tenderly placed it to his lips and gave it a light kiss. "You ain't so young anymore, babe, but you still got it."

He said the words to himself, but Vaughn could hear. He had seen his brother-in-law enact this ritual five times before with his older sister's photo, and it always made him uneasy. Jenkins slid the picture back into his pocket, technically a violation of the rules requiring they be "sterile" for this mission, carrying nothing that indicated in any way who they were, but Vaughn didn't say anything.

Jenkins turned to Vaughn. "Let's get ready."

Both reached down and lifted the MP-5 submachine guns lying on top of a mound of gear. Made by Heckler & Koch of Germany, they were the standard now for most Special Operations forces. These were specially modified with integrated laser sights, and had telescoping stocks allowing the entire weapon to be collapsed to a very short and efficient length or extended for more accurate firing. The worn sheen of the metal indicated they had been handled quite a bit.

Like warriors throughout the ages, the two men geared up for battle. The process was the same—all that had changed was the actual gear. In some ways, with the advent of advanced body armor technology, soldiers were harkening back to the days of knights, when protection was almost as important as weapons. It was a constant race between offense and defense, an axiom of military technology.

Vaughn was tall, just over six feet, and slender, wiry. The uniform draped over his body consisted of plain green jungle fatigues without any markings or insignia. Over the shirt, he slid on a sleeveless vest of body armor securing it tightly around his torso with Velcro straps. It was lightweight but still added noticeably to his bulk. On top of that went a combat harness festooned with holders for extra magazines for the submachine guns, grenades, FM radio, and knife. He wrapped the thin wire for the radio around the vest, placed the earplug in his left ear, and strapped the mike around his throat.

Vaughn slid an automatic pistol into a holster strapped on the outside of his left thigh. Two spare magazines for the pistol went on either side of the holster. Two more spare magazines were strapped around his right thigh in a specially designed holster. He then pulled hard composite armor guards up to just below his elbow, protecting his forearms from elbow to wrist, followed by thin green Nomex flight gloves. Whether handling hot weapons, forcing his way through thick jungle, or simply for protection against falling, he had long ago learned to cover the skin on his hands.

For the final piece of weaponry, he used a loose piece of Velcro on his combat vest to secure a set of brass knuckles that had been spray-painted flat black to his left side.

"You can take the boy out of Boston, but you can't take Boston out of the boy," Jenkins commented.

"South Boston," Vaughn corrected his team sergeant. Jenkins had grown up on a farm in Wisconsin and always found his wife's and brother-in-law's stories of big city life strange. As strange as Vaughn found Jenkins's stories of farm life.

"If you got to use those," Jenkins said, pointing at the brass knuckles, "you're in some deep shit."

"That's the idea." Vaughn looked over at him. "You carry that pig sticker everywhere," he said, referring to the machete Jenkins had just finished securing behind his right shoulder, the handle sticking up for easy access.

"It's for firewood," Jenkins replied.

"Yeah, right."

Finally came a black Kevlar helmet, not the same distinctive shape the rest of the United States Army wore, but simply a semiround pot with a bracket bolted to the front. Out of a plastic case, Vaughn removed a set of night vision goggles and latched them onto the bracket, leaving the goggles in the up and off position so they wouldn't obscure his vision. The amount of gear he wore limited his exposed flesh to a small patch between his eyebrows and chin, which was already covered with dark green camouflage paste. The entire effect was greatly dehumanizing, making the men seem like machines, not flesh and blood.

A third, similarly dressed figure walked up in the dimming light. "Sergeant Major, don't you think your wife knows how short you really are?"

"Shut up," Jenkins growled, but without anger. The same jokes now for months—it was almost a ritual. One that Vaughn wished would end.

Several other men loomed up, all equipped the same way, except for two who carried heavier Squad Automatic Weapon machine guns. Ten men. Vaughn's team. Across the field, in a long tin building, was the platoon of twenty-five Filipino commandos who were to accompany them on this raid. And in between, squatting on the field like man-made bugs, were five UH-1 Iroquois transport helicopters with Philippine army markings. Like wraiths in the darkness, the pilots and crew chiefs of the aircraft were scurrying around them, doing last minute flight checks.

Vaughn looked at his watch. "Time. Get our allies," he ordered one of his men, who took off at a jog toward the barracks. He turned to another. "Got the designator?"

The man answered by holding out a rucksack. "It's set for the right freq."

Vaughn took the backpack, slid one of the straps over one shoulder and the MP-5 over the other. "To your birds." He and Jenkins headed toward the lead helicopter while the others split up. The sound of excited Filipino voices now echoed across the field as the platoon of commandos also headed toward the choppers.

Jenkins suddenly froze, putting an arm out and halting Vaughn. With one smooth movement, Jenkins's right arm looped up over his shoulder, grasped the well-worn handle of the machete and whipped the blade out and down. The razor-sharp blade sliced into the foot high grass—and through something else.

Jenkins leaned over and picked up the still wriggling body of a beheaded snake. "Very deadly," he commented as he tossed it aside. "Got to watch out for bad things in the grass."

Vaughn stood still for a moment, then followed his

team sergeant. Without another comment they continued on to the helicopters. Jenkins slapped Vaughn on the back as he turned for the second bird while Vaughn turned toward the first. But then Vaughn paused and reached out, grabbing his brother-in-law by the arm and pulling him close.

"Hey, Frank," he whispered harshly. "This is the last mission for you. Don't do nothing stupid."

Jenkins smiled. "For sure, Jim. You watch your own ass. Linda will—" The smile was suddenly gone, and he didn't complete the sentence. The two stood awkwardly for a moment, then both of them nodded and turned toward their respective aircraft.

What Vaughn didn't mention was the promise he had made his sister to keep her husband out of any last mission—a promise he had known he couldn't keep as soon as he made it, because Frank Jenkins wasn't the type of man to be held back from doing his duty. But Vaughn had made the promise to give his sister peace of mind. She'd lost her first husband in the terrorist attack on the Pentagon on 9/11, and it was a testament to her love for Jenkins that she had married him though his job put him on the front line on the war against terrorism.

Reaching his helicopter, Vaughn scanned the other four birds and got the pilots' attention by circling his arm above his head, indicating it was time to power up. He climbed onboard the aging UH-1 Huey and sat on the web seat directly behind the pilots, facing outboard. Another Delta Force man took the seat next to him. Vaughn's MP-5 submachine gun dangled over his shoulder and he put the designator pack on the floor between his legs.

The turbine engine above his head came to life with

a loud whine. Vaughn checked his watch again. Three minutes before liftoff. Even though the aircraft were Filipino, the pilots were Americans, and like Vaughn, dressed in unmarked uniforms. They were from the elite Nightstalkers of Task Force 160, the best chopper pilots in the world. All the pilots selected for this mission were old warrant officers, as most of the newer 160 pilots had never flown a Huey, being brought up on the more modern Blackhawk. Vaughn grabbed a headset from a hook over his head and placed the cup over his ears so he could listen to the crew on the intercom.

"One minute," the pilot announced.

Vaughn looked up. He knew the pilots were ready to hit their stopwatches and would lift off on time. This entire mission depended on everyone doing their job at exactly the right second. The Filipino commandos filled out the rest of the space on the web seats in the chopper. In addition to the Delta operator on his left, there were two American "advisors" in the rear of each chopper to complement the Filipinos.

In fact, the Americans were running the show, and Vaughn was the senior U.S. Army man. A Filipino colonel was technically in charge of the commandos and the raid, since it was taking place in his country, but the older man had declined to participate, claiming it was more important that he remain behind to "supervise." Even though there was nothing to supervise. There would be no radio communication at all. The last thing anyone from here to Washington wanted was a recording of American voices in combat operations in a place where they weren't supposed to be.

Vaughn opened the backpack and pulled out a bulky object that looked like a set of binoculars piggybacked onto a square green metal box, with a glass eye at the front end and a small display screen on the rear. The manufacturer called it "man portable," and at thirty-two pounds, Vaughn supposed it was, but it was an awkward thing to use. Designated the LLDR— Lightweight Laser Designator Rangefinder—it could both tell the distance to an object viewed through the lens and, when needed, "paint" it with a laser beam, designating the spot as a target for smart bombs. A steady green light on the rear indicated the designator was on, although the laser was not activated. There was also a GPS—Global Positioning System—built into the device that would feed location information to the computer, in conjunction with range to the designated target, which then was transmitted to incoming missiles, directing them. It was a lot of technology designed for one purpose: to put a bomb on target within a designated three-meter spot.

Ten seconds. Vaughn heard the jet before he saw it. An F-114 Stealth Fighter roared by overhead, stubby wings wagging in recognition of the helicopters below it. Right on time. He pressed a button on the back of the designator—a double check to make sure the bomb carried under the wing of the jet and the designator were on the same frequency. The green light flickered as it made radio contact with the bomb, then returned to steady green. Good to go. Vaughn put the designator back in the pack.

The fighter pilot pulled the nose up, and the jet shot into the sky until it was lost from sight and sound. Which is where it would remain, at high altitude, out of visual range from the ground, for the entire mission. The fact that it was a stealth plane would keep it off radar screens. The pilot would never even see the island where the target was located. It was Vaughn's job to target the bomb the pilot would drop at the planned moment.

With a shudder, the Huey lifted its skids exactly on time. Vaughn turned to the Filipino commandos in his bird and gave them the thumbs-up. He noted that none of them returned the gesture, nor did they seem particularly enthused. They were going into the mouth of the dragon to rescue foreigners, not a high priority for any of them. The raid was headed to Jolo Island, controlled by Abu Sayef rebels, who he knew had a long history of kicking the Philippine army's ass. He'd worked with the Philippine army before, and found their enthusiasm level for combat muted at best. Most were in the army for the pay, three hot meals, and a bunk. Not to get killed.

Eight days ago, eighteen tourists, most of them Americans, had been kidnapped by the rebels off a sailing boat as it passed by the island. Six days ago, a video of the rebels executing one of the tourists, an American man, had been sent to a Philippine news station in Manila. The next day, Vaughn and his small group of Delta Force operatives were on a flight from Fort Bragg to the Philippines. Their participation in the raid was a violation of both Philippine and American law; thus the extreme requirements for secrecy.

He would have preferred that the entire raiding force be American—not out of any prejudice on his part, but because the Filipino commandos were not trained anywhere near the level of his men, especially at the most difficult military task of all: rescuing hostages. But compromises were a political reality that often crept into missions such as this one.

Vaughn leaned back in the web seat and closed his eyes. He could sense the fear coming off some of the commandos, especially those who had not experienced combat before. They were going to "see the elephant," the age-old military term for experiencing combat. He wasn't sure where the term came from, although he suspected it might stem from as far back as Hannibal crossing the Alps, elephants in tow to engage the Romans. He was a student of military history, and that explanation seemed to make as much sense as any other.

He mentally ran through the sequence of upcoming events, war-gaming the plan. It was too late to change anything, but he wanted to keep his mind occupied. He'd learned that it could drift to bad places if left to its own devices. The helicopters cleared the edge of the island they had been on, and the pilots dove toward the ocean until they were flying less than five feet above the waves.

Vaughn pulled the LLDR out of its pack and checked the small screen on the back to update their position, then he looked at his watch. Exactly where they were supposed to be at the exact time. He had worked with Nightstalker pilots before, and they were meticulous about their flight routes and timing.

"Ten minutes."

Vaughn relayed the time warning to the Filipinos while he flashed the number ten with his fingers.

The commandos nodded glumly and pulled back the slides on their M-16s, chambering a round. His own MP-5 already had a round in the chamber and the safety was off—the rule in Delta was that one's finger was the safety.

It was dark now, and he reached up and turned on the night vision goggles, letting them warm up but keeping them locked in the upright position for the moment.

"Five minutes," the pilot announced. "Landfall in sight."

The flight plan called for them to hit the north shore of Jolo Island, fly close to the terrain over the island, then split formation when they cleared a pass between two peaks. Vaughn's helicopter would go to the left, while Jenkins and the other four birds would go right, taking twenty seconds longer to get to the target. The reason for the delay was because Vaughn had the laser designator.

Satellite imagery had given them the location of the camp where both American and Filipino intelligence believed the hostages were being held. There were two tin buildings set in a treeline on the southern shoreline of the island, about twenty meters apart. The one to the east, according to intelligence, was the barracks for the guards; the one to the west, the prison for the hostages. The beach itself was about fifty meters wide at low tide, a factor they had taken into account while planning the mission since it was the only place in the area where they could land the helicopters. Intelligence also said there were only a pair of guards on duty at the holding building at night, while the rest—estimated at thirty to forty men—would be in the guards barracks. Vaughn had to wonder how intelligence had come up with this estimate, but the mission was based on it, so he hoped it was correct. He also had to trust that intelligence had the two buildings labeled correctly, because he'd hate to designate the one with the hostages in it.

He leaned forward in his seat and could see a dark mass ahead—Jolo Island. It was among the most southwestern of the thousands of islands that encompassed the Philippines. Not large, and not particularly important, except for the fact that the Abu Sayef made their headquarters somewhere on it and had expanded their sphere of influence over the entire island. There was no government presence on the island, and from what Vaughn had picked up from his Filipino counterparts, the two sides existed in tense pretend-ignorance of each other—that is, until the terrorists went out and kidnapped foreigners, bringing intense pressure on the powers-that-be in Manila. All in all, no one was happy with the current situation.

"Formation is breaking," the pilot announced as they passed between two black masses. The announcement wasn't necessary, since Vaughn could see that himself. But it was standard operating procedure for the pilot to call out all checkpoints, and he was a big believer in SOPs. Without them, little details tended to get screwed up, and enough little screwed-up details added together could lead to big mistakes. The other four helicopters, Jenkins's in the lead, vectored off to the right. They would arrive from the west twenty seconds after the bomb exploded. Vaughn watched the dark form carrying his brother-in-law disappear around the mountain.

It was hard for him to believe that Frank was retiring. They'd worked together for six years. Vaughn had introduced him to his sister five years ago, when she'd stopped by Fort Bragg for a visit. The two had hit it off, which had surprised him. Since her first husband died, she'd been raising her two boys on her own. Vaughn had tried to help, but he was deployed so much with Delta Force, his presence had been spotty at best.

He had not been happy about the blooming romance between his team sergeant and sister, primarily because he knew Frank's presence in his sister and her sons' lives would be as infrequent as his own had been.

But he'd kept his unhappiness to himself, partially because he had always lived in fear of his older sister. She'd bossed him around as long as he could remember, and that had never changed. But after seeing them together enough, he'd given in, realizing there was something special between the two. He was going to miss Frank, but was glad that in retirement his friend would be with his sister full-time.

Vaughn shook his head, clearing it of the stray thoughts. He had to focus on the mission. His chopper was swinging wide so they would come to a hover over the treeline next to the beach about a kilometer east of the target. The Stealth Fighter would be coming in from farther to the east and much higher up on its targeting vector.

They were flying just above the tops of trees, as close as they'd flown over the waves. He picked up the LLDR once more, checked the screen, and froze when he saw that the green light was no longer on. Had he accidentally turned it off? There was no time to even consider the question before he reacted, pressing the on button. Nothing. He ran his hands quickly over the casing to see if it had somehow been damaged, but the machine appeared intact.

He pressed the on button several times, hoping it was just a glitch, a ghost in the machine playing games with him. Not the slightest flicker.

The battery.

"Three minutes."

He slid open the cover to the battery compartment, pulled out the bulky green object, disconnected the leads, tossed the battery out of the chopper, then reached into the pack for the spare one that SOP dictated would be carried. He ripped the clear plastic cover off the replacement and shoved the leads in.

As he pushed the battery back into its compartment, he pushed the on button and was rewarded with a flickering green light, indicating that the system was powering back up. How long would it take to acquire a satellite? he wondered. He'd never timed it, but knew it was variable, depending on how close the nearest satellites were, cloud condition, and the vagaries of the machine's inner workings. He was at the mercy of the machine and the electronic forces inside of it.

"Two minutes. On final approach."

That meant that not only was his helicopter on final approach, but the F-114 Stealth Fighter over 10,000 feet above their heads was in its bombing vector, and the other four helicopters were heading in toward their landing zone on the beach.

"Missile away," the helicopter pilot announced as his stopwatch passed the correct moment.

Vaughn could visualize it all in his mind's eye. The pilot of the Stealth Fighter had just punched the release at the designated time and the missile was coming down. The fighter then banked hard left and headed home, mission done.

The green light on the laser designator was still flickering.

"On station," the pilot said as he brought the helicopter to a hover over the treeline and turned it sideways, giving Vaughn a perfect view of the terrorist camp almost a kilometer away on the shoreline. The ocean was off to his left, and a small mountain island about four kilometers in that direction visually confirmed their position.

He knew that someone awake in the camp might be able to hear the helicopter now in the distance, but they had expected that—it was supposed to be too late, since the missile would impact the guard barrack in less than a minute. Even if an alert were issued right now, there would be at least a minute or two of confusion as men awakened in the middle of the night searched for clothes, boots, and weapons, and tried to figure out what the heck was going on. And guards were usually slow to issue an alert for a sound at a distance. There were always those moments of uncertainty, of fear of waking up a superior officer for nothing, of wondering what exactly was going on.

But without laser designation, the missile was flying blind.

The green light became steady. Vaughn peered through the optics. He could see the two buildings now. He put the reticules on the barrack, pressed the designate button, and was surprised at a flashing red warning light that appeared in the scope.

In a second he realized his mistake as the specs for the machine ran through his brain—when the battery had died and the computer rebooted, the GPS needed to be reset or else the designator only broadcast its own position, awaiting confirmation of setting by the handler. Which meant the missile was heading directly toward the designator in his hands and the helicopter.

Worse, the other four helicopters were due to land on top of the camp twenty seconds after missile impact. Which meant they'd be sitting ducks for the guards who were supposed to be dead.

"One minute."

There was no time to consider courses of action. Vaughn jumped forward and slapped the pilot on the back. "Go for the camp. All out."

As befit his training, the Task Force 160 pilot didn't question the surprise order. He pushed forward on his collective and the Huey picked up speed. Vaughn leaned forward, as if by shifting his weight he could make the helicopter go faster. For him, time began to slow down, the helicopter moving in slow motion. All he could think of was the missile descending through the sky above and behind him.

They were picking up speed, but Vaughn knew it wasn't fast enough. The pilot had them low over the beach, trees off to the right, waves breaking to the left, sand below.

"Time?" he demanded of the pilot.

"Ten seconds to impact."

They were still a good two hundred meters from the camp, and he knew he had cut it as close as he could. He threw the designator out of the helicopter at the same time he yelled into the intercom: "Bank."

The helicopter turned hard to the left over the ocean.

Even though the missile was coming in at supersonic speed, Vaughn could have sworn he saw it flash by. There was no doubting the impact as it landed on the beach where he had dumped the designator. The explosion turned night into day for an instant as flames shot forty feet into the air, followed by a shower of sand. The shock wave hit the helicopter and it shuddered violently for a second, then held steady.

He had averted immediate disaster, but now things were preparing to go from bad to worse. "Put us down on shore," Vaughn ordered even as a string of green tracers punched through the darkness at them, narrowly missing. He flipped down his night vision goggles. He had a sick feeling in the pit of his stomach, which he had to ignore as the Huey landed hard about one hundred meters from the two buildings, to the west along the beach.

The other four helicopters appeared right on time, coming in low along the beach to the west, to be met not with a destroyed barracks and a few surviving terrorists in shock, but a wave of automatic fire from numerous Abu Sayef guerrillas pouring out of the barracks. Undaunted, the helicopters plowed toward their landing zone just short of the target.

"Come on," Vaughn yelled to the Filipino commandos as he jumped off. He had the extended stock of the MP-5 tight to his shoulder and fired twice, double-tapping a figure holding an AK-47, then continuing to run forward, killing two more terrorists and closing on the building where the hostages were supposed to be held.

The other four helicopters were flaring to land when an RPG round fired by a guard hit one of the choppers dead on, exploding as it penetrated the cockpit. Out of control, the helicopter banked and plunged into the surf. Upon impact, the blades ripped off, tearing through the rear compartment, killing those who had survived the initial blast.

The other three helicopters landed on the beach, and the men on board jumped out into the middle of the raging firefight. Vaughn was forced to dive to the sand as concentrated automatic fire tore through the air in his general direction, barely missing him. He had no idea if anyone else from his helicopter had followed him, and he was still a good fifteen meters from the hostage building.

Vaughn continued firing as he spotted targets. He estimated there were at least thirty or forty guerrillas opposing them—the result of failing to destroy the barracks. They had not planned for this. Military tactics dictated a three-to-one ratio in favor of the attacking force for an assault to be successful. The odds here were reversed.

As he sighted in on another target, a large flash lit the night and his night vision goggles blacked out. Then a hot blast of air lifted him up and slammed him down to the ground while a thunderous explosion deafened him. Sand and debris came raining down—among it, body parts.

Ears ringing, Vaughn slowly rolled onto his back. He blinked as the night vision goggles worked to regain their setting after the overload. He didn't really want to see. Didn't want to get up. Didn't want to confirm what he already knew. It was only a question of how truly bad this was, and he instinctively knew it was very bad.

As the ringing subsided, he could dimly hear firing, though not as much as before. Accepting his duty with the battle still going on, he tucked the MP-5 into his shoulder and got to one knee, scanning the area, though he knew they'd already failed.

The hostage shack was gone. A gaping hole stood in its place. The explosion had been so large, it also took out most of the barracks building, killed quite a few of the terrorists who had been arrayed around the complex, and cut a swath into the jungle behind the buildings. There was no way anyone inside could have survived the explosion.

As if on autopilot, Vaughn fired at an Abu Sayef guerrilla who was limping away from the scene of the explosion. He continued to scan, saw bodies everywhere, turned and looked behind him. A half-dozen Filipino commandos were tentatively moving forward. He could see the crashed helicopter burning in the surf.

Drawn by the flames, Vaughn walked toward it, the water lapping around his legs. A couple of his men were already at work, removing bodies from it, searching for survivors. He paused as he recognized one of the bodies laid out next to the helicopter—or partial body.

A helicopter blade had sliced through the man, cutting him in half. The upper half had been dragged above the waterline. There was no sign of the lower half. Most likely it was still pinned in the wreckage.

Trembling, Vaughn walked over to the torso and knelt next to Sergeant Major Jenkins. He ripped open the combat vest and body armor and, reaching into the breast pocket, retrieved the picture of Jenkins's wife—his sister. He looked at it for several moments, then at his friend and brother-in-law.

"I'm sorry," he said.

Over four kilometers away, on the side of a mountain to the southeast along the shore, an old man sat in a wheelchair. He was parked on a narrow ledge, less than five feet wide, that had been cut out of the rock. On the right arm of the wheelchair was a red button, which was depressed under the weight of his hand. He slowly released the pressure. To his right, a man stood behind a digital video camera set on a tripod. The video camera had a bulky lens—a night vision device. And it was pointed toward the clearly visible flames where the battle had just taken place. The sounds of shots still echoed across the water toward their location, but the number and frequency had dropped off considerably.

"Did you get it all?" the old man asked in Tagalog, the language of Filipinos.

"Yes, sir."

"Can you identify them as Americans?"

"The zoom on this is very good. There is no doubt they are not Filipino."

"Very good."

CHAPTER 2

The Philippines

The story ran less than six hours later on the largest news station in Manila, and was picked up internationally within twenty minutes. Video of a failed American-Filipino raid that cost the lives of all the hostages, a dozen Filipino commandos, a classified number of American soldiers, and an unknown number of guerrillas.

The U.S. Defense attaché in Manila was ambushed by reporters, and because he had not been clued in on the Delta Force participation, he denied it and then looked foolish as the footage was played for him. If it had just been the several Delta and twelve Filipino commandos dead, perhaps it could have been covered up, as other incidents in the past had been: terrible training accident, helicopter went down at sea, all lost.

But there was no getting around the dead hostages. Those people had families. They'd been in the news, with the Abu Sayef continuously releasing videos of them pleading for their release. It was the number one news story in the Philippines, and it spread like wildfire in the media around the globe.

No one seemed to know or even particularly care about who had videotaped the attack and how it had gotten to the Manila news station. The focus was on the illegal participation of American forces on Philippine soil in a raid that had cost the lives of not only Americans, but two Germans, an Italian, and a French citizen.

After all that had happened in Iraq, the United States government was gun-shy about negative military publicity. Heads began to roll.

Vaughn and his team were back in "isolation." It was a term used in Special Operations for the time when a team was completely cut off from the outside world in a secure location. It was usually done for mission planning. Now it was being done simply to hide the six Delta Force survivors after the mission.

They were locked in a compound far behind the gate of what used to be Subic Naval Base, now being run by the Filipinos. A team from the First Special Forces Group out of Okinawa had been their ASTs—area specialist team—for their mission isolation, and that team was now acting as both their jailers and protectors. No one had come in and said anything about what would happen to the six, but they did have access to TV in their building and they knew the hammer was going to come down.

Vaughn felt isolated inside the isolation. He'd been

honest about the problem with the LLDS at their first debriefing, and the other five team members had been surprised, and a bit skeptical. They had held their peace, though, due to the losses the team had sustained, especially knowing the bond between Vaughn and Jenkins.

The communications sergeant who gave Vaughn the LLDS and was responsible for making sure it was functioning had died in the raid, so he couldn't be questioned about the status of the original battery. Mission SOP was that all batteries to be carried on an operation were to be brand new. Had this one been forgotten about? Had it malfunctioned? The device had been destroyed when the missile hit it, so that couldn't be checked. It was just Vaughn's word that the battery had died.

The other five said they believed him, but Vaughn sensed an edge of uncertainty. He felt it himself. He couldn't get the image of Frank Jenkins's severed body out of his mind. He hadn't been able to sleep since they got back to Manila, and didn't think he would be able to sleep solidly for a while to come.

He knew he should call his sister, but no phone calls were allowed, and he was secretly grateful for that. The isolation would at least protect him from the emotional fallout. He also knew it could not continue indefinitely, even though a part of him wished it would.

With the debriefings done, the team was left alone to ponder their fate. Already, less than twenty-fours after the botched raid, the Undersecretary of Defense for Special Operations in the Pentagon had taken one for the team and tendered his resignation, claiming the authorization for Delta Force to be on the raid had come from his office and he had overstepped the limits of his power. Vaughn doubted that the raid had originated anywhere but at the highest levels. He couldn't remember the last time he'd seen someone who was truly in charge stand up and take responsibility for something they had ordered.

"It's bullshit."

He didn't realize that someone had come into the briefing room, where the imagery, maps, and overlays for the mission were still tacked to walls. He'd been sitting there alone, not wanting to be with the others in the small recreation room watching CNN scroll by, showing practically the same story every half hour, the graphic images of the raid video playing again and again. Whoever had been manning the camera caught the RPG hitting Jenkins's helicopter, and Vaughn could not help but dwell on his brother-in-law's last moments of life whenever he saw it.

The man who stood in the doorway wore civilian clothes: black trousers, black T-shirt, and white sport coat. A bit much for the climate, Vaughn thought, then spotted the bulk of a gun in a shoulder holster and knew that was the reason for the coat.

"Who are you?" he demanded of the man. "This is a secure area."

"It's a secure area because I secured it," the man replied.

"CIA." Vaughn said it with a tinge of contempt. "Clowns in Action," as they were well known in the Special Operations community. Stemming from when the CIA and Special Forces were both spawned out of the OSS—Office of Strategic Services—after World War II, there had been no love lost between the two organizations. The war on terror had not brought the two organizations any closer, as the CIA had tried to expand its paramilitary forces under the guise of fighting terrorism—an area that military Special Operations felt was their purview.

"No. I'm not CIA," the man said, surprising Vaughn.

"DIA?" His tone had shifted from fact to question.

"No."

"Are we going to play alphabet soup?" Vaughn asked, tired of the game. He figured this guy was here to deliver the bad news, whatever it might be.

The man shrugged. "Let's say NSA just so you feel better."

"Why would that make me feel better?"

"It seems important to you to know who I work for."

"I want to know who I'm talking to."

"My name is Royce."

Vaughn stared at him. He was older, in his later forties, maybe early fifties. The way he carried himself indicated he'd been in the military at one time, probably long ago, before disappearing into the covert world and landing wherever he had—NSA, or elsewhere. Royce's face was tanned from the sun and had plenty of stress lines etched into it, typical for his line of work. He was tall and thin with somewhat long dark hair with a liberal amount of gray in it. His face was clean-shaven and there was the slightest trace of a scar across his forehead, disappearing underneath the hair on the right temple. Vaughn recognized a kindred spirit in the shadow world, but that didn't make him feel any better, since it was a world where secrets were kept and motives were often questionable.

"What do you want, Royce?"

Royce indicated a chair. "Mind if I sit?"

"Yes."

Royce sat anyway. He regarded Vaughn with mild

interest, as if he were an exhibit in a zoo. Vaughn disliked the way this was going. "You always ask questions you've already determined the answer to?" he demanded.

"I know my answer," Royce replied. "I just wanted to know yours."

Vaughn sighed. He rubbed a hand over the stubble on his chin. "I don't want to play games."

"I'm not here for games," Royce said. He nodded his head toward the door that led to the rec room. "How come you're not watching the news?"

"I know what happened."

"But not what's going to happen," Royce pointed out.

"Neither does CNN," Vaughn said.

Royce leaned back in his chair, turning it sideways. He stretched out his long legs and put his heels on another chair as he continued to contemplate Vaughn, tipping the chair back, balancing it on the rear two legs.

"Why don't you tell me what happened?" Royce asked.

"Read the debriefing."

"I did." Royce waited, like a good therapist wanting the patient to expose himself more than he had, but Vaughn wasn't into it. He'd done all the talking and explaining he was going to. The silence stretched out for a couple of minutes.

Abruptly, Royce removed his heels from the other chair and slammed his chair to the ground with a bang. "All right. You answer me square, just a couple of questions, and I'll be out of here and leave you to your misery."

Accepting the inevitable, Vaughn nodded.

"Did you fuck up?" Royce asked.

There was no hesitation in the answer. "Yes."

Royce frowned, and Vaughn could see the scar more clearly. Royce leaned forward. "In the AAR you said that the battery in the designator died. It appears from that point you did everything humanly possible. And the dead battery was the communications sergeant's fault, who unfortunately is no longer with us."

"So?"

"So, doesn't that mean what happened is the communication sergeant's fault?"

Vaughn stared Royce in the eye, his gaze unblinking. "I was the team commander. Everything on that mission was my responsibility."

Royce abruptly stood. "All right." He headed for the door, then paused and turned. "If you had to do it all over again, would you?"

"I'd have a good battery in the designator."

Then Royce was gone.

Fort Shafter, Hawaii

In the early days of World War II, after the attack at Pearl Harbor, there was serious concern that the Hawaiian Islands would be invaded by the Japanese. Defensive preparations were made throughout the islands, including the digging of tunnels in the lava flows that made up most of the land. These tunnels housed various military organizations, from air defense headquarters to hospitals.

One such tunnel system on Fort Shafter was still in use. It housed an agency known as Westcom Sim-Center, which stood for Western Command, Simulation Center. It was the place where the major commands of the United States military in the Pacific theater played their war games using sophisticated computer simulations.

At the moment, inside the Simulation Operations Center—which mimicked the one at Western Command headquarters—a simulation involving the Air Force was being run. On the large video display at the front of the room a map showing North Korea and vicinity was projected. A blinking red dot was rapidly moving across the Korean peninsula from east to west, closing on a blue triangle.

The red dot represented a B-2 bomber, the blue triangle the principal North Korean nuclear plant that produced weapons grade material. Anxiously watching the dot were two dozen Air Force officers. Their billion-dollar toy was "in action," and the Sim-Center had a notorious reputation for what the officers would say—only among themselves—was "no bullshit." If the computer determined that the North Koreans had spotted the bomber—or worse, shot it down—the computer would play out the simulation that way. These officers had planned the mission using the best intelligence they had, and now the computer was taking their plan and testing it and the expensive high-tech toy they were employing.

At the very back of the room sat the scientist in charge of the Sim-Center, Professor Foster, who appeared to be the exact opposite of what he was: a computer programming genius. Foster was a hulking man, over six and a half feet tall and weighing in at a beefy 280 pounds. He'd played football at Stanford, where he'd received his undergraduate degree. He'd actually been good enough to be drafted by the Oakland Raiders and had gone on to training camp, where he blew out his knee on the first day, ending his professional career. Then he'd gone back to graduate school and focused on developing computer programs to simulate real events. He approached these simulations like they were the Super Bowl and the American military was the opposing team.

Today he was a bit disappointed. The flight route chosen for the B-2, the crew that was locked in a simulator at Wheeler Air Force Base "flying" the plane, and the intelligence used to plan the mission were all top-notch and working perfectly. Foster was tempted to throw a curve in, one of a dozen he had prepared. Perhaps an engine malfunction on the airplane, or a North Korean antiaircraft missile being moved into the flight path, or even the National Command Authority that had authorized the mission canceling it at the last minute. But he knew the probabilities of any of those happening were very low and it wouldn't be fair, although what was fair in warfare, no one had been able to pin down.

So the red dot reached the blue triangle without being spotted, dropped its bombs "destroying" the nuclear facility, and made its escape without incident, much to the delight of the military men in the room. After they had all filed out on their way to celebrate at the Fort Shafter Officers' Club, Foster sat alone in the Sim-Center, preparing the after-action review, which would be disseminated to the various commands involved.

Successful AARs were always harder for him to write, because there was little he could comment on. There were a few minor suggestions, but otherwise it was a pathetically thin report. And the problem with thin reports was that people then began to question the value of the Sim-Center. It was a Catch-22 that Foster had been fighting for over eight years.

The secure phone on his desk rang, and he frowned. It almost never rang unless a simulation was running. He stared at it through four rings, then reluctantly picked it up.

"Foster."

"Gambit Six."

The phone went dead, but Foster remained perfectly still, holding the receiver to his ear as if the voice would come back and retrieve the two words. They were words he had hoped to never hear.

CHAPTER 3

The Philippines

The hammer came down on the Delta survivors draped with the thin velvet sheen of secrecy. It didn't soften the blow, just kept anyone other than the team from being aware of it. They were to get the hell out of the Philippines without anyone knowing they had left, just as no one had known they'd arrived. Vaughn found it ludicrous, because the world certainly knew they'd been here. But he kept his mouth shut, said "Yes sir," and, with his gear in hand, climbed into the back of the deuce-and-a-half covered truck that had backed up to the door of their isolation facility.

It wasn't fancy transportation to the airfield, and he suspected that if the military had them available, the team would be put on a World War II era DC-3 cargo plane to fly them back to the States. And the hope would be the aircraft would fall out of the sky and everyone would disappear. But that damned video wouldn't disappear. Vaughn had to wonder about that. Who had shot it? The filming began even *before* the missile impacted, which disturbed him greatly.

Had the Abu Sayef been that ready? Having a camera continually running to cover themselves in case of attack? But if they had been that ready, the defense would have been stronger than it was. If the LLDS had not malfunctioned, Vaughn was confident they could have rescued the hostages.

He was concentrating on these questions because it helped keep his mind from darker thoughts and emotions. Somewhat. The vision of Jenkins wouldn't go away. His sister had to have heard by now. He had written her a letter, including the photograph, but had no guarantee that the officer he'd handed it to would make sure it was delivered. He knew when he got back to the States that he had to visit her, which made him none too anxious to be returning home.

The truck lurched to a stop, almost throwing the men off the wooden bench they were seated on and tossing their gear about. Then the gears screeched as the truck reversed. Vaughn knew the drill. They were backing up to either a C-130 or C-141 cargo plane's back ramp. They would be off-loaded quickly, straight from truck to plane without touching the ground, the ramp closed, and then be in the air as soon as possible. Just like cargo, except now they were cargo no one wanted. He could pick up the familiar stench of JP-4 fuel burning, and the engines on the plane were already whining with power.

The canvas cover over the back of the truck was pulled aside by an Air Force crew chief. As expected,

the back ramp of a C-130 cargo plane was waiting for
them. As they got up to grab their gear, the crew chief
held up a hand. "Just the major," he said, pointing at
Vaughn. "The rest of you will be taken to another
plane."

Vaughn frowned. He tossed his gear onto the ramp,
said his good-byes to his teammates, then hopped onto
the ramp. Even as his feet touched the metal, the crew
chief was closing it. The truck pulled away with a
belch of diesel exhaust, mixing with the exhaust from
the C-130's four turboprop engines. The back ramp
closed and Vaughn turned to the interior of the plane.
The cargo bay was empty except for his gear, which
the crew chief was stuffing into a bundle, the type used
for an air drop.

"What are you doing?" he asked, shouting to be
heard above the sound of the four turboprop engines
revving up to taxiing speed.

The crew chief pointed at a parachute strapped down
on the red webbing seating that ran along the outer
bulkhead of the airplane. "You got two hours until the
drop zone, so you figure out when you want to rig."

"Where am I jumping? What the hell is going on?"

The crew chief shrugged. "You're jumping onto Okinawa. Why, they don't bother to tell me those things.
We got orders, we follow 'em." He looked at Vaughn.
"You must be pretty damn important to get a whole
plane just to drop you."

Vaughn didn't bother to tell the crew chief it was notoriety, not importance. He sat down on the red web
seat as the plane lurched forward. He felt the absence
of his teammates with the emptiness of the large cargo
bay. The crew chief had finished rigging the bundle
and gone up front to the cockpit.

Abruptly he stood up and walked to the front of the cargo bay, then back to the ramp. Then back again. He paused at the right rear door and peered out the small circular window. The plane was roaring down the runway now, and he had to grab hold to keep from falling as the nose lifted and they were airborne. He spotted the deuce-and-a-half truck backed up to a C-141 cargo plane—a larger aircraft with jet engines, not turboprop. That indicated the rest of the team was going back to the States, since the 141 was a more logical choice for that long journey. Then he spotted the ambulance waiting its turn to deposit its cargo in the plane. Vaughn knew what was on that ambulance: the bodies of his lost teammates in flag-draped coffins.

He raised his hand, half in salute, half in farewell, and twisted his head, keeping it in sight as long as possible.

Jolo Island, Philippines

"Bring him in," Rogelio Abayon ordered the guard, his voice filtered by the speaker system. The old Filipino's wheelchair was in a room that was part of a tunnel system, the rock walls of the room semicircular from floor to ceiling, the room running straight and narrow, with doors set in steel walls on either end. Bisecting Abayon's desk and the room was a sheet of bulletproof glass, a speaker and microphone on either side to relay conversation. The glass was pitted in places, as if its strength had been tested sometime in the past and it had weathered the storm.

On the other side of the glass the guard swung open the steel door opposite Abayon and gestured. A middle-age Japanese man in a stained and rumpled black suit stepped in. Over the suit, the man wore a canvas vest with deep pockets. In those pockets were small charges of C-4 explosive with blasting caps stuck in them. The wires led from the blasting caps to a detonator set on a chain looped over the man's head. A blinking red light on the detonator indicated that it was armed. The man looked decidedly unhappy.

The guard immediately went back out the door, shutting it behind him, leaving Abayon alone with the visitor, albeit separated by the glass.

"Is this necessary?" the man asked in Japanese, indicating the vest.

Abayon nodded and replied in the same language, "Yes, it is." He lifted his hand from the right arm of his wheelchair, revealing a red button. "I press down on that, you explode. My men will be upset if I have to do that, because then they will have to hose out the room where you are standing, so you do not want to force me to do it." He placed his hand back over the button, and the Japanese took a step back, fighting to keep from showing his fear, working on his anger to replace it.

"I am an envoy and should not be treated this way."

"Who made that rule?" Abayon asked. He did not wait for an answer. "What were the rules for Unit 731?" This time he did wait, but the envoy was not to be drawn into such talk.

"You know who I represent—" he began.

But Abayon cut him off. "Do you know who you *really* represent?"

In reply, the envoy held up his right hand, fingers extended, showing that the pinkie on that hand was missing. "I am the right hand of the head of the Black Wind Society. He sent me here to negotiate with you."

"And who does he work for?" Abayon demanded.

"My master works for no one."

"You're a fool. Which means he's a fool to have you as his right hand."

The envoy's face tightened as anger made him forget about the vest he wore and where he was. "You had me blindfolded, stuffed in the bottom of a boat, dragged here—wherever this stinkhole is—and have treated me with no respect. My master will not—"

"Your master is a puppet whose strings are being pulled," Abayon said. "And your people built this place you call a stinkhole."

The envoy looked about, trying to understand that last comment.

Abayon sighed. "Give me your message."

"My master wants you to return what you stole from our country. He wants the Golden Lily back."

"You don't even know what the Golden Lily is," Abayon said. "It is not a thing, it was an event involving things. And stealing from a thief is not stealing. What does your master offer in return for what he wants so badly?"

"In return, he will use his connections in the government to pressure the Americans to remove all their military aid from these islands."

Abayon stared through the glass at the Yakuza envoy as he processed what this offer really meant.

Taking the hesitation as a negative, the envoy laid his next card on the table. "If you refuse, my master also told me to inform you that he will bring all his considerable resources to bear on destroying you and your organization."

"You should have stopped at the offer," Abayon said, "ridiculous as it was. You've given me the message you were meant to, even though you don't know what it was."

The envoy frowned. "What is your answer to my master's offer?"

"You were not sent here to ask me anything. You were sent here to tell me something, and I have heard you. However, I suppose I should respond." Abayon gestured with his left hand, and the video camera in the corner of the room behind him picked up the gesture. The door behind the envoy swung open. The guard walked in with a stool and a small tray on which were a syringe, a rubber piece of tubing, and an alcohol swab. He placed the stool down, the tray on top of it, and then left, shutting the door solidly behind him, the sound echoing into an ominous silence.

"What do you think you're doing?" the envoy finally demanded, eyeing the syringe suspiciously.

"I want you to take that needle and inject yourself with the contents."

"You're crazy."

"You either do that," Abayon said, "or I do this." He indicated the red button.

"What's in the syringe?" the envoy demanded.

"Something that will make you sleep while my men take you back to the main island. If I wanted to kill you, I could do it quite easily right now."

That made a weird sort of logic to the envoy as he worked it over in his mind. "But what of your answer?"

"Your master will know it, don't worry."

Reluctantly the envoy rolled up his left sleeve. He picked up the rubber tube and, using his right hand and teeth, tied it around his upper arm. Then he took the syringe and held the needle over his tattooed arm. He paused with the point pressed against his skin. He looked through the glass at Abayon. The Abu Sayef commander waved his wrinkled right hand ever so slightly above the red button.

The envoy slid the needle into his vein and pressed the plunger, pushing the clear fluid in the syringe into his veins. Then he removed the needle and pressed the alcohol swab against the small hole. Abayon gestured once more and the guard reappeared.

"Be very still while he gets that off you," Abayon advised.

The envoy was a statue while the guard turned off the detonator and carefully removed the vest.

Abayon gestured. "Go."

"But—"

"Go."

When the envoy and guard were gone, Abayon turned his chair around as the door behind him opened. The man who had run the video camera the other evening was waiting for him. The taper got behind the wheelchair and pushed Abayon along a corridor cut out of stone. At places the walls were natural rock, indicating that portions of the tunnel had been there before men had entered the cave complex. They went on for five minutes, passing several other steel doors and side passages, a sign of how extensive this labyrinth was, until they came to a room where there was a dialysis machine.

A nurse was waiting, and she efficiently set about hooking Abayon up to the machine while the taper moved a video monitor to a position where Abayon could see it. Displayed on it was a small open field cut out of the jungle with a six-foot-high wooden stake set upright in the ground.

As the dialysis machine began its work, several figures appeared on screen. The Yakuza envoy was strug-

gling between the grips of two guards. They slammed
him against the pole while another guard quickly secured the envoy to the pole by wrapping rope around
his body. The envoy's mouth was moving, obviously
screaming protests and threats, but the feed was video
only, which Abayon appreciated.

"It will take a while. A couple of days at least,"
Abayon said.

"I'm using time stoppage settings," the taper said.
"I'll be able to get the entire thing on one DVD."

"Very good. Let me know when it is done."

Okinawa

The back ramp of the C-130 Hercules transport
plane opened once more. This time, though, the plane
was airborne at 1,500 feet altitude and air swirled into
the cargo bay, buffeting Vaughn as he stood just in
front of the hinge for the ramp. He had a parachute
rigged on his back, and the static line was hooked to
the cable that ran the length of the plane on the right
side. On the left side was another cable, to which the
bundle holding his gear was hooked. The loadmaster
had one hand on the bundle and was holding onto the
hydraulic arm that lowered the ramp with the other.

Vaughn moved forward as the loadmaster briefly let
go of the plane and held up one finger, indicating one
minute until the drop zone. Getting near the edge of the
ramp, Vaughn could see blue ocean directly below. He
checked the waves and didn't see any whitecaps,
which meant the wind wasn't too strong.

He got down on one knee and stuck his head out to
the side into the 140 mile an hour slipstream. He could
see the familiar outline of Okinawa Island very close,

directly ahead. He'd jumped this drop zone before when he had done some work with the First Battalion of the First Special Forces Group, which was stationed on the island.

He spotted the clear field that was the drop zone along the track of the aircraft and got back to his feet, facing to the rear, his eyes on the set of lights high up in the tail section of the plane. The red light glowed, holding him in place. Land appeared beneath the aircraft, the coast of Okinawa that Marines had stormed so many years ago.

The strangeness of the situation was not lost on him. Why someone wanted him to jump and the airplane not to land, he had no clue, other than it seemed a secure way of getting him onto the island without anyone being aware—other than whoever was waiting on the drop zone.

It had crossed his mind that the parachute was rigged to malfunction. He'd checked it as best he could, along with the reserve. He figured if someone wanted him dead, this was a rather elaborate way to go about it. And it wasn't as if he had any other choice. Staying on the plane and not jumping would only delay whatever was awaiting him. He preferred to face it head on.

The green light went on and the loadmaster let go of the bundle. It slid off the ramp, the static line for its parachute playing out. Vaughn followed right after it, as he'd been trained. Stepping off the ramp, he free-fell for three seconds as his static line played out, pulling the deployment bag out and off the parachute, which opened with a snap. Vaughn had assumed a tight body position upon exiting the aircraft, hands wrapped around the edges of the reserve, chin tucked down to his chest, legs tightly together. The opening shock vibrated through the harness and his body.

He had done the routine so many times, he wasn't even aware as he looked up, checked to make sure his canopy was fully deployed and functioning, then reached up and took the toggle on each riser in each hand, gaining control of the chute. He'd stopped counting his jumps once he reached three figures and earned his master parachutist wings. He'd never understood civilians who jumped for fun. To him it was always a part of his job. He jumped for mission or pay. It was too dangerous a thing to do for fun.

He looked down, spotted the bundle floating toward the ground, and turned the chute so he was chasing it. This was what the Airborne called a Hollywood jump—no rucksack, no weapon. The easiest kind to do.

He looked past the bundle to see if he could spot anyone on the drop zone. There was a black Land Rover moving across the open field; like him, chasing the bundle. He turned his attention back to what he was doing—even if it was a Hollywood jump, he was still going to make contact with the ground hard. Military parachutes were not designed for soft landings. One did not want to float slowly to the ground when there was a chance of getting shot at.

Feet and knees together, toes pointed down, Vaughn stared straight ahead at the horizon. The voices of the "Black Hat" instructors bellowing that command through bullhorns as he did his first jumps at Fort Benning many years ago echoed in his head. Like most Army training, airborne school had been designed to build instincts, not develop deep intellectual discussion about the training. His toes hit, and in quick succession his calves, thighs, hips, and side, and he slammed into the ground.

He lay still for about two seconds, as he always did after a jump, savoring life. He could smell the tall grass he lay in, and layered on top of that, the nearby ocean. Adrenaline made all the senses more acute. Then he was up, unbuckling his harness before gathering in his parachute. He grabbed the opening loop in the top center and pulled it out to extend it fully, then began figure-eighting the material, looping it around both arms extended out to the sides. As he did so he noted that the Land Rover with tinted windows was already at the bundle. Whoever it was moved fast, because by the time he had the parachute stuffed in the kit bag, the Rover was coming toward him. It skidded to a halt and the driver's door opened.

Vaughn recognized the man who stepped out. "Mr. Royce."

"Just Royce will do." He jerked a thumb toward the rear of the Rover. "Throw the chute in. I got the bundle."

Vaughn did as instructed, then got in the passenger side. Royce threw the truck into gear and took off.

"Why am I here?" Vaughn asked.

"I've got a good battery for the designator," Royce said.

Hawaii

At the designated time, Professor Foster checked the "dead drop," as he'd been instructed upon receiving those two code words. There was a practically unnoticeable chalk mark in the right place on the side of the old loading platform in an obscure corner of Fort Shafter where antiquated military vehicles rusted away. Foster had half hoped the sign wouldn't be there, but he was a logical man and knew that action B would follow action A. And now he had to do C.

He got on his knees and reached under the rotting wood platform. His hand groped for the package that he had been told would be there. But there appeared to be a logic breakdown. He retrieved nothing but a couple of splinters that drew blood and curses.

He continued the fruitless search for several more minutes, to no avail. Why would someone put the mark but not the package? Reluctantly, he got to his feet and blinked at the figure standing less than ten feet behind him, wearing shorts, a Bermuda shirt, and sandals. The man's face was in the shadow of his broad-brimmed straw hat, but he had a fringe of white hair along the edge of the hat. There was a small backpack slung over his shoulder. Foster had neither seen nor heard him approach.

"I've got what you need right here," the man said, pointing at his head and then at the pack.

"Who are you?" Foster demanded, looking past the man, searching the area for anyone else. They were alone as far as he could tell.

"I'm David. I'm here to brief you on what you are to do." He gestured. "Come, walk with me."

Foster came alongside as the old man began to walk through the abandoned vehicles, planes, and assorted equipment.

David began: "Needless to say, this is top secret, Q classification and completely compartmentalized. The only one you will ever speak of this to, when needed, is myself and my replacement."

"Your replacement?"

"Don't worry about that right now," David said.

"You complete this task and there will be a promotion and reassignment in it for you."

Foster picked up the pace without even realizing it. "Reassignment to where?"

"The National Security Agency Headquarters at Fort Meade." David put out a hand, slowing Foster back to his pace. "The big show. Running simulations for the National Command Authority. Doesn't get any bigger than that."

Foster contemplated the offer, trying not to show his enthusiasm for something he had yearned for.

David gave him an appropriate amount of time, then removed the carrot and showed the stick. "You screw up, of course, and the little situation from your last year in college will have to come up. You remember. The bowl game. The trip to Tijuana two nights before? You did much more than break curfew."

Foster froze. No one knew of that. No one.

David dipped into his pocket and pulled out a couple of photographs. He fanned them like a short deck of cards in front of Foster's face, confirming his worst nightmare: the event had been recorded on film. But that was almost two decades ago.

"How did you get those? Who took them?"

"Come come," David said. "Let's be in the real world." He held up a hand as Foster started to say something. "We will not discuss it at all. Just be aware that your life is never as private as you think it is and that there are reasons why people are chosen for certain positions—good reasons and bad reasons, but reasons nonetheless. Which brings us to here and now." He slapped Foster lightly on the shoulder. "Look at this as a good thing. The glass is half full and you now have the opportunity to top it off."

David held out the backpack. "There's a laptop in there. Coded only for you. You'll see. It will only work when *your* palms rest on the pads below the keyboard. It has the information on what you are to do and links to data sources that will help you in accomplishing your goal. Do not let anyone use it, because if someone other than you tries to access the keyboard, the hard drive will be destroyed.

"Essentially," David went on as they continued to walk through the graveyard of rusting military gear, "you are going to run a simulation involving a covert strike onto Jolo Island in the Philippines to destroy the Abu Sayef."

"But—" Foster began.

"There are no buts," David said. "It will be a simulation to those who you bring in to do it, but in reality the mission will actually be going on. I think you understand how you would work such a scenario."

Foster blinked as the implications sunk in. And right away he did understand. It would be a delicate balancing act, but it could be done. But why? His thoughts were interrupted as David halted in front of a rusting hulk of an old UH-1 helicopter. "Did you know that when President Nixon ordered the halt to bombing raids during the Vietnam War, the order was so broad, it stated that there would not be *any* flights into North Vietnamese or Cambodian airspace? And that reconnaissance teams that had already been inserted across the border and were counting on helicopter exfiltration were abandoned? Simply abandoned."

"I'd never heard that," Foster said.

"It's in plenty of books," David said. "But most people do not care for the lessons of histories, especially those that killed people for political expediency." He put his hand on the nose of the helicopter. "You can go now."

Foster was confused. David pointed. "Go."

Foster turned and walked quickly away, as if by distancing himself from the messenger, he was distancing himself from the message, even though he had the pack holding the computer on his shoulder now. After taking a dozen steps, he paused and turned, a question forming on his lips.

But there was no one there.

Okinawa

"Isn't the definition of insanity doing the same thing twice and expecting different results?" Vaughn asked as Royce drove them down a road winding along the Okinawan coast.

"Stupidity is failing and accepting it," Royce replied. "Your job this time isn't to rescue hostages. There aren't any to be rescued."

Vaughn's face flushed red, but he didn't say anything.

"We want to make sure no more hostages are taken by the Abu Sayef. Ever."

"And how are we going to do that? It's a large organization."

"We cut off the head and the body dies." Royce glanced over at Vaughn. "Your task—your new team's task—will be to kill Rogelio Abayon, the leader of the Abu Sayef."

"What new team?" Vaughn asked as he absorbed this mission. "And isn't assassination against U.S. law?"

"This isn't an *official* mission," Royce said, emphasizing the word, "which also answers the question of legality since it will never have occurred. Your new unit is called Section Eight. Drawn from various organizations to fight terrorism on its own terms. No rules except don't get caught, and if caught you are denied by our government."

Vaughn considered this.

Royce continued. "Remember, although you blame yourself for what happened on Jolo Island, it was an Abu Sayef terrorist who fired the RPG that killed your brother-in-law."

"I was in command and I was the one with the laser designator," Vaughn said.

"You think a lot of yourself," Royce noted. "So all those missions you went on where everything worked and the team was successful—those were all your doing? You kept your brother-in-law alive on all those missions? All by yourself?"

"That's bullshit logic and you know it," Vaughn snapped.

"Yeah, it is," Royce agreed. "But you're denigrating your brother-in-law's sacrifice by beating yourself up. He signed up, he volunteered again and again—hell, you don't get into Delta Force without volunteering, what, how many times?" Royce ticked them off on his fingers. "Once to get in the Army. Then Airborne. Then Rangers. Then Special Forces. Then Delta. That's five." His voice turned harsh. "So who the fuck do you think you are to be so important, more important than the sacrifice he made in his willingness to serve his country? Get your head out of your ass, Vaughn, and take the opportunity I'm giving you. Direct your anger outward and not inward."

Vaughn didn't reply as the Land Rover bounced

along what was now a dirt road, heading toward a mountain. There was silence for a few moments, then Royce began speaking, almost as much to himself, as to Vaughn, as if reminding himself of something important.

"Did you know that Okinawa was the largest amphibious assault of the entire Pacific campaign? And that more people died here, on this island in the assault, than in the combined atomic bombings of Hiroshima and Nagasaki? Twelve thousand Americans killed. Over 100,000 Japanese military and conscripts killed. And over 100,000 civilians. At least those are the guesses. No one really knows what the true numbers were. The estimates were made by subtraction."

That got through to Vaughn. "What do you mean by subtraction?"

"They didn't count the dead after the battle because so many were buried by blasts or incinerated or otherwise wiped from the face of the earth. What they did was count how many civilians were still left. Then they subtracted that number from the prewar population and came up with their casualty estimate.

"And then there were the wounded. Almost half of the American wounded were caused by battle stress, around 26,000 men. That's almost two full divisions wiped out simply by the psychological stress of fighting here. Then there were the kamikazes off shore. Thirty-four ships were sunk and over 350 were damaged by them."

Vaughn tried to visualize war on that scale, but even his combat missions couldn't relate. Those men who had fought here, and the civilians caught in the middle, had truly seen the elephant. A damn big one.

Royce continued. "The civilians here were used to

typhoons. But the worst one that ever hit the island was nothing compared to the *tetsu no bow*—the storm of steel—that the U.S. Navy and Air Force unleashed on them."

Royce pulled the Land Rover up to a chain-link fence manned by two armed guards. They were next to a small river on the right. The dirt road beyond went to a tunnel entrance barely wide enough for the car. Beyond that there was darkness.

"This tunnel," Royce said, as the guards swung the gate open, "was a hiding place for motorboats that the Japanese loaded with high explosives—the *kikusui,* floating chrysanthemum—that they planned to bring out on railroad tracks, put into the river there, and send out to hit the American fleet. For some reason, that plan was never carried out. Maybe the Japanese naval commander had a fit of conscience. More likely they didn't have the fuel for the boats, since it was diverted to the kamikazes, who were considered more effective."

The gate was open but Royce didn't move the Rover. He turned to Vaughn. "Section Eight is classified far beyond anything you've ever been associated with. Only a handful of people at the very highest levels know it exists and what its mission is, which is to fight the bad guys with no rules. Gloves off. If you're successful here, you redeem yourself . . ." Royce paused. ". . . and you'll get revenge for your brother-in-law."

Vaughn sat still, but his mind felt as if it had gone over the edge he had experienced in isolation back in the Philippines. He was in free fall.

Royce continued the sell. "No bureaucracy. No staff officers interfering. Everything is tightly compartmentalized for security reasons. You will, of course, always be monitored, even when not on mission, but you'll have plenty of free time. The pay is five times what you made in the military and not traceable, so no IRS. In fact, when you join, you no longer exist in any data-base, anywhere. We make our own rules in this unit." Royce waited a few seconds. "Do you accept?"

"Do I have a choice?"

"We always have choices."

"I assume once I go black I can never come back out?"

"Good assumption."

"I'm in."

Royce didn't seem overjoyed. "It's not that easy."

Vaughn hadn't figured it would be, and he waited.

"You have to prove yourself first."

"How?"

"Do a little job for us. If you're successful, you join Section Eight. You fail . . . well, if you fail that means you're dead."

CHAPTER 4

Jolo Island, Philippines

"It is over."

Abayon looked up from the desk his wheelchair was behind. "It was faster than I thought it would be."

The taper shrugged. "His spirit did not fight well. Once he realized his fate, he gave up."

"You know where to send the DVD."

"Yes, sir."

Okinawa

Royce drove them into the tunnel. Lights tripped by infrared sensors came on, illuminating the way as he drove into the mountain. They went on for about a minute at a slow crawl until they came to a second barricade, this one manned by two Special Forces soldiers, which Vaughn found interesting. To put such highly trained men on a guard detail was unusual, to say the least.

This time Royce rolled down the window. One of the guards had his weapon trained on the vehicle as the other came up to it.

"Mr. Royce," the guard said. He looked past Royce at Vaughn. "And this is?"

"The last member of the team."

The guard nodded. "Proceed."

Royce drove on, and they reached a large circular cavern, with a half-dozen tunnels radiating out like spokes on a wheel. Royce stopped the Rover and got out. Vaughn joined him.

"This way," Royce said.

Vaughn shouldered his gear and followed Royce into one of the spokes. Royce opened a steel door twenty feet down the tunnel and gestured for him to enter. Vaughn hesitated, realizing this could as easily be a trap, but he went in.

Lights flickered on, revealing a small chamber, about twenty feet wide and long. A cot, a large table, a sink and toilet: an unsophisticated jail cell was the best way to describe it. Except for the papers piled on the table, which Royce went over to.

Vaughn dropped his gear and joined him. On top of the papers was a grainy black and white photograph of a man.

"Who is that?" Vaughn asked.

"The man you're going to kill tonight in order to make the team."

And with that, Royce walked out of the chamber, the steel door slamming shut behind him.

Japan

The flat screen TV was the largest and best model produced in Japan. The man who owned the company that built it sat on one side of the table among men who were as successful and powerful as he. There was one middle-age woman among the dozen in the room, the first of her gender ever to sit there, her place farthest from the head of the table. She was lean, her body tense as she listened and observed.

"Watch, please," the man at the head of the table ordered as he pressed a button and an image was displayed on the television. A man—the Yakuza representative who had been sent to negotiate with Abayon—was tied to a wooden stake set upright in the ground. He was bound to the stake with coarse rope.

"The time lapse of this DVD covers over twenty-six hours," the man informed them.

In a series of shots, the man tied to the stake went from struggling against the rope to struggling against whatever virus was spreading through his blood. The first indication was involuntary spasms. Then frothing at the mouth. Then vomiting blood. The spasms grew worse, to the point where it was obvious the man broke both arms in his convulsions, one a compound fracture with white bone sticking out of the skin of his forearm. More blood was vomited, then it began to trickle out of his eyes, ears, and nose. His mouth was often open, in what appeared to be a scream, but fortunately there was no sound to accompany the image.

Even with the advanced time lapse, it still took five minutes of video before he finally stopped moving. The man at the head of the table left that image on the screen as he turned to face the other eleven people in the room. Some of the men at the table had seen something like this before, long before.

"Meruta," one of the men muttered, which earned him a hard look from the man in charge.

"As we expected, the Yakuza have failed to resolve the Abayon issue."

One of the others nodded. "It was worth the effort, though. We have pushed Abayon off his center of balance."

The man across from him snorted. He was old, as was everyone in the room except two of the men and the woman. The nine oldest had all fought in World War II. Six of those had served in Unit 731, Japan's infamous biological warfare unit in Manchuria that had killed thousands in their experiments. They knew what message Abayon had sent with this video, since they had done the exact same thing to prisoners to test their various viruses at 731. The prisoners at the camp were called *meruta*—logs—dehumanizing them and putting them in their place as things to be used to perfect weapons of mass destruction long before the term became well known.

"Abayon is not a problem," the man in charge said. "There is a plan being implemented to remove him. This, however"—he jerked his finger at the corpse— "along with many other incidents over the past decade, proves we can no longer deal with our criminal associates. They have become incompetent and lazy. And too well known."

"The Yakuza are useful," one of the others argued. "They are a blunt instrument of violence that can be wielded when needed."

"The world is becoming a place," the man replied, "where blunt instruments of violence are as dangerous to the user as to the target. Worse, the government has been trying to penetrate the Yakuza for a long time. We have intelligence that they have managed to insert several deep undercover agents inside the Yakuza. The Black Wind is no longer secure."

That brought a quiet to the room. The man waited. One by one, each person at the table nodded their assent to his decision.

Except for the last person. The only woman not only nodded, she spoke. "I wish the honor of completing this task."

Every head in the room swiveled from her to the man in charge. He pursed his lips, deep in thought, and then his head twitched, almost imperceptibly giving his assent.

Okinawa

"Why do you want him killed?" Vaughn demanded as Royce came back into the chamber after an absence of over an hour. During that time, Vaughn had pored through the documents, which contained little more than a time and a place where the target could be "interdicted" later that day. There were photographs of a street intersection taken from numerous angles. And of the target—a middle-age Japanese man, always dressed in black suits and usually accompanied by several other men that Vaughn could tell were professional bodyguards. Sometimes, though, the entire group accompanied *another* man, who they all seemed to be guarding, which didn't make much sense to Vaughn.

"I don't want him killed," Royce said. "Section Eight wants him killed." He checked his watch. "We need to get you in the air if you're going to make the interdiction."

Vaughn had noted that the target was in Tokyo, several hours flight from Okinawa, and the time window was tight. He looked over at the pile of gear he'd brought from the Philippines.

"Forget that," Royce said. "Everything you'll need is on the plane. It's a simple job."

Vaughn followed Royce down the corridor and got in the Rover. "Who is the target?"

Royce continued driving, but he spared Vaughn a glance. "You don't get it yet, do you?" He didn't wait for an answer. "I've seen your service record. When you ran missions in Iraq, did you know the names of those you killed?"

"They were the enemy," Vaughn argued.

"Really? Were the insurgents wearing uniforms? Carrying little signs that read 'I am the enemy'?"

Vaughn already knew where this was going. "It was a combat zone."

"The world is a combat zone nowadays," Royce said. "You think those people in New York on nine/eleven thought they were in a combat zone?"

"So this guy is a terrorist?" Vaughn asked, holding up the picture.

The Rover was barreling down the highway toward the military airfield. "Here's the deal, Vaughn. I don't know his name. I don't know what he does. I don't know why Section Eight wants him dead. I get the mission, I task it out. This entire operation runs on cutouts. The way a true covert operation is supposed to. Certainly you understand that?"

Vaughn glanced out the window at the Okinawan countryside. A cutout was a person who knew both sides in a covert operation but was the only link between them. If the cutout was removed, then both sides were secure.

"I understand, but—"

"There are no 'buts' in Section Eight. You do the missions you're assigned. Right now that man is your mission."

They pulled into the airfield, where a Learjet painted black was waiting, engines running. Vaughn noted that there were no identifying numbers painted on the plane's tail. Royce rolled up to the boarding steps.

"As I said, everything you need to do the job is inside. You'll be taken around customs once you land. You've got the target and location. You have one hour to make it back to the plane, which will bring you back here. The plane is coming back whether you're on it or not."

Vaughn got out of the Land Rover and it pulled away. He stood for a moment, watching it, then looked at the stairs and the dark entry into the plane.

There was nowhere else to go.

Jolo Island, Philippines

Rogelio Abayon could hear his own breathing. The sound of air rasping in and out of his lungs. He felt like he would never get a clear breath. Never fill his lungs completely without hearing the sound of one of the simplest of human autonomic functions. And he knew he wouldn't. Of that the doctor was certain. Abayon knew his breathing would be the last thing he would hear, and that when he heard silence, there would be no more.

No words of comfort from family or friends. The former had been his wife, and she was long dead, over sixty years. He'd watched her die. The latter he could count on one hand with four fingers left over, and he was about to send that one person away from him and knew he would never see him again.

There was a tentative knock on the steel door, the sound muted and faint, stirring Abayon out of his dark thoughts.

"Enter," he ordered.

The door swung open, protesting on rusty hinges. Maintenance of his quarters was not what it used to be. There were more important chambers in the complex that demanded constant attention.

A young man dressed quite well for the environment entered. He wore a gray silk suit with highly shined black shoes. Abayon assumed his guest had brought the suit and shoes in a bag, since getting to the cave complex's secret entrance was quite an endeavor. The effort was not lost on Abayon, since it confirmed his decision to entrust a critical part of his plan with this young man.

"Ruiz," Abayon said, extending his hand.

Ruiz shook the old man's hand and then took the indicated seat.

"Are all the objects in place?" Abayon asked.

"Yes, sir. The last shipment arrived two days ago and they are in a secure location."

"And the auction?"

"The word is being put out discreetly to specific buyers. This is a very closed and elite world, and we've let enough information slip that the excitement and interest level is very high."

"It should be," Abayon said. "And the Chinese?"

"They are very happy with the shipment we gave them as payoff. They are providing us with security and support as requested. They believe our story about the Japanese, so they are more than willing to help us as there is no love lost between those two countries."

"Excellent," Abayon said. He raised his hand. "Go and do your duty."

Ruiz stood. "Yes, sir." He turned and walked out the door.

For several minutes Abayon was alone, then there was another knock. The second part of the plan. The time spacing between the meetings had been to ensure that Ruiz and the next man would not meet. Only Abayon knew the full extent of what he had spent years planning. He had not really needed Ruiz here, since he'd already known the answers to the questions he'd asked, but everything was coming toward the end, and throughout his life as the leader of the Abu Sayef, Abayon had always wanted to meet face-to-face with subordinates before they went to do tasks he had assigned them. He always wanted to look his men in the eyes and get a feel for their state of mind and emotion, while at the same time letting them know that he was taking full responsibility for their orders. He never delegated responsibility. It was a lesson he had learned during the Second World War fighting the Japanese.

The second man who entered was Abayon's age but in much better physical condition, although he was missing three fingers from his right hand—the result of a machete blow from a Japanese officer during World War II. The two had known each other since childhood.

"My old friend," Abayon said.

Alfons Moreno walked up to Abayon, took his hand and kissed the back of it before sitting down. "Is it time?" Moreno asked.

Abayon nodded. "The dark ones are stirring the nest to see what comes out. We must make sure our sting is much worse than they ever feared."

"The man was from the Yakuza, and the assault was pushed by the Americans," Moreno pointed out. "Two different directions."

"Yes, but we know someone was pulling the strings in the background, just as they've been since—who knows how far back they go? We have never been able to determine that."

"We have not been able to determine much at all about our enemies." Moreno frowned. "But the raid failed and the envoy did not succeed."

Abayon shook his head. "But I don't think either was designed to succeed. Whoever is behind all this plays games with people. To see how they react. They are trying to draw me out so they can have their Golden Lily back. They have tried before and they are patient, but now they rightfully fear me, so they are taking action first."

Moreno sighed. "It is all too complicated. This game."

Abayon knew that Moreno considered him a bit of a paranoid. To survive this long, he'd had to be paranoid. "Yes, it is complicated, but it is necessary because our opponents also are complicated and shift identities. And it is no game. Much is at stake. The future of everyone. Most people around the planet are living as slaves and don't even see their shackles or who controls their lives."

"I know it is not a game," Moreno said. "But remember that there are good and evil people on both sides. The Americans helped liberate us in World War Two. Colonel Volckman taught us much of the tactics we still use."

"Volckman was a great man," Abayon agreed, "but he is long dead and the new world is much different.

The Americans seek to crush all who do not believe as they do, and that seems to be in our enemy's interest. So perhaps they are one and the same."

The two had had many similar discussions. Moreno had long ago accepted that Abayon had a much larger vision than he did. Moreno had always been the practical one, while Abayon was the great thinker. They had made a formidable team over the years, surviving despite large bounties being put on their heads. They'd also survived several attempted coups by younger members of the Abu Sayef.

It bothered Moreno at times that his old friend did not simply concern himself with their goal of an independent Muslim state among the islands surrounding Jolo. Abayon's vision had always extended far beyond the borders of the Philippines and beyond the stretch of the immediate future.

"You are ready?" Abayon asked.

Moreno nodded even though the question was mainly rhetorical. "The last repairs were completed three days ago. I would have liked to do a practice cruise, but it is too dangerous." He smiled. "Let us hope everything works, or I might submerge and never come back up."

"You will come back up, my old friend. And when you do, our enemies will howl from the pain you will inflict." Abayon lifted his hand, gesturing for Moreno to come close. When Moreno did so, Abayon half lifted himself out of the wheelchair, wrapping his still strong arms around Moreno.

"You are my secret weapon," Abayon whispered. "I will never forget you no matter what happens. I will miss you, my friend."

Okinawa

Royce had stopped the Land Rover in the shadows of one of the hangars and watched the Learjet carrying Vaughn take off. He checked his watch impatiently, then nodded as a similar jet came in from the west and landed. He waited until the door opened and a short, stocky man got off, a duffel bag hoisted over one shoulder.

Royce drove the Rover up to the man, who threw the duffel in the back and got in the passenger seat. The two exchanged nods but not a word. Royce drove to the same spot he'd been in and parked. The other man finally spoke as Royce turned off the engine.

"Who are we waiting on?"

"A member of your new team." Royce pulled a file out of his case and passed it to the other man.

"Fuck," the man muttered as he opened it and saw the black and white photo on top of the military personnel file. "A woman?"

"She's good, Orson," Royce said.

"Since we're waiting on her," Orson said, "I assume she passed her test."

Royce nodded. "Six hours ago in Bangkok."

Orson checked the file. "Captain Layla Tai. Weird name. She a keeper?"

Royce turned and looked at Orson. "That's to be determined."

Orson laughed. "As always."

A third jet came in for a landing, and Royce turned his attention to it, ignoring Orson. If there was one thing that had impressed him in all the years he'd been working for the Organization—the title he had made up for the unnamed entity that issued him his orders—it was that it never lacked for money or resources.

The plane pulled up to the stairs and the door opened. The woman whose file Orson had been perusing stepped out. She had a white bandage taped to the left side of her forehead and looked disoriented. She was a slender, tall woman with dark hair cut very short. Her eyes had a slight angle to them, indicating Asian genes in her bloodline.

"The test was a little rough?" Orson commented, glancing up from the file as Royce started the truck.

"Looks like," Royce said. "But she's still breathing and mostly in one piece. She'll do. You bring her in. I have to go to Hawaii on that plane to get support for your team's mission rolling."

Orson frowned as he flipped a couple of pages. "Captain Tai was Military Intelligence?"

Royce didn't reply, since the answer was on the printed page.

"What's our leverage on her?"

"Her sister. And prisoner abuse in Iraq."

Orson flipped through and read. "I don't think that's good enough. I don't think she'll be a keeper." He snapped the file shut as Royce brought the SUV to a halt at the base of the stairs.

CHAPTER 5

Hong Kong

Ruiz came out of the jetway into the vast expanse of Hong Kong International Airport. The other passengers on his flight gave him a wide berth as he walked up to two men wearing long black leather coats and sunglasses—despite the temperate climate inside the terminal and the fact that it was night outside. Ruiz had to assume these agents of the government had watched too many western videos and adopted their attire based on those images. It was a problem he saw everywhere he went—the American way of life was corrupting the world in ways most people didn't even notice. On the other hand, he also realized that it was a very nice way of life if one was on top of the pyramid of power.

"Ruiz," one of the men barked, holding up a badge.

"Yes."

"We are your escorts," the man said, snapping the badge shut and sliding it into his pocket. "Come with us."

"My luggage—" Ruiz began, but the men got on either side of him and by sheer momentum began moving him.

"It will be taken care of."

The two moved him along, walking in step. They bypassed customs with a flurry of badge-waving. By the way everyone deferred to the two guards, Ruiz had to assume they were not merely underlings sent to escort him. Perhaps the leather coats and sunglasses were more than just an affectation, he thought as they exited the terminal and the man who had shown the badge gestured for him to get into a waiting limousine.

Ruiz noticed there was someone already in the back as he slid in, trying to let his eyes adjust to the dim lighting inside. The two escorts got in the front, separated from the rear by a thick plate of what Ruiz assumed was bulletproof glass. The limousine moved away from the curb.

"I have been to the holding area," the man in the shadows said.

Ruiz waited.

"It is as you said it would be," the man continued. "Very impressive."

"Then we are set?" Ruiz said.

The man nodded. "Yes. I don't suppose you will tell me how your group came into possession of these articles?"

"That is not a story I am authorized to tell," Ruiz said. "As I informed you earlier, we were not the ones who stole them initially. We appropriated them from the original thieves. And now we are trying to make things right."

"And make money."

"For our trouble, yes."

"Let us hope there will be no trouble."

Tokyo

A limousine was waiting outside the Learjet. Vaughn was dressed in black slacks, black T-shirt, black leather jacket, and in his right hand had a metal case hiding a sniper rifle. All had been waiting inside the plane. He felt overwhelmed, but impressed with the efficiency of Section 8.

He'd thought when he went into Delta Force that he had gone as deep into the world of covert operations as one could go. Now he knew he'd just seen the tip of the iceberg. He—and his teammates—always suspected there was more out there. They'd seen too many things, too much that was unexplained, to accept that they were as deep as it went.

The driver got out of the limo and went around the near side near the foot of the stairs, opened the door and waited, still as a statue. Vaughn went down the stairs and inside. The door slammed shut and they were off.

Vaughn leaned back in the plush comfort of the limo. Between the Learjet and the limousine, there could be no more startling contrast between this and the way he had always gone on missions for Delta Force, via military cargo planes, helicopters, and parachuting.

He ran his hands over the metal case and noted in a distant way that they were shaking slightly. Exhaustion? The stress of the past week? The uncertainty of the future? He didn't know. Probably all of the above, he thought.

This was the first time he'd ever gone on a mission

without a team. In the infantry, the Special Forces, and Delta Force, he'd always been part of a team. He'd always been able to count on the support of others to achieve the mission. He looked around the spacious interior of the limousine and longed for the cramped quarters of the back of a Combat Talon aircraft.

He'd made the decision on Okinawa because of lack of other paths.

He couldn't go back to the States and face his sister after letting her down so terribly. She'd had a hard life, particularly after the death of her first husband, and he had made that damn, stupid promise that he knew he never could have held Frank to. And now he was gone.

He also knew his career in the Army was over. To succeed in the Army, an officer didn't have to be good, as much as avoid bad. Any hint of screw-up or scandal and the faceless committees that determined one's future simply saw what was in the paperwork and axed a person's career.

Vaughn leaned forward, elbows on the case, and put his head in his hands, as if he could press his scattered thoughts and feelings into some form of sanity and normalcy.

Off Jolo Island

The conning tower of the old diesel submarine cut through the water. Moreno shared the tight space on top with two lookouts. They had no running lights on and had to be wary of fishing boats that might be anchored for the night. At the fore and after of the top deck of the submarine were two strange contraptions shaped like large twenty-foot-high horseshoes welded to the deck upside down.

Moreno looked to his left, toward Jolo. He could see the outline of Hono Mountain silhouetted against the sky. He reached into his shirt pocket and pulled out a cigar. Ignoring security for the moment, he cut off the end, flicked his lighter and puffed away.

Several seconds later there was a corresponding small flicker of light, high up on the mountainside. Moreno smiled. While he smoked the cigar in his left hand, he brought the tip of the surviving fingers of his right hand to his forehead in a salute.

Hawaii

After ending his business with Orson, Royce had landed in Oahu and was helicoptered to Fort Shafter, where he entered the simulation center. He stood in the back of the room and quietly watched as Foster brought in his team of computer experts and military liaisons. Royce was surprised that David wasn't here. After all, his boss, and friend—insofar as one had friends within the organization—had requested this highly unusual personal meeting. Upon entering the Sim-Center, Royce had been given a note with some coordinates on it, and right away knew where David was waiting for him—but first he had to make sure the "simulation" got off on the right foot.

Foster stood behind a podium, which had the crest for Western Command on the front. Royce had seen such briefings before. The key for Foster was to get everyone in the room, particularly the military staff, to make the transition from thinking they were playing a simulation to some semblance of belief that this was a real mission. Which, in fact, it was going to be, but no one in the room other than he and Foster knew that. In essence, Foster was the cutout to make sure Orson's team had the military support it needed to conduct the mission.

Royce was concerned about Foster, but they had enough leverage on the computer expert to ensure his complete cooperation and discretion. Royce had no doubt that David had played Foster perfectly. David was too old a hand and too much of a professional to do anything less.

Foster read from a prepared script. "Forty-five minutes ago, Western Command headquarters received a warning for a covert operation in its theater command. This warning order was relayed to subordinate headquarters, resulting in your presence here at the operations center." He turned to the senior officer seated in the center, front seat. "Brigadier General Slocum, Commander Special Operations, Westcom, is in charge of this mission. He will give you the mission tasking."

Foster took a seat and the one-star general took his place. Slocum had a Special Forces combat patch sewn onto the right shoulder of his camouflage fatigues, and the Combat Infantry Badge and the Master Parachutist Badge on his chest, above his name tag. He was all business as he barked out the tasking.

"Westcom Special Operations has been ordered to conduct a direct action mission to destroy a terrorist cell on Jolo Island, the Philippines. The primary target is the elimination—" Slocum looked up from the paper. "Gentlemen, 'elimination' is the word used in the order. You and I need to talk in plain English. We're going to kill this son of a bitch Rogelio Abayon, the head of the Abu Sayef.

"I'm going to say something, and I'm only going to say it once," Slocum continued. "We know this is the

Sim-Center, not the war room at headquarters. So we know this mission isn't real. But I want every one of you to act like this is real. That flesh and blood soldiers are going to be out there putting it on the line. I hear or see any of you acting with less than your best effort, I'm going to put my boot so far up your ass, when you land, you'll be eating kimchi in the worst hellhole I can slot you in South Korea.

"Questions?"

The room was still.

Slocum nodded. "Let's get going. Time's a-wasting. G-2. Briefing. Now."

The intelligence officer stood behind the podium. Royce noted that a digital camera was aimed at the man, and he knew that the briefing was being forwarded to Orson in Okinawa, where it would be stored so it could be replayed for the team—once it was assembled.

"There's a lot of disinformation being disseminated about the Abu Sayef," the officer began. "Which might be part of a deliberate effort on the group's part to keep itself shrouded in confusion. According to media reports, the Abu Sayef only came into being in 1991 when it split off from the MNLF: the Moro National Liberation Front. But classified intelligence reports indicate the opposite is true: the Abu Sayef has been in existence since the end of World War Two under the control of Rogelio Abayon, and the MNLF was actually subordinate to it for many years.

"The Abu Sayef kept a very low profile for decades, funding and supporting other groups that got more attention, such as the MNLF. The stated goal of the Abu Sayef is to establish an Iranian-style Islamic state in the islands of the southern Philippines."

"What does Abu Sayef mean?" Slocum asked, interrupting the officer.

"Bearer of the Sword," the officer said. "It's only in the past ten years or so that the Abu Sayef has gotten in the news, which is a credit to Abayon's ability to conduct covert operations and use other organizations as a cover. That changed after 9/11. There are credible reports of financial links between Abu Sayef and Al Qaeda. Since Islamic fundamentalism is so much in the news, it was inevitable that some word on Abu Sayef would come out, so it seems as if Abayon accepted the inevitable. Another factor could be that Abayon is getting old. He's in his late seventies, and there's some speculation among analysts that he wants to go out—for lack of a better term—with a bang.

"The first major action directly linked to Sayef was in 1991 when they conducted a grenade attack that killed two foreign women suspected of being missionaries. Then, the next year, Sayef terrorists threw a bomb at a ship docked at the southern city of Zamboanga. The ship was an international floating bookstore crewed by Christian clergy. Right after that, there were a series of bombings against Roman Catholic churches throughout the Philippines. In 1993 the Sayef bombed a cathedral in Davao City and killed seven people."

The officer checked his notes. "That's the same year the Sayef began their campaign of kidnapping foreigners. Initially it was believed that they did it for the ransom, but it is more likely they did it for the notoriety. In 1995 the Abu Sayef attacked a Christian town on Mindanao, razing it to the ground and killing fifty-three civilians and soldiers."

Royce turned as Foster entered the control room.

The scientist stared at him for several seconds, until Royce finally spoke. "I work with David."

Foster was about to say something when the intelligence officer continued and both turned back to the operations center to listen.

"No group like this comes into being in a vacuum. This goes back hundreds and hundreds of years. Islam came to the Philippines in the thirteenth, fourteenth, and fifteenth centuries. While in Indonesia and Malaysia, Muslims became a majority, in the Philippines they've always been a minority, about five percent of the population, concentrated in the southern islands. Catholicism is the dominant religion in the Philippines by far. After all, the Philippines were a Spanish colony from 1565 to 1898, and then we took over after the Spanish-American War. However, despite the small numbers, for centuries some islands, including Jolo, were essentially independent sultanates with a predominant Muslim population.

"It was me, the United States, who forced them into becoming part of the rest of the country. Both before and after World War II, most of those people did not even consider themselves Filipino but rather Moros. The central government in Manila always considered the Moros a threat and has made forced resettlement of Christians into Muslim held territory a national policy, which has not pleased the Moros. As much as the central government pushed, the Muslims have reacted and pushed back.

"This came to a head in 1946 when the Philippine Republic was established and the United States relinquished control of the islands. Choices had to be made. Surprisingly, some of the elite and powerful Muslim elders actually aligned themselves with the central government and even supported the resettlement of Christians in historically Muslim territory.

"Essentially they sold out. Or they bowed to what they viewed as an inevitable reality. But not all. Not Abayon. He tried to make things work between the two sides and almost succeeded. In the sixties he was able to broker a truce between the government and the Muslim extremists, but he couldn't keep it going. In 1968 a group of Muslim army trainees were massacred by their own Christian leaders. Then in the 1971 elections, Marcos and the ruling party gained so much power that they no longer felt they had to appease the Muslim minority. Outright war broke out between Christians and Muslims."

The officer continued. "Marcos declared martial law in 1972. In reaction, Muslims declared themselves independent. Thousands were killed in the fighting and hundreds of thousands were displaced. Libya provided sanctuary for some of the Muslim leaders during this. But"—the officer glanced up from his notes—"Abayon never left the islands like many of his contemporary leaders in the revolt did.

"In 1976, under pressure from Libya and the OIC—the Organization of Islamic Conference, mainly made up of other Muslim countries—the Tripoli Agreement was negotiated. This brought a cease-fire and autonomy to thirteen southern provinces in the Philippines where the majority of Muslims lived.

"Of course it didn't work out," he continued. "The Muslims began fighting among themselves over who should control their territories. The MNLF, the BMLO—Bangsa Moro Liberation Organization—and other splinter groups fought for power. And in the background, Abayon and the Abu Sayef remained aloof from the infighting.

"Fighting between the central government and the Muslims broke out in 1977. The various Muslim groups also were fighting among themselves, which must have delighted Marcos. When Marcos fell in 1985, the new government held out the olive branch to Muslims. It seemed that everyone was tired of the fighting. A peace process was begun. But a serious schism was beginning to form between moderate Muslims and extremists. This is when the Abu Sayef began to come to the forefront, espousing jihad, violent struggle, versus the government policy of nonviolent mobilization, known as dawa."

General Slocum stood up. "This just reflects what started happening everywhere in the world in the nineties and into the new millennium. Abayon is the head of the Abu Sayef and the group is just one of the many tentacles of this movement, just like Al Qaeda. They are a threat to our way of life, and our job is to take down one of those tentacles."

Slocum wasn't done. "These people use terrorism as their weapon against civilization. They took the war to us on 9/11. Now we're taking the war to them. Let's do it."

Royce was impressed with Slocum. The general didn't seem to be acting. His musings on the simulation were interrupted by Foster.

"Why are we playing this game?" the scientist demanded. "You heard that. The Abu Sayef are terrorists and Abayon is their leader. We shouldn't have to be playing this hide and seek game to—"

"Shut up," Royce said. He realized Foster wasn't as bright and aware as he had thought.

Foster appeared not to hear him. "This is a simulation center, not a real operations center. I can't be held responsible for—"

Royce pulled out his pistol and pointed it at Foster. That got through, and the scientist's mouth snapped shut, his eyes getting wide.

"David explained your situation, correct?"

Foster nodded.

"Let me explain it more clearly since you haven't gotten the message." Royce pressed the muzzle of the gun against Foster's forehead. "I don't give a shit about your job at the NSA. Or the blackmail from college. You pull your weight here, get the team the support it needs, do what I tell you to do, or else I kill you. Is that clear?"

Foster swallowed hard. He tried to nod, then realized the cold steel against his forehead precluded that. "Yes," he managed to get out.

Jolo Island

Abayon smiled for a moment, but it passed quickly as the cigarette smoke reached his lungs and he doubled over in his chair, hacking and coughing. He cursed as he stubbed out the cigarette on the armrest of his wheelchair. This one vice had been taken from him by the frailties of his aging body.

He watched the small dot of light that represented Moreno move through the strait between Jolo and Pata islands into the open sea until it disappeared around the headland. Then he wheeled himself inside the complex, the camouflaged steel door sliding down behind him. He rolled down the corridor, the only sound the rhythmic hiss of air being moved through the large pipes bolted to the ceiling. It was a sound he had lived with for many decades so it went unnoticed. Somewhere in the distance another steel door clanged shut.

Abayon reached an elevator. The doors slid open and he rolled inside. Reaching up, he could just barely reach the buttons. They had faded Japanese writing next to them. He punched the one for the lowest level of the complex. With a slight jerk, the old elevator slowly began descending into the bowels of Hono Mountain. It took over two minutes for him to get to the level he wanted.

The doors opened, presenting him with two of his men armed with submachine guns standing in a small anteroom. They snapped to attention upon recognizing him. One turned to the control mechanism for the door behind them, sliding a large metal key into one of the slots. Abayon wheeled to the other side of the door, pulled out his own version of the large key and slid it into the slot on that side.

"On three," Abayon said. "One, two, three." They turned their keys in unison.

With a squeal of reluctance, the heavy steel door began to rumble open. Whatever was on the other side was bathed in darkness. When the doors stopped moving, Abayon rolled himself into the darkness. He paused as the door shut behind him. Then he reached out to his right, his hand finding the familiar switch. He threw it and large lights spaced along the ceiling of the huge tunnel he was in came on.

The light was reflected back many times as it struck six-foot-high piles of gold bullion stacked on either side, the entire eighty-foot length of the tunnel.

And this was just the beginning of what was hidden here. A steel door at the far end of the tunnel beckoned, and Abayon rolled his wheelchair toward it. It was the front end of an air lock. The chamber beyond was climate controlled, with three backup generators on constant standby to ensure that the system never failed. Abayon went past the gold without a glance at it. After decades of seeing it, the yellow metal had lost its hold on him.

However, what lay beyond the air lock was a different story. Abayon opened the closest door and entered the lock. He impatiently waited as the humidity and temperature were brought in line with the chamber beyond. The red light on the door turned to green, and Abayon leaned forward in the chair, turning the wheel that unlatched the door. It swung open and he pushed himself inside, turning on the lights as he did.

It was the museum a pack rat might put together—a pack rat with exquisite taste. Paintings lined the walls, frame-to-frame, competing for space. Statues and sculptures were lined shoulder-to-shoulder. Tables covered with exquisite artifacts were in front of the statues. It was a treasure that matched in potential wealth the bullion in the preceding chamber. It was actually more valuable, though, in emotional terms, because almost every piece of art in the room was ancient and irreplaceable, and long believed lost during the mayhem of the Second World War as the Rising Sun spread across the western Pacific Rim.

There were artifacts in this chamber from every country the Japanese had invaded. This was the result of the rape of those cultures under the guise of the Golden Lily Project, a most misleading name. In several places there were gaps on the wall and floor, where some of the treasure had recently been removed. A small but significant portion.

There was something else in the chamber. Bodies. Dozens of them. Mummified in the room's dry air. Still garbed in their Imperial Army uniforms. Abayon moved into the room until he was in front of one of the bodies. The rank insignia indicated he was a colonel. A sword was still buckled around his waist. A faded red gash across his throat indicated how he had died.

Abayon had made that cut. He remembered the event like it was yesterday.

CHAPTER 6

Jolo Island, the Philippines, 1942

They had known only defeat and retreat ever since answering General MacArthur's call to arms. Then MacArthur ran away in the middle of the night to Australia, and the Americans surrendered at Bataan. Rogelio Abayon and his comrades had watched from the jungle as the tattered prisoners—American and Filipino—were marched by. What they saw convinced them that their decision to take to the hills and not follow the order to give up had been the right one.

The route to the prison camps was lined with the bodies of those who could not make it and those the Japanese guards randomly executed. There seemed to be no rhyme or reason to delineate those whom the guards bayoneted or shot. The brutality combined with the shocking collapse of the apparently invincible

American military left the young band of thirty-odd former Filipino recruits bewildered. For a week after the last prisoners had been marched by they lived in the jungle, content to hide and afraid to move.

Abayon was only nineteen years old and a private. There were several noncommissioned officers among the group, but none seemed eager to take charge. They'd had an American officer, but he disappeared during the last days of the fighting. After the week, with their food supplies running low, it was Rogelio who took command. He knew it was too soon to take action against the Japanese. Indeed, from the few reports they received from frightened civilians, it appeared as if the Japanese might actually win this war. There were rumors that the Japanese had destroyed the mighty American fleet in Hawaii and even invaded those islands, taking them over. If that were true, Abayon had his doubts whether the Americans would once more establish their presence in the Pacific. After all, it had been obvious to all even before the invasion that the eyes of the white men were turned toward the war in Europe, not Asia.

On the morning marking the seventh day since they had run into the jungle, Abayon gathered the men around him. He proposed that they leave the main island and go to the island he had grown up on: Jolo. It was remote, and he knew he could find support among the people. He had family there, and a young wife whom he longed to see once more. His best friend, Alfons Moreno, who was with them, also was from Jolo, and seconded Abayon's suggestion.

Most of the others agreed, more out of a lack of any better suggestion than an eagerness to follow him. A few headed off to their own villages. Abayon led the rest through the jungle to the coast. He organized a raid where they seized a small fishing boat. He and Moreno, who had been a fisherman before being inducted into the army, captained the boat, traveling only at night to avoid the Japanese patrol boats and planes. It took them over ten days to make it to Jolo.

They put in at Abayon and Moreno's village. Abayon was overjoyed to be reunited with his wife, but they were not greeted with open arms by most of the villagers. The Japanese were on Jolo, the village elder told Abayon late at night. There were Japanese soldiers on Hono Mountain, and they had conscripted every able-bodied man they could capture for some construction project. What exactly was going on at the mountain, the elder did not know, since no one who was captured had come back, and the one road that had been built leading to the mountain was guarded by soldiers.

Abayon made a pact with the old man—he would take his group into the jungle and hide, as long as the village provided them with food. Anxious to be rid of the group—and the threat of Japanese reprisal—the elder agreed. With his wife accompanying him, Abayon led the men into the center of the island, to a place he knew of, next to a stream that supplied them with drinking water.

For several months they lay low, not wishing to draw attention to themselves, while more ex-soldiers and men avoiding the Japanese labor conscription filtered into their camp. Eventually over one hundred men, along with a handful of their women, were living there. It was a number the food supply could not sustain much longer.

The presence of the Japanese on his island bothered

Abayon. Even more than that, he was curious about what they were doing on Hono Mountain. What did they need the slave labor for? His and Moreno's relatives were among those who had been taken. All that, and the growing pressure to take some sort of action against the invaders, led Abayon and Moreno to leave their hidden camp on a reconnaissance mission to Hono.

It turned out that what was happening was not on the mountain, but in it.

They spent a week scouting in the vicinity of the mountain, discovering where the Japanese were boring a tunnel. They found unmarked graves where the slaves who had died had been summarily buried. And from what they could see, they were the lucky ones. Men and women went into the black hole on the side of the mountain each day. The only ones who came out were those carrying rock and dirt, who immediately went back in, and the dead, who did not.

The tunnel entrance was about two hundred meters up the side of the mountain, at the farthest place where a vehicle could climb up the track cut through the jungle and up the slope. Abayon and Moreno were puzzled. They could think of no tactical reason to build such a complex in Hono Mountain. Their puzzlement turned to rage during their second week of surveillance when the Japanese soldiers lined up all the surviving laborers and machine-gunned them, the bodies tumbling into ditches the doomed had been forced to dig before their execution.

As they watched helplessly from the jungle, the people they knew were being killed; Abayon had to hold Moreno back. A group including Moreno's brother had been lined up in front of the smoking barrels of the machine guns, and there was nothing they could do for them, except get themselves killed. He told his best friend as much, while restraining him, but it did little to comfort either of them.

"Vengeance will be ours," Abayon whispered in Moreno's ear as the machine guns spit death, sending the bodies tumbling on top of those who had been killed before them.

"Vengeance," Abayon repeated again and again to Moreno, trying to contain his friend's white hot rage. "Whatever they have built in the mountain, it must be important. They are killing all who know the way in and what was built. But we know. And we know what they have done here. We will have vengeance."

Moreno was shaking his head, tears streaming down his face. They were on a hill across the valley from Hono, well hidden, but with an excellent view of not only the mountain, but the valley where the executions were taking place. "What good is vengeance?" Moreno asked. "It will not bring back the dead."

"It is all we have," Abayon said simply. "It is what we must feed on. Until every last Japanese soldier is dead."

The distinctive chatter of the Japanese machine guns echoed once more as the last group of laborers were executed. Abayon pointed. "See that officer?"

Moreno blinked away his tears and nodded. The man had an ornate samurai sword strapped to his side, and the rank insignia on his collar indicated he was a colonel in the Imperial Army.

"I have been watching," Abayon said. "He is in command. Every soldier and other officer he comes in contact with defers to him. He will be dead within the month. I promise you that. All of them will be dead."

"How?" Moreno asked. They had counted at least three hundred Japanese soldiers on the mountain. Even though most of them appeared to be engineers and not infantrymen, there were still too many for their poorly armed and equipped group to take on.

"I will think of a way," Abayon promised.

Surprisingly, it was the officer he had pointed out who gave him the means.

The next day, as the corpses of the Filipino men and women who had worked in the mountain rotted in their shallow graves, the colonel led a large contingent of his men to the beach to greet a Japanese ship that appeared in the water to the south. They had cut a rough road through the jungle from the mountain to the beach, and now drove a half-dozen small trucks to the edge of the ocean, where they lined up on the sand.

Crate after crate was off-loaded from the ship, brought ashore, and loaded onto the trucks. Abayon and Moreno watched as the trucks made over two dozen trips, hauling crates to the mountain, where the Japanese soldiers man-handled them into the gaping black opening.

"What do you think they are hiding?" Moreno asked as the last load disappeared into the mountain. The ship had already departed, gone over the horizon even as the trucks made their last trip back from the beach. In its place, a small patrol boat was at anchor offshore.

Before Abayon could reply, they heard the chatter of machine-gun fire echo out of the black hole across from them.

"What is going on?" Moreno asked. "Were there more of our people in there?"

The Japanese colonel appeared in the mouth of the cave with three men. Two of them were firing machine guns back the way they had come. Abayon frowned, trying to make sense of it. The colonel gestured to the third man who was unreeling wire. The man attached the wire to a small box, and it was suddenly clear to Abayon.

"They're sealing the entrance," he said.

The man pushed down the plunger, then dust blew out of the tunnel entrance, the rumble of the explosion drifting across the valley to Abayon and Moreno. A second explosion followed, and the mouth of the tunnel crumbled, leaving behind a tumble of rocks blocking the entrance.

"But where are the rest of the Japanese?" Moreno asked.

Abayon simply pointed. The colonel had his pistol out. He lifted it and fired three times, killing the men who had been with him.

"My God," Moreno muttered. "What is going? Has he lost his mind?"

"A secret," Abayon whispered, realizing the import of what they had just witnessed. "He's the only one who knows this location. The jungle will grow over those rocks." Abayon nodded grimly. "But we know." He stood. "Come."

His eyes were no longer on where the tunnel had been, but on the Japanese officer who was walking down the thin dirt road, unreeling more wire, stopping every so often to attach the leads to charges on trees. The demolitions must have taken days to prepare, Abayon realized as he and Moreno headed into the valley. And the engineers who had prepared them were now trapped inside the mountain, either already dead or dying.

They heard three explosions as they headed toward

the road. The colonel was blowing trees on the side of the road. Like the tunnel entrance, it would not take long for the jungle to reclaim the road, hiding what had been there.

They reached the valley floor as a fourth explosion rumbled through the forest, followed by the sound of trees falling. It was not far from their location, less than half a kilometer away, as near as Abayon could tell. He tried to imagine the rationale for building something inside the mountain and then immediately destroying all trace of it and blocking the way in. What had been in those crates? And why was the colonel hiding them even from his own people?

They climbed up out of the stream bed, and the double track trail was in front of them. Abayon signaled to Moreno, and the two took up hidden positions alongside the rutted track. After several minutes the Japanese colonel appeared, hooking up the detonator to fused charges he'd placed on a half-dozen trees spaced out along the way. He did the last one less than one hundred meters from their location and unreeled about half the distance in wire before kneeling and pushing the plunger.

The explosion thundered through the jungle, trees from both sides collapsing across the path, making it impassable for vehicles. The dust-covered colonel retrieved as much of the wire as he could, reeling it up, then turned to continue his destructive journey toward the beach and the waiting patrol boat. Abayon had no doubt what the fate of that crew would be once the colonel returned to civilization.

But that was not going to happen.

As the colonel drew even with their position, Abayon gave Moreno the signal. The two men leapt out of the brush and overwhelmed him as he hooked up the wire to a charge on a tree opposite their location. They had him pinned to the ground within a second, Abayon tying the man's hands securely behind his back. The colonel struggled and fought, but the two guerrillas were too much for him.

Abayon rolled the Japanese over on his back as he unbuckled the samurai sword from around the officer's waist. The colonel kicked out, catching Moreno in the stomach, doubling him over. Abayon drew the sword and placed the point against the man's chest.

"Do not move," he ordered.

The colonel glared up at him, but did as ordered. Moreno got to his feet, cursing. He pointed the muzzle of his rifle at the colonel, his finger curling around the trigger.

"Not yet," Abayon ordered his friend.

Instead of a bullet, Moreno spit, the glob splattering on the officer's face.

"Keep him covered," Abayon ordered as he put the sword down and quickly went through the prisoner's pockets.

He drew out a leather wallet that contained identification and papers. "Colonel Tashama," Abayon read. "From the Kempeitai."

Moreno hissed as he heard the name of the infamous military intelligence branch of the Japanese army. They had led the way in rape and torture on the main island.

"What did you put in the mountain?" Abayon asked.

Tashama just glared at him. Abayon stared back, thinking it through. "You are the only one who knows where the entrance to the tunnel is. In fact, who probably even knows what mountain you tunneled into."

He knelt down, the edge of the sword resting across Tashama's neck, and smiled. "Except for my friend and I."

Muscles on Tashama's face twitched, but still he remained silent.

"Whatever you buried there must be very important," Abayon continued, "for you to have killed so many of your own men. For you to go to such extreme lengths to keep this place secret." Abayon shrugged. "It does not matter."

Even as Tashama frowned, Abayon drew the blade across the man's neck, the razor-sharp edge easily slicing through skin, cartilage, and arteries. Blood spouted and Tashama gasped, his body spasming as his life poured out of him.

"He could have told us things," Moreno said disapprovingly, his initial rage having subsided.

"He was Kempeitai," Abayon said, wiping the blood off the blade on Tashama's uniform blouse. "He would never have spoken. Besides, we know where the tunnel is. We can find out for ourselves what is in there."

In the years after, Abayon often reflected that Moreno was right, that in immediately killing Tashama, he'd been too rash that day. They could probably have learned more from the man.

In the days that followed, Abayon led a group that swam out to the patrol boat one dark night, slaughtering the sailors on board and scuttling the boat, effectively cutting off any Japanese contact with the island and the tunnel. Then the gathered guerrillas went to work digging through the debris into Hono Mountain.

When they managed to break through, Abayon, mindful of what they'd witnessed, ordered everyone except Moreno to remain outside as the two of them went into the complex. What they found there stunned them so much that they remained inside for three days before returning to the anxious group of men who awaited them.

Abayon had the men block the entrance once more. He knew with the war still raging there was nothing that could be done with such treasure, and he feared the return of the Japanese. The priority right now was the war.

Within the year, they had gone on the offensive against the Japanese, returning to the main island and hooking up with a handful of American officers, including Colonel Volckman, who were organizing the resistance. They fought for over six months before the base camp that Abayon was in charge of was overrun by Japanese soldiers led by a traitor. Moreno was wounded but escaped. Abayon, in charge of the rear guard action, and his wife, who stood by his side, were knocked unconscious by a mortar blast and taken prisoner.

Given what happened next, Abayon often looked back and thought it would have been better if both of them had been killed by that mortar round.

Now, over sixty years later, with one last glance at the mummified body of Colonel Tashama, Abayon turned his wheelchair around and headed back out the way he'd come. Since he had not been killed then, all that was left to him was vengeance. It had taken decades, but the time was now at hand to pay back those who had done such terrible things to his family and his people.

CHAPTER 7

Tokyo

The target window was tight. Vaughn checked his watch one more time. He was in a hotel room, using the key card he'd been handed by the driver when they pulled up to the service entrance in the rear. The driver had not said a word, just tapped his watch and held up a single finger—one hour—which confirmed the parameters in the packet Vaughn had received.

Upon entering the room, he had assembled the rifle, a round ready in the chamber. He pulled the dresser over to a position about three feet inside the open window, so the muzzle of the weapon didn't extend outside, a sure giveaway and sign of an amateur. He was seated in a chair, the stock of the rifle against his shoulder.

He put his eye back on the scope and scanned the

well-lit street below. There had been no sign yet of the target.

The target. Vaughn considered that term. Royce's logic notwithstanding, he knew he was now far out on the thin ice of covert operations. He had no idea who the target was, why he was killing him, or whether that limo would actually be there to take him back to the airfield. And he wasn't even sure which of those problems should be his priority.

One of the first lessons Vaughn had learned in his Special Forces training was to expect the worst, and in this case the worst was that he had been abandoned here. However, he saw no reason why Royce would do that—after all, it did make sense that this was a test to gauge his abilities and commitment to Section 8 in order to join the team.

Vaughn mentally shrugged, still watching the street. He'd been in worse places. At least this was Japan, and if push came to shove, he could try to make it out on his own—although, as he thought about it, he realized he was here illegally, with no passport, no identification, no money, on a mission to kill a Japanese national.

Not good, but doable.

As long as he was on the good-bad track, he considered something else: he had never even heard a whisper of a unit called Section 8. And he'd conducted several top secret, real-world missions for the United States in various places around the world. In a way, that was good, because it meant the unit's cover was solid. But as with all the other aspects of his current situation, it was also bad, because he was operating off very scanty intelligence.

The sniper rifle felt heavy in his hands, even though

most of the weight was supported by the bipod on the dresser and the stock pressed against his shoulder.

He lightly ran his finger over that edge, experiencing the yawning darkness he'd felt seeing his brother-in-law's body. He folded the picture, slid it back in his pocket, and checked his watch. Twenty-five minutes left in the target window. He picked the rifle back up and scanned the street, trying to shut out all thoughts other than the mission at hand.

Still, there was a part of him that hoped the target window would pass without having to shoot and—

The subject walked out of a building, exactly as in the surveillance photographs. He was flanked by two men, both with the hard look of professional security personnel, and seemed to be in a rush. A car with tinted windows pulled to the curb and he was headed for it.

No time to consider.

Vaughn centered the reticules on the target's head, his finger on the trigger. He exhaled, felt the rhythm of his own heartbeat, and in the pause between beats he smoothly pulled back on the trigger.

The round hit the target in the head, snapping the man back with a spray of blood and brain. Vaughn automatically shifted the scope to the guard closest to the target and almost pulled the trigger, but stopped.

His orders had been to kill the one man, not anyone else. He broke the rifle down, shoving it in the case. Then he left the room, walking quickly, taking the rear fire stairs. When he reached the door leading to the alley, he paused for a second, taking a deep breath, then shoved it open.

The limousine was exactly where it was supposed to be, engine running, rear door open and waiting for him.

Oahu

Done with Foster and confident the "simulation" was on track, Royce slipped out the back. He slowly walked down the long tunnel to the outside world. From the rack just inside the tunnel entrance, he took a set of keys for one of the Humvees parked outside. He climbed in and started the large four-wheel-drive vehicle. He drove off Fort Shafter and turned to the north, toward the ridge of mountains along Oahu's west side.

The road went from four lanes to a well-maintained two lanes to two lanes of dilapidated hardtop to dirt as he got farther north and west. He took a turn onto an overgrown dirt trail, trees and bushes on either side scraping the sides of the wide Humvee. The path wound upward, traversing back and forth along the steep side of a mountain. Several times Royce had to back up and cut the wheel hard to make the sharp turns. It had been an easier drive in a smaller Jeep. The wider wheelbase of the Humvee compelled him to edge his way in between trees lining the track. Sometimes, he reflected, improvement wasn't better.

He finally broke out of the foliage into a clearing near the crest of the hill. A Land Rover Defender was parked there. Royce smiled as he saw the other four-wheel-drive vehicle. It was painted gray and tricked out with all sorts of useful additions, such as snorkel air intake, roof rack, winch, extra gas cans, shovel, and axe. Everything the consummate four-wheel-drive enthusiast would want. He had been in that vehicle on trips all over the island. It had also worked well in picking up older female tourists for drives to remote beaches on the island, off the beaten track. The driver of the Defender was sitting on the roof rack, a pair of binoculars trained to the north. Royce got out of the Humvee and walked over.

"Have a seat," David said, tapping the metal grate next to him. He was seated on a piece of foam rubber, and he slid another onto the rack.

Royce climbed up the narrow ladder to the roof and took the indicated spot. The view was magnificent. They could see the ocean to the north and west and even the faint outline of the next island in the chain.

They sat in silence for several minutes. David finally put the binoculars down. "How's the op going?"

"Slocum is perfect for his role to run the simulation," Royce said.

David nodded. "We shoehorned him in there a year ago."

Royce wasn't surprised. Headquartered here in Hawaii, David had run operations here for the Organization for over fifty years. The two had worked together for the past two decades, ever since Royce had been recruited by David into the Organization after several tours in the military.

"Foster is flaky," Royce added. "I had to motivate him."

David laughed. "I figured he'd need a little stimulation. Short attention span." He stopped laughing. "He's expendable."

"I figured as much." That gave Royce an idea how important this Section 8 mission was: if they were willing to get rid of Foster, that was a significant cutout being removed.

"The Jolo Island thing by Delta was a major screwup," David said.

"Was it?" Royce asked, earning a hard look from his boss, then a laugh.

"Always the suspicious one," David said. "That's a good trait in this line of work."

Royce didn't expect David to give him any information on the botched raid. As a consummate professional, he would never speak "out of school."

"How's the team?" David asked.

"They have the skills needed if they all make it."

"Carefully worded answer," David noted.

"I question their motivations," Royce said.

David's eyebrows rose. "Their motivations are what we use to get them to do the mission."

"A good fighting unit is cohesive and shares the same motivations," Royce said. "This is a collection of fuck-ups and failures—and that's what we're using to get them to do this."

"It's not like they have to win World War Three," David said. "They've got one mission."

"So they're expendable?" Royce thought of Orson's comment while looking at Layla Tai's file.

"We're all expendable."

"You know what I mean."

"Yes, I do."

Royce's satphone buzzed and he pulled it out, checking the text message. "The last Section Eight member passed his test. He's on his way back to Okinawa."

"Good."

"Why'd you pick Section Eight as the name for the team?" Royce asked.

"Ever watch MASH?" David asked. "We need to keep our sense of humor."

Silence settled over the clearing once more. The two were used to their roundabout discussions. But in a world where secrecy ruled supreme, they both enjoyed their time together. It was as close to a real conversation about the job they had devoted their life to that either man was ever going to have with someone they wouldn't immediately kill afterward.

Royce finally got down to business. "Why am I here?"

"To run the op," David said.

"I'm the field agent. You run the ops."

"Not anymore." David reached into the pocket of his khaki shirt and pulled out a postcard. It showed a tropical beach with a beautiful woman in a skimpy bikini.

"No shit?" Royce had known this day was coming, but he'd never dwelt on it.

"No shit," David echoed.

"When?"

"In a couple of days. Which is why you're here. This is your op. One hundred percent from this moment on out."

"Where is this?" Royce asked, pointing at the card.

"Well, that beach is Kaui," David said, "and I don't happen to know the young lady's name." He put the card away and became serious. "Of course, I'm not going to Kaui. Symbolism is what I was shooting for.

"I'd heard about this place. Where they send people like me. Out of the way. In the western Pacific. Isolated but nice. Out of harm's way, able to enjoy our last years, courtesy of the Organization, for our years of service."

"You've still got plenty of work in you," Royce protested. "You—"

David shook his head. "I'm tired, Royce. Bone tired." He grabbed the ladder and slid down to the ground. Royce followed.

David pointed to the north, where they could still see the ocean. "They came from that direction so many years ago. My brother was on this hill that morning. Eighteen years old."

David had never mentioned a brother to Royce, who had always assumed they met up here because it was remote and safe.

"Pearl Harbor?" Royce asked.

David nodded. "December seventh, 1941. We got hit hard and were surprised. Same as 9/11." David sighed. "Makes you wonder."

"About?" Royce asked.

As he expected, David changed the subject. "Everything's compartmentalized in our Organization," he said. "I know who I answer to but I don't know who he answers to. You answer to me, but I don't know who you have working for you most of the time. It's been the key to our success. Someone takes out a link, they can only go so far in either direction before they hit a dead end. It's kept me alive and it's kept you alive."

"I'm going to miss you," Royce said.

David smiled. "Thanks. You know, us meeting here—it should have never happened. I was wrong to meet you here that first time so many years ago."

"I know." Royce paused. "Then why did you?"

David looked at his friend. "Honestly? Because I was lonely. I'd been alone for thirty years running ops. I went through two wives. They thought I worked for the Department of Defense inspecting food service at military bases. Real exciting stuff. I lived a lie with them and it ended both marriages." He put his hand on Royce's shoulder. "I never lied to you. I withheld the truth a lot, but I never told you a lie."

"I know," Royce repeated. Ever since being recruited, he'd relied on David, his only contact with the Organization. In fact, the term "Organization" was what they had come up with to call the group they worked for—they had never been given an official name. Section 8 was the term that David had given him for the team for this mission, since people seemed to want to hang a label on things.

"Who do I—"

"Don't worry," David said, before he could finish the question. "The Organization will be in contact with you. Finish this mission. You know what needs to be done."

"But with you gone—"

"You'll be all right. Just do what you're ordered."

David pulled his car keys out, indicating that the meeting was over. Royce walked with his mentor to the Defender, stood by the door as David got in and started the engine.

David rolled down the window. "I'll leave this—" he tapped the steering wheel—"in the parking lot at Kaneohe Air Station. You've got your keys. Take good care of her."

"I'll . . ." Royce wasn't sure what to say.

David reached out the window and gripped his forearm. "Be careful. There are always wheels turning within wheels."

With that, he let go and drove off, leaving Royce standing alone in the clearing.

Tokyo

The Black Wind Society of the Yakuza was controlled by a middle-age man who looked like he would be comfortable standing behind the counter of the local pharmacy, smiling at customers and dispensing medicines to make them feel better. Atio Kasama had a slight smile almost permanently entrenched on his face, a look that had disarmed many he'd come in contact with over the years—to their great disadvantage, for Kasama was anything but a happy or pleasant man.

He harbored dark thoughts and ambitions, and had ever since watching his father, a strict disciplinarian who ran the family with an iron hand, butcher his mother with a knife, and then commit suicide—after tying him to a tree in their small backyard in suburban Tokyo many years ago. Kasama spent eight hours getting himself free of his father's knots, all the while watching the bodies of his parents go into rigor mortis in front of him and their blood coagulate in the mud that had formed underneath.

Even at that age, traumatized by what he'd witnessed, he knew he did not want what was going to come next if he stayed. His parents had been only children in their families, so he would become a ward of the state, an institution he saw as simply a much larger version of his father. As he worked his way free of the bonds, he decided that for the rest of his life he would make his own rules and live his life his own way.

He'd escaped from the knots and the dead household and disappeared into the Tokyo underworld. Subsequently, he learned the reason for his father's despair—he had owed a large debt to a bookie who worked for the Yakuza. Kasama went to visit the bookie—not to wreak vengeance, as one might suppose, but rather, to learn. He considered his father weak for giving up to a force outside of himself, and he wanted to understand such power. So he learned the trade of exploiting the weakness of gambling in others—others like his father. He also learned how to exploit other weaknesses in people, in the form of running prostitutes, lending money, and dealing illegal drugs.

By the time he was eighteen, Kasama had already

made his mark in the criminal underworld. Then the Black Wind had come calling. It brought him into its fold and gave him the security he had never known within his own family. His determination never to give in to any of the vices he helped ply made him different from most of those around him and allowed him to rise quickly in the ranks. Added to that was a ruthlessness that had no boundaries. He would do whatever his superiors demanded of him, because he knew it was the quickest way to get to the point where he would be the one giving the orders.

He became the right-hand man to the head of the Black Wind over six years ago, and when his boss passed away in his sleep from a heart attack, Kasama assumed power, just one year ago. There had been a few squeaks of protest from others high in the organization, but he'd crushed those squeaks with direct and violent action, brooking no dissent to his rule. There were even rumors that the heart attack had not occurred naturally. Kasama knew the truth, which was that he had nothing to do with the death, but he allowed the rumor to circulate unchecked, since fear was the most effective tool for keeping his people in line.

Now he was in his armored limousine and on his way to an afternoon meeting with some rich industrialists at a location they had designated near the port of Tokyo. He was not happy. He had inherited a problem from his predecessor: nine rich businessmen who used the Black Wind's darker talents in some of their shadier negotiations around the world. His predecessor had made the deal in exchange for political influence and money, but somehow—Kasama wasn't quite sure when it happened—the balance of power had shifted too far in the businessmen's favor.

This past month he had gotten involved in brokering some sort of deal between this group and the Abu Sayef guerrillas in the Philippines. There had been similar dealings in the past, most of the time over the return of hostages taken by the guerrillas. Kasama usually sent people with the money to negotiate the release, and in the process kept a generous broker's fee. But this last encounter with the Abu Sayef had been different.

He sent a man with a message, and the reply had been a slap in the face to the Black Wind. Kasama watched the DVD of the killing of his man just once. He'd had it explained to him that the man was given some sort of virus that slowly killed him. He understood the message because he understood the old men with whom he was working: many of them had been involved in Unit 731 during the Second World War. The name of that infamous unit made even Kasama think twice about who he was dealing with.

So when the limousine pulled up to the nondescript warehouse where he was to meet some of the old men, he waited for a few moments, as three sport utility vehicles with tinted glass pulled in, one in front of his car, two behind. His men. Armed to the teeth. They were in an alley next to the port. Warehouses lined the alley and all the doors were shut. There was no one in sight.

It bothered Kasama that he had to make such a show of force for a meeting. It was a loss of face. But the DVD had made an impression on top of his feelings about those who had once been part of Unit 731. Something was going on, something he was not clued in to, and that bothered him more than the loss of face and made him wary. It also bothered him that his chief bodyguard had not been there to meet him. That was most unusual, and Kasama planned on severely disciplining the man—another finger removed would be a fitting punishment.

He remained in the car as a man got out of each SUV and took up position near the doors of the appointed place. They had automatic weapons, which they openly brandished. Kasama had never been here before. However, he'd met with the old men before in such out of the way places several times.

One of the men tried the door. It did not budge. Kasama frowned as he watched through the armored side window of his limousine. Who did these people think they were?

His cell phone rang and he flipped it open. "Yes?"

It was one of his assistants, informing him that his chief bodyguard had not shown up because he was dead, gunned down in the streets. Kasama snapped the phone shut.

"Take me back," he ordered his current bodyguard, who relayed the order to the driver.

At that moment at each end of the street, container carriers that serviced the port appeared. Each one had a container held high in its crane, and the heavy objects were dropped to the ground, blocking both ends. The sound of metal thudding on pavement echoed through the alley.

Kasama sat back in his seat and took a deep breath as his bodyguard screamed orders into his radio. He knew it was already too late. It was a strange experience, realizing he would soon be dead. The only other time he'd felt like this was the interim between his father stabbing his mother to death and using the knife on his own stomach. Kasama had never understood why his father didn't kill him too.

A rocket-propelled grenade streaked into the alley, and one of the SUVs exploded, showering the narrow space with metal and body parts. Then a second SUV was hit, and Kasama caught a glimpse of the rocket being fired from the rooftop just before it hit. Everyone was piling out of the third SUV, firing at the rooftops.

The limousine jerked forward, the driver trying to make them a moving target within the confines of the kill zone. There were four sharp, loud cracks, and then the sound of thousands of steel ball bearings splattering against the side of the limousine. A series of claymore mines had been hidden along both sides of the alley, and their effect upon detonation was to kill every man who was outside. Their riddled corpses were splattered about the alley, and the limousine jerked as the driver ran over one of them.

An effective combination, Kasama thought as he was thrown against his seat belt when the driver threw the limo into reverse. Someone had anticipated possible defensive reactions. He was almost curious to see what would come next. His head bodyguard thrust out a spare submachine gun toward him; he looked at it, then shook his head. Enough face had been lost.

"Stop," Kasama ordered.

The limousine came to a halt. The frightened driver looked over his shoulder to the rear. His bodyguard stared at Kasama in confusion. The confusion turned to fear as Kasama reached for the door handle.

"Sir! You cannot."

Kasama ignored him. He pushed the heavy door open and stepped out of the armored car. He could smell the distinctive odors of explosives and human viscera. He slowly turned, looking about, trying to see his enemies. His body was tense, expecting a bullet to impact at any second, but all was suddenly quiet.

He spotted no one. His bodyguard exited the car, weapon in hand, and was promptly killed as a bullet from a hidden sniper hit him between the eyes, taking half his head with it as passed through. The limo driver took that as his cue and accelerated away, leaving Kasama, even though there was no escape route. The car made it about forty feet before rockets from either side of the alley hit, almost ripping it in two.

Kasama folded his arms and stood tall.

A door across from him opened up and a figure stepped out, a samurai sword in hand. Kasama's eyes widened as he made out the feminine body outline underneath the black one-piece suit. The ultimate insult.

CHAPTER 8

Okinawa

The Humvee that had picked Vaughn up at the airfield
came out of the tunnel into an open chamber where
several other vehicles were parked, including three
more Humvees. Various mounds of supplies were
stacked here and there. The driver still had not said a
word to him, indeed had not looked at him once, either
in the rearview mirror or by turning around. As soon as
the engine was turned off, as if on cue, the door to the
right swung open and people began stepping out, all
wearing sterile camouflage fatigues. Vaughn slowly
got out of his Humvee, and as soon as he was clear, it
departed, back the way it had come.

My new team, he thought as he looked at them.

Several things struck him right away about his new
teammates. First, one was female. A slender woman of

Japanese descent with dark hair shorn tight against her skull and a white bandage on her forehead. One of the men was Korean. Vaughn had served long enough in the Far East to tell the ethnic differences among the races. Another was African-American. The other two were Caucasian, one a tall man with graying hair, the other short and powerfully built, with what appeared to be a permanent scowl on his face. And they all had the aura that Special Operations personnel carried. A sense of confidence without a need to press it upon anyone.

The short man stepped forward. "I'm the team leader. Name's Orson." Only five and a half feet tall, Orson looked like a human fireplug. "I spent some time in the SEALs," he said vaguely. "Including Team Six."

Vaughn knew that Team Six was the SEAL version of Delta Force—an elite counterterrorist unit. He'd worked with elements of Team Six several times on training missions but had never met Orson.

Orson turned to the others. "Gentlemen—and lady," he said. "Our latest and last addition to the team. Vaughn, formerly of Delta Force."

The "formerly" resonated in Vaughn's ears. For some reason, the way Orson said it made the finality of his decision strike home. There was no going back. He'd heard of people who, rumor said, had been recruited for covert units and then simply disappeared into the world of black ops. Vaughn also noted that Orson had not used his rank—another indicator that things were going to be very different. He followed as Orson led him down the line, introducing his new teammates.

"Hayes," Orson said, stopping in front of the black man. "He spent most of his childhood in the Philippine Islands, so he is our area expert. Also qualified on weapons and demolitions."

As Vaughn shook the man's hand, he had to wonder why his Delta Team hadn't had access to Hayes as an area specialist. They certainly could have used more intelligence about the setup on Jolo. He also noted that there was a tremor in Hayes's hand, so slight it was almost unnoticeable. Almost.

"Vaughn," Hayes said, the greeting noncommittal. He stepped back with a glance at the Japanese woman next to him.

"Tai." Orson said her name so sharply that Vaughn was uncertain for a moment if it was her name or some expression, but the doubt disappeared as she put her hand out.

"Welcome to the team, Vaughn."

"Tai is expert in demolitions, but her particular expertise is in intelligence and counterintelligence with a specialty on terrorism, particularly in the Pacific Rim."

Orson had already moved on to a tall gray-haired man. Before he could say anything, the man stuck his hand out. "Hey. Sinclair's my name. Spent some time in Fifth Group and the schoolhouse at Bragg teaching at SWC." He pronounced it "swick," which was what Special Forces people called the Special Warfare Center at Fort Bragg.

"Nice to meet you," Vaughn said, feeling a bit strange. Every other time he'd gone to a new unit, he'd at least known someone there, since the U.S. Special Operations community was still a relatively small one. Here he had no advance intelligence on these people and had to assume, or hope, they had none on him. He'd never met Sinclair, as far as he could remember, but Special Forces had grown into a large community in the nineties, and once he was in Delta Force, he'd little interaction with the Special Forces groups.

"Kasen," Royce said, stopping in front of the Korean. "Formerly of the First Ranger Battalion."

Kasen's grip was strong and the skin rough, toughened; Vaughn assumed it was from a rigorous martial arts routine. Kasen said nothing, staring at him with no apparent emotion, but Vaughn felt a coldness in the man. Vaughn had gone to Ranger school but never served in one of the battalions. He had a lot of respect for the soldiers who did, since they were the most elite infantry in the U.S. Army and perhaps the world. But there was a much different attitude between soldiers in the Ranger battalions and those in Special Forces: the former were more action oriented and thought in the short term, while the latter tended to be more cerebral and considered long-term missions.

"We're glad you're finally here so we can proceed," Orson said, giving Vaughn a cold look. With that, he spun about and headed back to the door.

"Hey," Sinclair said, slapping Vaughn on the back, "I'll give you a hand with your gear."

Orson led the other three inside, leaving Vaughn with Sinclair to haul the contents of the bundle that had been left there from his previous time in the tunnel.

"Friendly fucking lot, aren't they?" Sinclair said as he hoisted a duffel bag.

"You been here long?" Vaughn asked as he threw one strap of his rucksack over his shoulder and they headed for the door.

"Six hours," Sinclair said. "I was the third one here. I guess we've been waiting on you to get the show going."

"So everyone is new to the team?"

Sinclair shrugged. "I am. You are. You'll have to ask the others."

"Did you have to—" Vaughn hesitated, not sure how to phrase it.

"Pass a test?" Sinclair nodded. "Yeah, but we ain't supposed to talk about that. Everything's a big secret here. Hush-hush and all that good shit."

Vaughn had wanted to know how long Sinclair had been in Section 8, but he knew better than to ask too many questions right away. There would be time for that later. Sinclair's answer, though, did indicate this was a newly assembled team, which meant he wasn't the outsider. That was both good and bad: good, because he wouldn't have to be accepted by those who had already formed bonds; bad, because it meant they all would have to quickly form the bonds of trust and training that the upcoming mission was going to require. The thought of going on a mission with a group of people who had just been thrown together didn't sit well with Vaughn.

They stepped through, and the steel door slammed behind them. Vaughn looked around. A typical setup for isolation. Plywood boards with maps mounted on them along with satellite imagery and lists of supplies. Two more doors at the end that Vaughn assumed led to their bunks and latrine. "Functional" was the word that applied.

The other three Section 8 members were seated in folding chairs, Orson standing in front of them, waiting with impatience. Vaughn and Sinclair dropped the gear and sat down in the two remaining folding chairs. Orson had a remote in his hand, and a multimedia projector had been set up, attached to a laptop on the lectern in front of him. Orson took a thumb drive out of his coat pocket and plugged it into the USB port of the laptop. He worked the keyboard for a few moments, bringing up whatever he was going to show on the projector.

"Our mission," he began, "is to kill the leader of the Abu Sayef, a man named Rogelio Abayon." The face of a middle-age man appeared on the screen over Orson's right shoulder.

Vaughn felt a surge of adrenaline as Orson confirmed what Royce had promised—this was the real deal. No more pussyfooting around. No more reacting. They were going to take the war to the bad guy.

Orson tapped the screen. "This is the last photograph we have of Abayon, and it was taken over twenty-five years ago."

"No one's seen this guy in twenty-five years?" Sinclair asked with disbelief.

"No one's taken a photograph of Abayon in that time," Orson clarified. "He's been seen, but rarely. It appears he hasn't left Jolo Island in all those years. And outsiders aren't welcome on Jolo."

Orson looked at Hayes, a not too subtle prompt.

The black man nodded. "I saw Abayon on Jolo once, eight years ago. Only in passing. From what I managed to pick up, he has a hiding place on Hono Mountain, which pretty much dominates the entire island. There's supposed to be a set of tunnels built up there connecting natural caves. Only his closest people know where the entrance is."

Tai spoke up. "If Jolo is controlled by the Abu Sayef, what were you doing there?" she asked Hayes.

"My father was in the U.S. Navy. My mother was Filipino. I grew up mostly in Manila, but when I was twelve I—" He paused, as if figuring out how to say it. "—I traveled around the islands a lot with my friends. There are a lot of people like me, people of mixed race, in the islands. So although I don't pass as a native, since I speak the language and know the ways of the land, I can go pretty much anywhere."

"Eight years ago you were on Jolo?" Tai prompted.

Hayes nodded. "Yes."

She waited but he didn't elaborate.

"Your teen years seem long gone," Tai finally said. "What were you doing there?"

Hayes stared at her. "I was working."

"Doing?" she pressed.

Vaughn glanced at Orson and noted that he wasn't stepping in, giving tacit approval to Tai's line of questioning. Vaughn had noted that while Orson had given the background of certain members of the team, for others he'd been rather quiet.

Hayes didn't blink. "I was negotiating the transfer of funds for illicit drugs. Does that make you feel better?"

"No," Tai said. "You're a drug dealer."

"Was," Hayes said. "And do you want to know who was supplying me with the money to buy?" He didn't wait for an answer, and Vaughn half expected the answer that was coming, based on his experiences in Afghanistan. "The CIA. They wanted intelligence on the Abu Sayef and they recruited me to get it for them. What do they call it? Humint. Human intelligence. That was me. Of course they denied it, said I was just a drug dealer."

"Doing it for money," Tai said.

"What?" Hayes asked. "You do it for free?"

"I do it for my country," Tai said.

"So you hand your paycheck back?" Hayes asked.

Sinclair got them back on track. "When was the last time you were on Jolo?"

"Two years ago," Hayes said.

"Shit," Sinclair said. He looked at Orson. "And we're supposed to trust this guy?"

"Yes," Orson said. "Hayes has his reasons for being here. As you all do."

Sinclair wasn't satisfied. "So we're to take your word for it?"

Orson eyed him. "Would you like to explain to the others why you're here?"

Sinclair glared at Orson but didn't respond, which was answer enough. Vaughn shifted in his seat and picked up the sense of unease that Orson's question to Sinclair had generated in all of them.

"But you didn't see Abayon?" Tai asked Hayes.

"Only in passing, as I said."

"If I may continue." Orson made it an order, not a question. "As you all know, the Abu Sayef were recently responsible for the deaths of eighteen tourists of various nationalities."

Vaughn once more shifted uncomfortably in his chair. But no one turned to stare at him, so he had to believe they didn't know his role in the recent debacle on Jolo.

"With the exposure of American involvement in the failed raid on the compound on Jolo Island," Orson went on, "the normal covert, albeit unofficial, channels of going after Abayon and his organization are closed. No other organization dare touch this, and the Philippine government, which has jurisdiction, wants nothing more to do with Abayon, the Abu Sayef, or Jolo Island. We believe they have negotiated an informal truce."

Hayes snorted. "They've had an informal truce for a long time."

Orson continued. "Unfortunately, we have intelligence that the Abu Sayef have been making contact with various other terrorist organizations, including Al Qaeda. Such a linkage is unacceptable. There are also vague but substantiated reports that the Abu Sayef are planning a major terrorist operation against the United States. Therefore, we are taking the fight to the terrorists, not waiting for them to bring it to American soil again."

"Who is we?" Tai asked.

"Our team designation is Section Eight," Orson said, deliberately misinterpreting her question. "We have an AST team for support but they have no idea—nor should they—what our mission is. All requests for support will be encoded and passed through the AST, who will coordinate whatever you need.

"Questions?"

"Who is we?" Tai repeated. She amplified the question. "Who do we work for? If we're Section Eight, what is the designation of the organization we fall under?"

"Who we work for," Orson said, "is none of your business. Remember, an essential part of this is deniability."

"So what do we say if captured?" Tai asked.

"Don't get captured," Orson said.

Tai was not giving up easily. "If our bodies are found, what will be the cover story?"

"We'll be operating sterile with no indications of our nationality," Orson said. "We won't need a cover story."

Vaughn wasn't sure he bought that, but Tai seemed to have exhausted that line of questioning in the face of Orson's stone wall.

Kasen, the ex-Ranger, raised his hand and Orson acknowledged him with a nod. "Will killing Abayon destroy the Abu Sayef?

"Abayon founded the Abu Sayef after World War Two. He's the only leader it's ever had. Our estimate is that without him, the organization will splinter into ineffectual pieces that will spend most of their energy fighting among themselves. Without Abayon they'll be vulnerable. At that point it might be possible to get the Philippine government to take a stronger role.

"There is intelligence there"—Orson pointed at a row of laptop computers—"on both Abayon and his organization. As much as we know, which isn't much. One thing to know is that during World War Two Abayon fought with the Filipino guerrillas against the Japanese."

"So he was on our side," Vaughn said. He hadn't even heard of Abayon during the previous isolation for the raid. "Just like Ho Chi Minh was during the same war."

Orson didn't rise to the bait. "Gentlemen—and lady—we need to start planning."

"Is there a time limit on this?" Tai asked.

"We have five days to come up with a plan," Orson said. "We'll brief-back then and either get a go or you start over. So let's make it a good plan."

Like we'd want to come up with a bad one, Vaughn thought.

Orson scanned the other five section members as if assessing them with that simple look. "Tai, you are intelligence. There's a taped briefing on the Abu Sayef in the computer—I want you to distill out critical points in two hours. Hayes, you assist her with what you know about both the group and the locale, and also start giving me ways to infiltrate and exfiltrate Jolo Island and an idea exactly where our target is.

"Sinclair. Weapons. Find out what everyone is familiar and comfortable with. But I want at least two heavy guns—Squad Automatic Weapons. One shotgun for breaching if needed. Also, any trained snipers?"

Vaughn raised his hand, as did the Ranger, Kasen. "All right, draw two sniper weapons just in case we take that path. Kasen, explosives and mines. Vaughn, work on how we're getting from here to there and back again. Tai, you also have medical training, correct?"

The woman nodded. Vaughn had noted that other than giving her expertise, Orson had not divulged her background during the introductions.

"Good. Draw medical kit and make sure you check everyone, blood types, personal gear, and all that. Vaughn, you help Tai on targeting. I want you to lock down Abayon's position."

Orson glanced at his watch. "We will gather back here in two hours for a briefing on Abayon and the Abu Sayef. Tomorrow I want initial thoughts on targeting, tactical possibilities, infiltration and exfiltration."

The six scattered to the various equipment and sources of intelligence in the room. Vaughn logged onto one of the laptops set up on a plywood table and began searching through the classified database, looking for information about Abayon's hiding place.

He was engrossed in the data when the sound of two voices raised in confrontation interrupted him. He immediately recognized Tai's. Looking up, he saw her and the Ranger, Kasen, standing face-to-face, inside each other's personal space.

"What's the problem?" Vaughn asked as he stepped over. Sinclair was watching with interest from his position, making no move. Hayes also seemed to want to have nothing do with it. Orson was nowhere to be seen, having gone out to coordinate with the ASTs.

"The little girl wants one of the machine guns,"

Kasen said. "I told her to leave the big guns to the men."

"I can handle a SAW," Tai insisted. "We're a team. I—"

"Why not just carry a submachine gun?" Kasen asked, making it a taunt. "Something small and delicate, like you."

Tai's left hand was a blur, the knife edge of it striking Kasen in the neck. The Ranger staggered back, coughing hard. He wasn't off balance long, going into the attack, hands a blur of blows aimed at Tai. Vaughn was impressed as she fended off every one of them with blocks, twisting and turning, getting inside Kasen's range and hitting him two hard blows in the solar plexus, doubling him over, before she skipped back out of range.

"You bitch," Kasen cursed as he slowly straightened and considered his adversary. "You were lucky."

"I don't think so," Vaughn said, stepping between the two.

"I don't need you to intervene," Tai said. "Let the pig come at me. I'll teach him the meaning of pain."

"As you said," Vaughn said, "we're teammates. We—"

He was caught off guard as Kasen leapt past him, going for Tai's throat. Kasen was left grasping air as Tai ducked underneath him, then spun about, her left boot toe leading, striking Kasen on the side of his head and dropping him unconscious to the floor.

"Shit," was Sinclair's take on the TKO. "Seems to me the lady wants the machine gun."

"Seems to me we ought to give it to her," Vaughn said as he knelt and checked Kasen. The Ranger opened his eyes, the pupils unfocused for several moments, then realization set in and he tried to jerk to his feet.

"Enough," Vaughn said, putting an arm across his chest.

"What's going on?" Orson demanded, his short bulk filling the open door.

"A slight disagreement over equipment," Vaughn said, helping Kasen to his feet and glancing at Tai, who stood perfectly still without saying a word.

"If we kill each other," Orson said, "there won't be much of a mission. Back to work."

Vaughn helped Kasen to his place, then went over to Tai.

"I don't need you to help me," Tai hissed.

"We're teammates," Vaughn said again. "We're supposed to help each other. You going to be able to work with Kasen?"

"He's a pig," Tai said. "As long as he does his job and doesn't insult me again, I'll have no problem."

"What martial art was that?" Vaughn asked. "I didn't recognize some of the blocks."

"Something my father taught me," Tai said vaguely. She looked at him. "You were on that team that screwed up the hostage rescue, weren't you?"

"Yes." Vaughn waited for more.

"Interesting," Tai said, a surprising response. "Royce approached you after that, right?"

Vaughn nodded.

"An undercover team of terrorist hunters?" Tai asked.

"Yes."

"Do you believe him?"

"Why shouldn't I? We're here."

"Hmm," Tai mused.

"How did he recruit you?"

"How is not important," she said. "*Why* is."

"Then why?"

"Because of my sister."

Vaughn felt like he was pulling teeth to get anything out of these people. "What about your sister?"

"She was killed in the attack on the Pentagon. He promised me vengeance against the Abu Sayef, who we believe are allied with Al Qaeda."

"That was years ago," Vaughn said. "You've been working for Royce all this time?"

"No. He approached me two days ago. There was something else."

"And that is?"

"I was accused of prisoner abuse in Iraq."

"And you just passed a test to get on the team?" Vaughn asked.

Tai's head jerked and she reached up and placed her fingers lightly on the bandage. "Yes. And you?" Her eyes met his, and they were locked in a stare that lasted several seconds, each appraising the other.

Finally Vaughn nodded. "Yes." He broke the stare and looked at the other members of the team, wondering what in their past had caused them to be recruited and what they had just done recently in order to be allowed on the team.

His thoughts were interrupted by Orson. "Briefings in one hour."

Then the team leader left the room once more.

"So everyone here is new to this team?" Vaughn asked Tai, trying to confirm what he had suspected upon entering isolation.

She shrugged. "As far as I know. Makes sense if they want to keep it covert."

"But Royce told me that this was a one-way ticket,"

Vaughn pointed out. "We'll never go back to our previous assignments."

"And?"

"Do you think we're the first ones ever to get booked on this kind of thing?" he asked her.

That gave Tai pause. "What are you trying to say?"

"I don't know," Vaughn admitted frankly. "But . . ."

"But . . . ?"

Vaughn looked at the photo of Rogelio Abayon. Eyes on the target—it was an axiom of planning. "Let's get this son of a bitch."

Tai nodded. "That's the idea."

Tokyo, Japan

The death of a Yakuza boss was big news. But for the moment that news was being held very tightly. Both ends of the alley where Kasama had been killed were still sealed by the containers. The police had used ladders to climb over the trailers blocking one end and then get down into the alley. Upon ascertaining who the victims were, a special police unit had been called. The head of that unit, working on a classified alert bulletin he had been given just a few days before, then made another call, this one to the Public Security Intelligence Agency, the Japanese version of the CIA.

Within fifteen minutes an unmarked helicopter appeared overhead and landed as close as possible. Two old men got off. They brushed their way past the police under the escort of the head of the special unit. Laboriously, they clambered up the ladder and then down another ladder into the alley. They walked up to Kasama's body, ignoring the smoke still drifting out of the SUVs and the other bodies and body parts littered about.

The Yakuza boss's head was resting on his stomach, neatly severed from his body. His dead hands cradled the head, as if protecting it. Lifeless eyes stared at his feet. The two men stood there for several moments, not speaking.

The head of the police special unit on the Yakuza cleared his throat, then said, "We do not think this was done by a rival faction. There have been no reports or rumors. Someone would be boasting of it if they had done it. And the preparations"—he indicated the three destroyed vehicles, the two trailers, the bodies—"we would have gotten some wind of it if some other part of the Yakuza were involved."

" 'Wind,' " one of the old men repeated. "The Black Wind blows no more," he added, nodding toward Kasama's body.

His partner turned toward the policeman. "This is our problem. You are correct—it is not internal Yakuza conflict."

"What is it?" the policeman asked. "Who did this?"

The first old man considered the question for several moments, as if trying to decide how much to say, then shrugged. "We don't know. That's why we're here. But we know the Black Wind has been involved in things that extend beyond the borders of our country. Far beyond. And strong as Kasama and his organization were, there was something stronger than them. As we can obviously see."

The other man turned to the policeman. "You can go now."

The policeman beat a hasty retreat.

"Should we call the group?" one asked the other.

He nodded. "Let them in on the confusion."

Okinawa

It had been a long day, the team getting slowly into gear processing the intelligence they had been given. Each member had watched the briefing from Hawaii on the Abu Sayef, and Tai had added a little to it.

Now Vaughn lay on the hard bunk staring up at the rock. He could hear the breathing of his teammates, each different. Orson snored, which Vaughn noted—a potentially dangerous thing on a mission. Tai, on the next bunk, was motionless and her breathing so shallow he had wondered for a few moments if she'd died in her sleep. Kasen tossed and turned, occasionally muttering, another trait that was not good if they had to go on an extended mission. Sinclair seemed the most normal of the bunch, sleeping soundly and without much noise.

Hayes was not asleep. Nor was he in his bunk. Vaughn had watched him get up and make his way to the latrine in the darkness, stepping carefully to avoid making any noise. But even with the latrine door shut, Vaughn could hear the muffled retching and coughing.

After ten minutes, Hayes crept back into the room and slid into his bunk. Vaughn turned his head. And saw Tai looking right at him, the dim light glinting off the whites of her eyes. They held each other's gaze for several moments, then she closed her eyes.

Vaughn did the same. But sleep was a long time coming. And before it did come, he heard Hayes make two more trips to the latrine.

CHAPTER 9

Okinawa

"Hono Mountain, on this side," Vaughn said, pointing at the imagery tacked to the plywood. He had managed a few hours sleep, but got up before dawn, poring through the intelligence on Abayon and Jolo Island.

Orson stared at him silently for several seconds. Vaughn was behind the podium, the rest of the team arrayed about in their seats facing him.

"That's it?" Orson finally asked.

"There's not much intelligence on the Abu Sayef on Jolo," Vaughn said, which was an understatement. "Reversing the videotape that was taken of the failed raid indicates it was shot from the mountain." Vaughn turned to a satellite image of the mountain and marked out a large area with a pointer. "Somewhere on the southeast side."

Orson turned to Hayes. "You have any idea where Abayon hides out?"

"Like I said yesterday, in the mountain," Hayes said. He shrugged. "No one except those in Abayon's inner circle are allowed anywhere close to the mountain. What I heard when I was on the island was that there are tunnels and chambers throughout it and that's where his lair is. And he almost never comes out. That's why there is no recent photo of him."

Orson got up and walked to the imagery. "It's a big damn mountain. And the area is crawling with guerrillas. Not only do we need to pinpoint how to get into the tunnel system, but we also have to figure out how to kill him once we're in. Whether it's a shot to the head or taking out the whole complex."

"There's a third issue," Sinclair said.

"And what is that?" Orson demanded.

"Getting out."

Vaughn smiled but didn't say anything. He could tell that Sinclair had indeed served in Special Forces. It was always an issue on A-Teams that higher command had great plans for getting a team into its target area but was always vague on getting them back out.

"We'll get out," Orson said.

"That's about as specific as where the entrance is to the tunnel complex," Sinclair pointed out, "and you weren't too happy with that."

"One thing at a time," Orson said. "First, we have to pin down exactly where Abayon is. According to everything we have and our asset"—he nodded at Hayes—"he's in the tunnel complex. So we have to figure out how to get in there."

"Why?" Tai asked. She didn't wait for an answer. "If we can figure out how air is pumped into that place, we could gas everyone in there. Wipe them out without entering. Get Abayon and a bunch of his people in one attack."

Orson shook his head. "We have to confirm that Abayon is dead. Doing what you suggest won't accomplish that."

Tai frowned but didn't say anything more. Vaughn also wasn't satisfied with Orson's answer. If they were so sure that Abayon was in the complex, then what she'd suggested made sense. Yes, they wouldn't be able to bring back Abayon's head, so to speak, for confirmation, but the odds would be that they had succeeded. He also knew, though, that ever since 9/11 and the failure to nail Bin Laden, there was a strong emphasis on having bodies in hand rather than best guesses on termination. The last thing anyone wanted was to report Abayon dead and then have him pop up somewhere.

"What about thermal imagery?" Orson asked.

Vaughn nodded. "I ordered an intelsat to do some shots when it goes overhead. We should be getting those in shortly."

"The other thing to factor in," Hayes said, "is that Abayon has money. Lots of it. He's put a lot of it into the infrastructure on the island and also bought a lot of space from the Philippine government with bribes. When I was on the island, I heard rumors of large piles of gold that Abayon had from the war."

"Yamashita's gold," Tai said.

"Whose gold?" Vaughn asked.

"Gold is not an issue here," Orson said. He tapped the photo tacked to the plywood. "Abayon is the target." He turned to Tai. As he was about to speak, there was a tap at the door.

Vaughn went over and opened it. One of the ASTs

was there with a large manila envelope with a red top secret seal. Vaughn took it and went back to the podium. He ripped it open and looked at the thermal imaging while the others waited impatiently.

"The complex must be deep," he said as he scanned the pictures. "There's not much . . ." He paused as he noted something. "There's a hot spot on the side of the mountain. Northwest side. Looks like it might be a ventilator exhaust, since hot air is flowing out of it."

"Just one?" Tai asked. "A complex as big as what were talking about should have more than that."

Vaughn shook his head. "According to some historical records I found, there were originally numerous caves and caverns on Hono, which the natives used hundreds of years ago. So we have to assume that the complex is mostly natural, with some artificial enhancement—cross tunnels, enlarging of natural chambers, and so on. I checked online with an expert on underground bunkers and he told me that in such a situation it's possible that the complex doesn't need an extensive air system, that air might flow through fissures and other natural openings. They could place generators for power in caverns that have the most air flow to cross ventilate.

"There's even the possibility," he continued, "that used air and exhaust could be pumped out into this river"—he tapped the imagery, indicating the valley in front of Hono Mountain—"and be dispersed in the water. So we're lucky to get at least one hot spot."

Kasen spoke up for the first time. "Pretty sophisticated setup for a bunch of terrorists."

Hayes cleared his throat and everyone turned toward him. "The rumor is that the original complex was built by the Japanese during World War Two."

Vaughn frowned "I didn't find anything on that."

Hayes shrugged. "That's just the rumor on the island. I never saw anything either to substantiate it. An old guy I met did speak, though, about Japanese soldiers killing some of the villagers, but he said they weren't around very long."

"If the Japs initially built this thing," Sinclair said, "any chance of getting their blueprints or whatever?"

"I found no record of the Japanese building anything," Vaughn said. He tapped a very thick folder. "The NSA, CIA, and various other agencies have spent a lot of time putting this material together, and there's nothing in it on that."

"So all we have is one hot spot and a big mountain?" Sinclair asked. He got up and went to the map. "Nice talk, but there's six of us, and we have to get onto this island, find this old man hidden in a tunnel complex we don't even know how to get into, kill him, and then— even though you don't seem overly concerned about it—get back off the island and home without getting our heads blown off. We could use a little help here."

"We have to find him ourselves," Orson said.

Vaughn glanced at Tai. He found it curious that Orson had cut her off so abruptly earlier about the Yamashita gold thing, and that he also didn't seem interested in the Japanese connection. Even though it was long ago, it made sense that the Japanese might have done something on the island.

"And how do you propose finding him?" Sinclair asked.

"We send in a recon team ahead of the target window to pinpoint Abayon's location," Orson said. "To check that hot spot and see if it's a way in."

Since it seemed that his part of the briefing was

over, Vaughn went and took the seat that Orson had vacated. He glanced around the room. They were all considering the suggestion.

Sinclair was the first to voice an objection. "If this island is run by the Abu Sayef, then it's going to be hard not to get discovered and give the enemy a warning, never mind losing the recon team."

Orson held up a hand. "We're getting ahead of ourselves here. Let's back up and stick with the original briefing plan. We've determined we can't pinpoint our target—Abayon—so we'll have to come back to that." He turned to Hayes. "It's your island. I tasked you with infiltration and exfiltration planning."

Hayes stood. He ran a hand along his upper lip, wiping off a thin sheen of sweat, then went to the maps. "Either into the water or the jungle is the best way. You want to avoid the villages, naturally. Any strangers will immediately be reported to the Abu Sayef. And none of you are going to pass for locals."

"We land in water," Vaughn noted, "it's a bit of a walk to the mountain."

Hayes nodded. "True, but the closer you come down to the mountain, the more eyes will be watching. One thing the Abu Sayef are constantly warned about during their training is to watch the sky, that the government troops would come in helicopters or by parachute from a low flying airplane. You can be sure that there are antiaircraft missiles hidden somewhere on that mountain."

Vaughn remembered the RPG that had killed his brother-in-law. Things would have been much worse if the terrorists had used surface-to-air missiles. For this mission, he had entertained thoughts of landing right on top of the mountain and working their way down to find the entrance. Military dogma dictated taking the high ground.

"You said a low flying plane," Vaughn noted. "I think we can get in at night using HAHO with offset." He was referring to a high altitude, high opening parachute operation. It was a procedure where the plane flew very high, sometimes at an altitude of over 20,000 feet with the jumpers on oxygen, exiting at that height. The aircraft would not only be high, but offset laterally from the drop zone. After exiting the aircraft, the jumpers would immediately deploy their parachutes and then "fly" them to the drop zone. Offsets of ten to fifteen miles were common using such a technique, but the aircraft never got close enough either in altitude or lateral distance to raise suspicions.

Orson nodded. "HAHO definitely for the recon team. The question is, who here is qualified to do that kind of jump?"

Vaughn raised his hand. Then Tai. That was it.

"We have our recon team," Orson announced.

"When do we go?" Vaughn asked.

"As soon as we can get a plane to drop you," Orson said. He tapped the map. "You pick your drop zone. You HAHO onto the island. Check it out. Radio back to us how the rest of the team will get in. And you find Abayon. Let us know how we can get to him, and we'll do the mission prep for the actual kill. You let us know what we'll need to bring."

How about a tactical nuke? Vaughn thought. He didn't think much of the plan. It put him and Tai into enemy territory in an exposed position. "And if we're compromised?" he asked.

Orson's dead gray eyes fixed Vaughn with their gaze. "Then you're dead. Do not allow yourself to be taken alive, because we're not coming to get you, if that's what you're asking."

Vaughn took the thermal imagery and went over to the map of the island. "I say we land here," he said, tapping the very top of Hono Mountain, where there appeared to be a small clearing. "That all right with you?" he asked, looking at Tai.

She nodded. "Fine."

Orson almost seemed disappointed. "All right. I'll arrange the aircraft. You go in tonight. Get your gear ready today. The rest of you, back to work."

Fort Shafter, Hawaii

The request to send in a reconnaissance team had generated a great deal of debate among the staff officers who were working the simulation. Most were against it and argued instead that more assets be allocated. The operations officer even sent a request to the National Command Authority for more troops and some Air Force assets with greater firepower. General Slocum, part of the old school that believed in using a sledgehammer when a hammer might do, signed off on the request, adding in an appendix the alternate plan for a recon element to be sent in early to try to pinpoint Abayon's position and the attendant risks of doing so.

It only went as far as Foster's computer, which was acting as National Command Authority. He denied the request for more assets, on the grounds that the operation was to be conducted clandestinely. Then he gave the go-ahead for the reconnaissance element to be sent in. The operations officer then turned around and, after having Slocum sign it, sent the tasking for a C-130 transport to conduct the HAHO drop that night, thinking it was all part of the simulation. In fact, Foster sent this tasking with the official signature block and proper code words to the designated Air Force squadron in Okinawa.

It was a shell game, one that only Foster knew the extent of and controlled. He had his own ideas about why he was being used to do this. He assumed that he was the "cutout," the link between those doing the mission and those ordering it.

Foster wasn't naive, though. He also knew that things were done in certain ways to allow for deniability. No one would be able to prove who gave the orders. While he yearned to work for the National Security Agency, he also knew that he'd be traveling much further into the world of covert operations than while working military simulations here in Hawaii. Not that the thought bothered him. If one wanted to play in the big game, they had to be willing to take big risks. And there was also the issue of the threat the NSA representative had held over his head. He was still shaken by the revelation that the secret he had assumed was buried in the past was not only known by others, but well-documented.

When he was in college, during his senior year, the football team had been invited to a bowl game in San Diego. Two nights before the big game, Foster had gone with a group of teammates across the border into Tijuana. They'd consumed vast quantities of questionable alcohol and finally ended at the desired location: a whorehouse. The group had split up into various rooms as directed by the madam, and to his surprise, dismay, and—to be honest—titillation, he had walked into a room occupied by a young girl. A very young girl. One who not yet made it to double digits in age.

In the years since then, he'd always regretted not turning right around and walking out. But he'd been drunk, he'd been horny, and he'd been in Mexico.

And now he wondered if he'd been set up. He doubted it, given the years that had passed since with nothing happening, but when the mysterious David showed him those photos, he'd wondered.

Foster shook off his concerns as he worked both sides of the supposed simulation. He had to accept that he was on the inside now. He was what he had always aspired to be—a player—and he was getting ready to move to the big leagues. He looked out the window of his office at the Sim-Center, at all the men and women in military uniform "playing" their parts, and shook his head. They were fools, ignorant of the way the world really worked.

There was another aspect of this that told him he was already at another level. The intelligence he was forwarding to the team in isolation was not only top of the line from the NSA, CIA, and other alphabet soup organizations in the United States government, but some of it was coming from agencies that worked for foreign governments. He assumed that the NSA had tapped into these sources somehow and was coopting them.

Foster ran through the message traffic being generated on Okinawa. Most of it was mundane, the normal stuff that was to be expected from a team in isolation, and it mirrored what his computer was generating for the staff in the simulation. There were some minor differences, however. For example, the team was asking for two Squad Automatic Weapons, while the simulation had not anticipated such a request. Foster pulled that message out of the flow and sent it on to the appropriate facility on Okinawa, giving it the proper authorization from Westcom headquarters. He did the same with the request for sniper rifles and the equipment for the HAHO jump. It was almost a ballet of data, he thought, and he was into it, playing both sides with the expertise he had built up over the years. Those being tasked did as ordered, as far as supporting the mission, while those giving the orders as part of the simulation didn't know that some of the orders were actually being implemented.

Foster paused as he noted a message directed to an address he didn't recognize. He checked his database and found out it was being sent to ARPERCEN: Army Personnel Center, headquartered in Fairfax, Virginia. The message seemed innocuous enough: a request from Captain Lee Tai to be considered for an ROTC teaching slot in her next assignment. Not exactly an earth-shattering message, and one that could easily have been lost in the volume of traffic.

But it was wrong because it had nothing to do with the mission. The written instructions he'd received on the laptop had been explicit: any unusual message traffic was to be diverted to a certain address to be reviewed. He was sure there was nothing wrong with Captain Tai's request, but after his most recent encounter, he was now a big believer in following Royce's rules. Foster stopped the message and did as instructed.

As General Slocum took the podium at the front of the Sim-Center, Foster paused in his work and turned on the intercom so he could hear what the general had to say.

"People, listen up," the general began. "Apparently, the big wigs in Washington think they know how to run this operation better than we do. They've denied our request for more air power, but they have given the go-ahead for the reconnaissance element to go in tonight. Regardless of how you feel about that, I want you to support this with your best effort." Slocum paused and looked about the room. "Is that clear?"

The reply was a thunderous, "Yes, sir."

In the control room, Foster shook his head. It was as if they were still in college, playing on the team. He had left the team behind a long time ago.

Okinawa

"What is this Yamashita's gold thing you mentioned?" Vaughn asked Tai. The two of them were in the corridor outside the main isolation room, packing their rucksacks for the upcoming mission. Vaughn could tell that Tai had been on airborne missions before, because she was going through the same process he was: packing and repacking, each time leaving something out to lighten and tighten the load. You took a whole different view about what you packed when you had to carry it on your back.

For example, they were carrying a week's worth of food—just in case—even though they planned to be on the ground for only a few days. But they were cutting down the meal packages, taking out unnecessary and "heavy" items such as extra plastic spoons. To an outsider it would seem ridiculous, but it was almost a ritual of mission preparation in Special Operations. Of course, a week's worth of food for a mission was only seven meals. On the other hand, they both were going heavy on items such as ammunition.

Tai looked up from her gear, which was laid out on

a poncho liner. "General Tomoyuki Yamashita was the commander of Japanese forces in the Philippines during the Second World War. It's been well-documented that the Japanese conducted a systematic pillage of the countries they conquered during the war. They took all the riches they could get their hands on, particularly gold—the accumulated wealth of twelve Asian countries. Not only gold, but other treasures, such as pieces of art.

"There were special teams accompanying Japanese forces in the early days of the war, when the Rising Sun spread around the western Pacific Rim. They were tasked with emptying banks, treasuries, art galleries, museums, palaces—even pawnshops and private homes—of anything of value. It was a special branch of the Kempetai—the Japanese military intelligence service."

Vaughn didn't find that very surprising. He'd been to Kuwait during the first Gulf war and seen what the Iraqis had done there. Plundering was an age-old companion of military conquest. Sometimes it was done officially, and often unofficially. He knew the Nazis had done it in Europe and Russia during the Second World War, so it didn't take a great leap of logic to figure the Japanese had done it too.

"There's a lot that's not known about the entire thing," Tai continued, "but there are some facts. The overall plundering project was called *kin no yuri,* which means Golden Lily, named after a poem written by the Emperor Hirohito." She snorted. "That's one war criminal who got to skate. He professed ignorance of Golden Lily after the war and said it didn't exist. Yet his brother, Prince Chichibu, was in charge of the project. You don't think they chatted about it over a meal?

Of course, Hirohito also expressed ignorance about the rape of Nanking. Seems everyone always gets memory failure or they weren't really in charge when bad things that occurred under their watch are brought up."

"I don't get it," Vaughn said as he refolded his Gore-Tex waterproof jacket and stuffed it once more in an outside pocket on his rucksack, trying to have it take up fewer square inches of room. "Why do you think this treasure ended up in the Philippines and not Japan? Seems like the emperor would have wanted those riches close at hand."

"Because the U.S. Navy instituted a submarine blockade of Japan very early in the war," Tai explained. "Many ships heading back to the homeland were sunk, and Chichibu didn't want to take the risk of losing the treasure. It was easier—and more secure—to send the ships carrying the loot to the Philippines. The Americans were leery of sinking ships in that area because some of them carried American POWs. In fact, a couple of POW ships were accidentally sunk late in the war, with great loss of friendly life."

Vaughn considered this as Tai began loading magazines with nine-millimeter rounds for her MP-5 submachine gun. He noted her precision as she made sure each round was properly seated.

"Why do you think Orson didn't want to talk about it?" Vaughn asked.

Tai paused, bullet in one hand, magazine in the other, and looked at him. "As he said, the target—our target—is Abayon."

"But if Abayon has some of this Golden Lily treasure—"

"Listen," Tai said, cutting him off. "There's no doubt Yamashita received a lot of the Golden Lily shipments in the Philippines. Hirohito's cousin, Prince Takeda Tsuneyoshi, was stationed in the Philippines to oversee the secreting away of the treasure. Some say there were over 175 sites prepared all over the islands. No matter how good they were at secrecy, word of this leaked. Some have been found. But the rumor is a couple of the truly key ones, containing hundreds of millions—if not billions—of dollars worth of gold and art are still hidden.

"When Yamashita surrendered on September second, 1945, he was charged with war crimes, but there was no mention of plundered treasure—not a single mention of it in the trial transcripts. Yamashita was convicted and sentenced to death. He was hanged. Pretty damn quickly too. War was different back then. None of this bleeding heart stuff you see these days." She said this with a tone of contempt that even Vaughn found striking.

"But . . ." She drew the word out. "Have you ever heard of Operation Paper Clip?"

Vaughn shook his head. He had stopped packing and, while focused on what Tai was saying, felt as if he were at the edge of a vast, dark chasm, the ground on which he stood not exactly secure.

"Operation Paper Clip has also been well-documented, yet no one ever talks about it," Tai said. "And when they do, they focus on Europe and the German rocket scientists. Paper Clip was instituted in the last years of the war, when the tide had turned and we were pretty confident we were going to win. Some smart person figured out that there was going to be a wealth of technical information to be gained from those we defeated. After all, the Germans had built V-2 rockets capable of hitting London.

"Operation Paper Clip, a rather innocuous name for a rather devious endeavor, was started in 1944 as those at the strategic level started looking beyond the end of the war. The Japanese and Germans might have plundered the lands they conquered of their physical riches, but in the States there were those who realized that there were other, more valuable riches which needed to be harvested." Tai tapped the side of her head. "Brain power."

Vaughn nodded. "Yeah. I read about that. A lot of the scientists who worked on the early space program were ex-Nazis."

"Ex-Nazis who we could use," Tai said. "They hanged Yamashita in the Philippines for war crimes, yet they welcomed into the United States Nazi scientists who had done terrible things, because they had knowledge we wanted. Like the Kempetai, we sent intelligence officers from the JIOA—Joint Intelligence Objectives Agency—with our frontline troops as they swept into Germany. There are actually recorded instances where the JIOA officers almost got into firefights with officers from the war crimes units as both groups went after the same people, but for very different reasons. And when official decisions had to be made over jurisdiction, the JIOA almost always took precedence. And this was despite the fact that President Truman signed an executive order banning the immigration of war criminals from the Axis powers into the United States."

"How do you know all this stuff?" Vaughn asked.

"My specialty is intelligence."

"Yeah," Vaughn said, "but all this history. World War II. I mean, that's old stuff."

"Old stuff that still has repercussions today," Tai said. She put another bullet into the magazine in her hand, held it up to check that it was full, then slid it into a pocket on her vest. "Abayon came out of the Second World War. Everything has a history. The best way to understand things now is to examine where they came from. Most Americans have little sense of history, and because of that, they have little sense of why things are the way they are."

Vaughn held the thought. His brother-in-law had died on a mission to free hostages. The justification for the mission had been enough for Vaughn's team in isolation. But they had never examined *why* the Abu Sayef had taken those hostages. It was an axiom of guerrilla warfare that few openly discussed anymore, but one man's terrorist was another man's freedom fighter.

"Listen," Tai said. She had stopped loading bullets. "You know the saying, 'Those who don't learn from history are doomed to repeat it'? Well, those who don't learn from history end up not making it, but being footnotes in it. Bad footnotes. And for everything that's written down in history books, think about all the things that aren't written down.

"You said you heard of the German rocket scientists we used after the war. But what about the German chemical and biological scientists? No one ever wrote about them or talked about them. But the Germans were the world's foremost experts on chemical warfare by the end of the war because they used it. On an unimaginable scale in the concentration camps. Tabun. Soman. Sarin. They invented them all."

Vaughn held his hand up. "Wait a second. Let's not go off on a tangent here. This"—he pointed down at the rock floor—"is Okinawa, not Europe."

Tai nodded. "I know. I was just using examples. But

don't you think we did the same thing out here in the Pacific at the end of the war? You have to admit that despite the war crimes trials, overall, we were pretty lenient on both the Germans and the Japanese after the war."

"Okay," Vaughn acknowledged. "Getting back to the Golden Lily project . . . wasn't a lot of treasure recovered after the war?"

"No. Some say Marcos came to power because he had some of Yamashita's gold. Then there's the rumors about the Black Eagle Trust." Tai paused and shook her head. "You're right. I'm going too far afield. We have to keep our eye on our ball: Abayon. He's the target, and we're going in tonight to figure out how to terminate him."

Vaughn was tempted to ask about the Black Eagle Trust, but knew it was time to focus on the upcoming mission. There was still some last-minute planning before they headed out to the airfield.

He went into the latrine and stopped in surprise when he saw Kasen seated on one of the open toilets, a rubber tube around one arm and a syringe in the other hand, the needle sunk deep into his arm. Kasen looked up and saw Vaughn but pushed the plunger anyway.

"What the hell are you doing?" Vaughn demanded.

Kasen slid the needle out of his arm, removed the rubber tube, and flexed that hand several times. He stood, sliding the gear into a small black pouch. "None of your fucking business."

"We're on a team," Vaughn said.

"So?"

"I don't want to be on a team with a junkie."

"Oh, fuck off," Kasen said, trying to push past.

Vaughn put an arm out, blocking him. "Wait a second."

Kasen swung and Vaughn ducked the blow, backing up. "The others need to know about this."

"Why?" Kasen asked, pausing, looking at Vaughn as if he were speaking to an idiot. "Everyone here has secrets. At least you know mine. Tell Orson. Tell the others. You don't think Orson and the people he works for know about this?" He held up the black case. "Shit, it's the *reason* they recruited me."

With that, he pushed past Vaughn and left the latrine.

Oahu

Royce read the message from Tai to ARPERCEN twice, then closed the lid of David's laptop. He was seated in David's Defender, which he'd parked along the side of a road overlooking Kaneohe Marine Corps Air Base. He put a set of binoculars to his eyes and looked down at the runway. A Gulfstream jet painted flat black was parked near the tower, door open and stairs down.

Royce adjusted the focus as a half-dozen people emerged from the building below the tower and made their way to the plane. Even without the aid of the binoculars he would have been able to spot David's figure among them. The other five were around David's age, but Royce had never seen any of them before. They were all dressed aloha style and seemed quite excited.

The heat was reflected off the tarmac, intensifying the effect of the sun. David put a hand over his eyes to shade them and looked up at the mountains to the west. He knew Royce was up there somewhere. He was going to miss his friend. He dawdled, letting the others pass him on the way to the plane. There was a distinct sense of anticipation among them—the payoff after decades of hard work in the trenches was at hand. It wasn't a normal retirement, but none of them had lived normal lives. The other five were from the mainland and had been flown to Hawaii the previous day. David had never met any of them before, though he knew it was possible he'd worked on missions in conjunction with some if not all of them. The Organization was big, its tentacles spread around the planet.

As he reached the steps up to the plane, he paused, looked past the mountain where he knew Royce was and to the sky. As his brother must have looked at the sky that morning over sixty years ago, he reflected. His last dawn. He and his older brother had been close for all of his fourteen years, before his brother enlisted and was shipped out to basic and then to Hawaii.

David had visited the Punchbowl the previous day and stood at his brother's grave, one of many with the same final date etched on the stone: 7 DECEMBER 1941. Leaving the grave for what he knew was the last time had been difficult, harder than leaving the small house on the east shore he'd called "home" for the last ten years. People in the covert world never really had homes.

A flash of light on the hillside caught his attention. He knew it was Royce, shifting his binoculars, the sun striking the lens. David waved, sighed, then stepped into the plane. As soon as he was on board, the door was pulled up behind him and the jet engines revved with power.

Royce tracked the Gulfstream down the runway and into the air. It was gaining altitude fast, rocketing up into the blue sky and banking to the west. He kept the craft in sight until it disappeared into the blue haze, then slowly lowered the binoculars and put them back in their case.

He glanced at the laptop lying on the passenger seat, feeling the pull of duty and work, but didn't pick it up for a while. The laptop was his link to David's—and now his—handler in the Organization. It was also the address where all information on the operation was collated. Royce had spent the morning recovering from the hangover that was the result of his and David's last night on the town, and then going through the computer after David disappeared in a cab to head to the Marine base. Royce had offered to drive, but David nixed that idea, saying they had kept their relationship secret all these years, there was no point in him showing up at the gate of Kaneohe with Royce at the wheel.

So Royce had checked what had been bequeathed to him by his old friend: an old truck and a new laptop. The setup inside the laptop was efficient. There was an address book with numerous points of contacts, each labeled with a code word and a brief summary of what that POC was responsible for. It was specific and extensive. If he needed weapons up to and including heavy machine guns and rocket-propelled grenades in Chile, there was a phone number and a code name. If he needed access to the Defense Intelligence Agency's most deeply held files, there was an e-mail address, a phone number, and a code name for that. There were even access points for most other country's intelligence agencies.

Royce had his own code name. Like the others, it was a six letter/number combination. An annotation told him that the code cycled every forty-eight hours, which required him to sync the computer to the satellite wireless system it automatically picked up every time it was on, at least every two days. He had no doubt he was hooked in to Milstar, the secure satellite system the Pentagon had circling the planet.

Since the satellites were linked to each other, Milstar provided initial security by requiring no ground relay, which could always be tapped in to. And the satellites used frequency hopping to transmit their encrypted messages. When he checked into Milstar after first using it several years ago—and he always checked everything he used, since his life depended on it—he discovered that the Air Force claimed there were five working satellites in the system, even though six had been launched. The publicity page on the Air Force website claimed that a mistake was made on the third launch in 1999 and the satellite had been placed in a nonusable orbit.

He very much wanted to know where that satellite was in geosynchronous orbit. He had a feeling it would tell him a great deal about the Organization he worked for, because he doubted that the orbit for that one had been a mistake. Perhaps from the Air Force point of view it had not gone where they wanted, but he believed that someone else was very happy wherever that satellite had ended up.

Royce sighed. All this thinking was keeping him from doing what had to be done. He opened up the laptop and read Tai's request to ARPERCEN one more time. It was either bullshit, stupidity, or something else. Because he had told Tai, as he'd told the others, in no uncertain terms, that she was no longer part of the big green machine and could never go back to it. So why was she sending an e-mail concerning a next assignment that would never happen?

She was not stupid. He had her file. Tops in her class at the University of Arizona. While on active duty, she had somehow managed to earn a Ph.D. in military history. Every efficiency report sparkled and glowed with that extra bit of effort that indicated her commanders had not been just routinely punching her ticket, but truly impressed with her. Until she was accused of abusing prisoners in Iraq, a strange departure from her straight and narrow record to that point.

Since she wasn't stupid, that meant the ARPERCEN request wasn't bullshit. Which meant it was something else, and the only thing Royce could come up with was that it was some sort of coded message Tai had sent to someone on the outside.

According to the file, she'd been recruited because of the prisoner abuse charges—and her personal motivation after losing her sister on 9/11. Her test—like those of all the others—had been to assassinate a target designated by the Organization. Even he had no idea why these people have been targeted. She had killed the target as ordered, so there was some degree of security in that—she'd crossed a line.

But . . .

Royce brought up her 201 personnel file once more and began reading it, searching for the thread he must have missed the first time through, now that he suspected that Captain Tai was more than she appeared to be. He glanced at his watch. The C-130 for the recon team should be ready on Okinawa by now. And Tai and Vaughn should be heading to the airfield.

Royce pulled out his secure satellite phone and punched in a number.

Okinawa

Vaughn could see that Orson wasn't one for rah-rah premission speeches. "We don't hear from you on your initial entry report in twenty-four hours, we'll consider your mission compromised."

Orson was standing in the entrance to the tunnel, looking up into the back of the truck. Tai and Vaughn sat on benches across from each other, their packed rucksacks on the space behind them.

"Roger that," Vaughn said. He hadn't told anyone about his encounter with Kasen—at this point it would make little difference, if any. The mission was on, and he had to make the best of it.

Diesel fumes from the idling engine wafted through the enclosed space. He felt a curious sense of detachment as he pushed away the thoughts and feelings about the coming mission.

"Is the primary mission canceled if we're killed during the recon?" Tai asked.

Orson stared at her. "What do you care? You'll be dead."

Vaughn and Tai met each other's eyes. He wasn't sure what he read in hers. Anger? But there was something else. He turned to Orson. "What if we're captured? Twenty-four-hour rule?"

He was referring to the concept that a prisoner could hold out against torture for twenty-four hours, then even the best would give up everything they knew. But twenty-four hours was enough time for every plan the prisoner knew to be changed, and for damage control to begin.

"Don't get captured," Orson growled. He slapped the side of the truck to let the driver know it was ready to go, then turned and walked away.

Vaughn pulled down the canvas flap covering the back of the truck. "Friendly."

"This isn't a friendly business," Tai said.

Vaughn wondered if she knew about his brother-in-law. Frank and he had discussed the problem of serving on the same team, but in the end they had decided they'd rather fight with someone they knew and trusted. That had not turned out well.

As the truck rumbled its way toward the airfield, Vaughn began preparing for battle. Both he and Tai wore sterile camouflage fatigues of a make easily bought anywhere in the world. He put his body armor on, securing it with the Velcro straps. He then slid on the combat vest bristling with extra magazines, grenades, a knife, and the FM radio with which he could talk to Tai. He put the earpiece in, secured the mike around his throat, and when Tai had done the same, turned his radio on and moved to the front of the truck bay, as far from her as he could get.

"Read me? Over."

"Roger that," Tai responded. "Over."

"Let's keep the radio off until just before jump to conserve batteries," Vaughn said. "Then operate only on minimum settings. Over."

"Roger. Out." Tai turned off her radio and Vaughn did the same. He returned to the rear of the truck and checked his pistol, making sure there was a round in the chamber. Then he put on his composite armor forearm guards.

Tai noted that. "What's your training in?"

Vaughn knew she was asking for a specific martial arts discipline. "Killing."

Tai laughed. "Know enough of a bunch of various styles and master of none?"

Vaughn shrugged. "I don't have a black belt in anything, but I have trained in a variety of styles. What about you?"

"Black belt in hapkido and tae kwon do. And trained in a variety of styles."

Vaughn had expected as much, given the way she took down Kasen. He pulled his flight gloves on, flexing his fingers to ensure a tight fit, then secured the brass knuckles to his combat vest.

Seeing that, Tai raised an eyebrow. "That's a new one."

"Something from my childhood," Vaughn explained. He felt a flush of sadness, remembering Frank at the assembly area in the Philippines before the botched raid also commenting on the knuckles.

Tai pulled something long and thin, wrapped in black cloth, out of her pack. "Something from *my* childhood." She unwrapped the object. A wooden scabbard and hilt appeared. Tai drew the blade. It was a shoto, a Japanese short sword, the blade about eight inches long.

"May I?" Vaughn asked.

Tai paused and then handed it over, handle first.

Vaughn took it. He was surprised how light it was. He turned it and looked at the edge. Razor sharp. "How many times was the metal folded?" he asked, referring to the process by which such blades were handmade.

Tai smiled, holding her hand out to take it back. "You know something of swords?"

"I spent time in the Far East," Vaughn vaguely answered.

"The making of this is a family secret," Tai said as she slid the blade back into its sheath. She then put the sword inside her combat vest, on top of the body armor, straight down along her chest, between her breasts.

"Interesting placement," Vaughn said. Tai shot him a sharp look. He held his hands up defensively. "Sorry,"

"You get one mistake," Tai said. "And you've made it."

Vaughn nodded. "It was stupid."

Tai relaxed. "A man who can admit he's wrong. That's something new."

The truck lurched to an abrupt stop, then gears grinded as the driver threw it into reverse. Vaughn lifted the canvas flap covering the rear and saw the back end of a C-130, ramp open.

"We're here."

CHAPTER 10

Jolo Island

The report of Kasama's execution reached Abayon while he was once more hooked up to the dialysis machine. He was not surprised. Abayon knew the power of the Yakuza. And he knew that anyone who could do what had been done to Kasama was even more powerful. He had seen this before. A powerful organization struck by some group that lived in the shadows, one that seemed able to wield power with impunity. Not for the first time—or, he knew, the last—he wished he had not been so quick to cut Colonel Tashama's throat. In the six decades since that event, he had come to realize that it was as close as he'd ever gotten to someone who might have known what this shadow organization was. However, given the security levels he had run into whenever he tried to penetrate his enemy, he realized

Tashama had probably known little more than he needed to hide this part of the Golden Lily here.

The nurse pulled the needle out of his arm and smiled at Abayon. He nodded his head in thanks. The dialysis was not a cure—it was a stop-gap measure designed to keep death a handsbreadth away. Time, the most valuable of all currencies, was what he needed. Just a little more time. And then he would embrace death. He had faced it many times before and he did not fear it—he only feared not completing what he'd set out to do so many years ago.

The issue of whether there was life after death had plagued mankind since the beginning of consciousness. For some people, usually those in the bounty of their youth, such a question was often considered in theoretical terms. For those in his situation, pinned to a wheelchair and hearing his life leave him molecule by molecule with each breath, it was a very real consideration.

He had managed to get the doctor to be honest with him, and Abayon knew that he would not be alive that long. What was beyond that increasingly occupied his mind. He was not one of the Muslims who believed heaven was a bountiful place of all the food one could eat and all the beautiful women one could take for one's own pleasure. Those were the naive dreams of ignorant men. A strict reading of the Koran indicated that man could have no concept of heaven because it was so far beyond anything experienced here on Earth.

Abayon liked the concept of something he couldn't conceptualize. It was a spiritual existence, not a physical one. There would be a birth of a soul from his own soul. And that new soul would reap the benefits of the type of life one had lived on Earth. According to his interpretation of the Koran, Heaven and Hell existed in the same place but on a different dimension. It was all relative, depending on what one could perceive and one's state upon death.

Abayon planned for his state upon death to be one of equilibrium. He had suffered much in life and spent decades building himself up to a position of power in order to equal out the scales. It had required tremendous patience, the need to hold back when there was a burning desire to strike out against his enemies and those who had done him tremendous wrongs over the years.

There was evil in the world. The evil of the material world. And looming behind that evil was the United States and its corrupting influence. In that, he agreed with Al Qaeda and the other extremist Islamic groups. But Abayon sensed something more. A power behind the power. He had seen and heard and interpreted too many unsettling things over the course of his life.

Finding this complex and its contents had been disturbing enough over sixty years ago. But it had only been the first of several events that changed his view on the world, just as his learning of Islam had changed his view of the afterlife.

A guard wheeled Abayon from the medical center to his office. Abayon checked the in-box, signing off on the minor details that kept the Abu Sayef running its day-to-day operations. He smiled as he thought it was not much different running a guerrilla organization than a corporation.

Okinawa

Wheels up. Vaughn felt the plane depart from the runway. A small pile of equipment was tied down on the

ramp: two parachutes, night vision goggles, and helmets. He loosened the straps and removed one of them.

"I like to pack my own," Tai said as she grabbed the
other one.

"I do too," Vaughn said, but they both knew that was
impractical in the back of the aircraft. They checked
the rigging on the outside as best they could. Everything appeared to be in order.

Vaughn turned to the crew chief, the only other occupant of the cargo bay. "How long until the drop?"

The crew chief spoke into his headset, listened and
then turned to Vaughn and Tai. "Two hours, twenty-six
minutes."

Over the Pacific

Everyone else appeared to be asleep to David. They
were several hours out of Hawaii, and looking out the
window, all he could see in the moonlit night was the
ocean far below. He reached into his pocket and pulled
out his satellite phone, then hooked his PDA to the
phone. He brought up a small keyboard display on the
PDA, held the stylus over it, and began to enter a text
message:

   ROYCE
   THERE WERE SOME THINGS ABOUT THE OR-
   GANIZATION WE NEVER TALKED ABOUT. I AM NOT
   SURE IF

David paused, the words reflected back at him. He
smiled. He still wasn't sure whether he should write
and send this message to his old friend. A lifetime of
lies and deceptions had wormed its way so deeply into

his mind, he wasn't sure anymore what was the right thing to do. A harsh lesson he had learned early in his career in covert operations was that sometimes ignorance was indeed bliss.

He leaned his head back on the seat, the message incomplete, and closed his eyes. Within minutes he had joined the other retirees in slumber.

Jolo Island

Abayon paused in his paperwork when there was a knock on the steel door, a dull thud, repeated in a pattern he recognized. He pressed the release for the heavy door and it swung outward.

A young Filipino woman who had just passed her twenty-second birthday stood in the entranceway. "Come in, Fatima," he called out to his goddaughter.

She smiled as she walked toward him, and Abayon felt some of the weight that had been pressing down on him lighten. It was always a pleasure when Moreno's granddaughter visited him. Even if it involved business. She was the light he was leaving behind to shine for the Abu Sayef.

"Have a seat," he said.

There was an old, overstuffed chair set against the wall about four meters from Abayon's desk. Visitors often glanced at it strangely, since it seemed inappropriate for both the office and the occupant. But it was Fatima's chair, one she had occupied as a child in Moreno's home when his wife—Fatima's mother— was still alive. When Moreno's wife died, he'd burned the house down in his grief, but Abayon, anticipating his friend's strong reaction, quickly had the chair removed and brought here.

Now, Fatima settled into it and tucked her legs up beneath herself. She looked small and childish, but Abayon had long ago seen past the outer facade. She was brilliant, and as tough-minded as her father. For years Abayon had watched the younger ranks of the Abu Sayef for someone who might take his place. It took him a while to accept that Fatima was the most qualified, and the one he most trusted with his legacy.

He knew that announcing a woman as his heir would not go over well with most of the members of the Abu Sayef, but he didn't care. She was the best person, and would have to make her own way. It would not be easy, but he felt she was up to it. And he knew the power struggle would make her stronger in the long run, and that he was leaving her a powerful legacy.

"My father is gone," Fatima said.

Abayon nodded.

"Will he return?"

Abayon did not hesitate in answering. "It is not likely."

Fatima slowly nodded. "I could tell by the way he said good-bye."

"He is going to strike a great blow for our cause."

"And Ruiz?"

Abayon liked that Fatima wasted no time on emotional subjects. He could tell by the dark pockets under her eyes that she had probably spent the entire night crying over the departure of her father, but she was not going to bring it up now.

"Ruiz is in Hong Kong," he said.

"With some of the treasure from the vault." It was not inflected as a question, but he answered anyway.

"Yes."

"Why?"

"To auction it."

"Do we need the money?"

"The cause always needs money. Whatever he can get for the objects he took, however, will not come to us, but rather to our brethren in other countries."

"Al Qaeda."

Abayon nodded.

Fatima considered that. "It is dangerous."

"Yes, it is," Abayon said. "However, it is better that some other group keep the forefront in this war than us, because whoever is in the forefront will take the most casualties."

"The Bali bombing," Fatima said.

"That's one example."

She crossed her arms and regarded her godfather. "There's something more going on than what you're telling me."

Abayon tried to hide his smile. She was indeed the one who should take his place. "Yes, there is."

"And what is it?"

He didn't have to try to hide his smile anymore, because it was gone. "I don't know exactly." He sighed. "People think there is a war between Islam and Christianity. I do not look at it that way. I have known, and fought beside, many Christians who were good people. And I have met some very bad people who were Muslims. Islam and Christianity have the same roots, just different paths from those roots." He shook his head. "No, the war is between the haves and the have-nots. Between those who control the world's economy and those who are controlled by it."

"Between the established nations and the third world," Fatima said.

Abayon nodded once more. "Yes, except the gap is

getting wider instead of narrower. The western world, particularly the United States, is so focused on itself that it fails to even acknowledge what is going on in the rest of the world."

"Unless made to."

Yes," Abayon allowed. "That is what 9/11 was. A wake-up call."

"But the United States attacked Afghanistan and Iraq. I do not see how that was good for the third world."

"It got attention, and everyone did not react as the Americans. Even now there is a backlash in that country over Iraq. And when I say 'western world,' that isn't quite accurate. Perhaps the better term is 'industrialized world.' For certainly Japan, and to an extent Korea, are part of this. It is those countries that consume at the expense of the rest of the world."

"There are so many countries like that, though," Fatima pointed out.

"Many countries, but . . ." Abayon lapsed into silence.

Fatima waited for a little while before speaking. "But . . . ?"

"They are connected at some level, some secret level," Abayon said.

"How do you know this?"

"The gold and art that was hidden here. Most think it was just the Japanese. The Golden Lily project. But I heard something a long time ago that I've often thought about."

"And that is?"

Abayon felt old and tired. He did not want to tell this story but knew he had to. Fatima needed to know it if she were to make the right choices after he was gone. And with what he had planned shortly, he knew he would soon be high on the target list for his known and unknown enemies.

"You know my wife and I were captured by the Japanese during the war. What you—and everyone except your father—do not know, is what happened to us. How my wife really died. And no one, not even your father, knows what I learned from an American I met during my captivity."

"An American?" Fatima was confused. "But you were sent to Manchuria, to . . ." She paused, unwilling to say the name.

"Unit 731," Abayon said.

"I have never heard of any Americans being sent there."

"A handful were," Abayon said. "A special handful. What I am going to tell is part my story and part his story, so please bear with me."

Fatima nodded. "Yes, Godfather."

Abayon looked around. "Take me up to the observation platform. I'll tell you there."

Fatima got up and went behind the wheelchair. She pushed it to the door, opened it, pushed him through, and shut it behind her. Then she began the long journey to the platform, pushing Abayon in front of her.

Over the Western Pacific

"Thirty minutes," the crew chief yelled into Vaughn's ear.

He acknowledged the time warning and glanced across at Tai. She was lying on the red web seat on the other side of the plane, eyes closed. He doubted, though, that she was sleeping. No matter how many jumps one had, there was always a sense of anxiety.

Vaughn went over and tapped her on the shoulder. "Thirty minutes. Let's rig."

Over the Mid-Pacific

David's eyes snapped open as the screech of an alarm bell resounded through the interior of the plane. Oxygen masks dropped from the overhead, dangling on their clear tubes. Instinctively, he reached for the mask, then paused. He could see the other passengers grabbing the masks and slipping them over their heads.

David's nostrils flared as he sniffed the air. Nothing seemed amiss. He took a deep breath and was rewarded with lungs full of oxygen. The alarm was still clanging but there was no other sign that anything was wrong. The plane was flying straight and level.

The man to David's left, across the aisle, slumped forward, head bouncing off the back of the chair in front of him. Within seconds all the other passengers were also unconscious. David reached out, took the mask that hung in front of him and stared at it. He was tempted to take a sniff, but didn't know how powerful the knockout gas obviously flowing through the plane's backup air system was.

The pilots. David unbuckled his seat belt, made his way forward and knocked on the metal door separating the passengers from crew. He waited a few seconds, the moments weighing heavily on him, then knocked again, harder. Then he pounded, slamming his fists against the unyielding metal.

"Stop." David said the word out loud to make it very clear to himself. He did as he ordered himself. He slowly turned, went to the nearest person and checked his pulse. Still breathing, albeit very slowly. He nodded. It made sense. They would be killed when the plane crashed. On the very slim chance that a body was recovered, cause of death would be crash trauma. A smart plan.

There was no retirement. There was only oblivion. He had suspected as much. In fact, he now realized he'd known this was coming. It was the logical solution. Everyone on this plane was a loose end. And the Organization had never tolerated loose ends. Something else also struck him with startling clarity. There was no way the Organization was going to put this many of its members together and allow them to swap their stories, even it was on some remote island in the far Pacific. Pieces could be put together that were never meant to be put together.

David slowly made his way down the passenger compartment, searching for a tool to use to try to breach the door to the pilot's compartment. Since 9/11, planes had been hardened to make getting into that compartment nearly impossible. He held on to the word "nearly"—there was always a way around things.

CHAPTER 11

Jolo Island, Philippines

"It was just five months after the American disaster at Pearl Harbor," Abayon said. He and Fatima were near the top of Hono Mountain, in the same place where Abayon had watched the failed American raid to rescue the hostages just days before. "Smoke was still rising from some of the ships sunk in Pearl Harbor, and oil has been leaking out of some of the hulks to this very day.

"The Rising Sun of Japan seemed to be spreading without check throughout the western Pacific Rim. At least, so it appeared to all of us back then. The day after the assault on Pearl Harbor, the Japanese launched attacks on the Philippines in preparation for invasion. Despite having had over fourteen hours of warning about what had happened at Pearl Harbor, the great Douglas MacArthur, the overall commander here in the Philippines, did not have his forces on alert, and most of his planes were destroyed on the ground, lined up at the airfields around the islands.

"It got worse. On the tenth of December, 1941, the pride of the British Pacific fleet, the battleship *Prince of Wales* and the battle cruiser *Repulse,* were sunk by Japanese torpedo planes. It was a stunning defeat for the British, who had always looked down on the Japanese as an inferior race and not a foe worthy of serious consideration. That loss would soon be followed by another even more devastating blow.

"Singapore was considered by the British to be their Gibraltar in the Far East. Unfortunately for the British, and fortunately for the inferior Japanese, most of the defenses were oriented toward the ocean, where the British naturally assumed the attack would come. They were shocked when the Japanese landed on the Malay peninsula and fought through swamp and jungle toward the city. Despite being outnumbered by the British almost two to one, the Japanese rapidly advanced. They were under the command of General Tomoyuki Yamashita, who, as you know, would later be in command of the occupation of the Philippines."

Abayon was looking out to sea. The lights of a few anchored fishing vessels were visible, but otherwise there was no sign of man. He continued his story.

"The Japanese advance was swift and brutal. No prisoners were taken. Wounded men were executed. Locals who assisted the British were also killed. On February the eighth, 1942, the Japanese captured Singapore, taking over 100,000 Allied troops prisoner. A tenth of those would later die building the Burma-Thailand railway, much as many of those captured here died.

"The beginning of 1942 was a dark time for the Allies in the Pacific. The Japanese seemed invincible. Hong Kong had fallen. Darwin was bombed. China, Burma, Borneo—the list of places the Japanese were advancing through was almost endless. And with those advancing troops came the Kempetai, the secret police, and within the Kempetai an even more secret unit that began the systematic looting of the conquered lands."

"Golden Lily," Fatima said.

"Yes," Abayon said. "We will get back to that. But let me continue so you understand as much of the big picture as I do. In the United States, morale was at an all-time low. President Roosevelt ordered his Joint Chiefs of Staff to come up with something to hit back at the Japanese homeland. It was a daunting proposition, given the vast width of the Pacific Ocean. The plan that was developed was daring: launch medium bombers off an aircraft carrier.

"Sixteen B-25 Mitchell bombers were loaded on board the *USS Hornet*. The crews of the bombers, despite having spent weeks practicing short takeoffs, did not know their target or mission as they boarded the carrier. The Americans used to be very good at keeping secrets, a skill they've lost to a large degree since then. The ship set sail from California and headed west.

"Also on board the ship were three men who were neither part of the flight crew or the ship's complement. They had orders signed by General Marshall himself . . . very strange orders that simply directed any U.S. Military officer who was shown the orders to do as the bearer instructed."

Fatima stirred as if to say something, but Abayon continued without acknowledging her.

"I am sure Colonel Doolittle, the commander of the bomber group, was none too happy to have these orders shoved in his face shortly after the fleet took sail. But Doolittle was a good officer and he would do as ordered.

"The launch was set for April nineteenth, when the *Hornet* would be around five hundred miles from the Japanese islands. The planes would fly to their targets, drop their bombs, then continue onward to land in China. That plan, as with most military plans, went out the window on the eighteenth of April when one of the escort ships was spotted by a Japanese picket boat. The Japanese boat was sunk, but it was assumed it had gotten a warning message out.

"As dawn broke on the eighteenth, the public address system on the *Hornet* called the Army pilots to man their planes. For the first time since boarding the ship, the three men who had been snuck aboard in California during darkness came up onto the deck. They made their way to aircraft number sixteen, named *Bat Out of Hell* by its crew. Unlike the other fifteen bombers, this plane, as ordered by the man who carried the letter from Marshall, carried no bombs. Instead, the three men climbed into the bomb bay, where their equipment awaited them—parachutes, weapons, grenades, a wireless, and other equipment indicating they were going somewhere to do something dangerous."

Abayon was on a roll, telling the story almost as if he had experienced it firsthand, which surprised Fatima.

"The lead plane, piloted by Doolittle, lifted off the deck of the *Hornet* at 0820. The other planes followed as quickly as they could be moved into position. An hour after Doolittle had taken off, *Bat Out of Hell* roared down the wooden deck and into the sky. As soon as it was clear, the *Hornet* began a wide sweeping turn to head back east.

"Inside the last plane, the man with the letter made his way to the cockpit. The plane's original target was supposed to have been Kobe. The man's orders, backed up by his letter, changed that. *Bat Out of Hell* headed on an azimuth to make landfall just north of Tokyo.

"When the navigator estimated the plane was an hour from the Japanese coast, the three men rigged their parachutes and gear. At the designated location, the bombardier opened the doors on the bottom of the aircraft and the three men threw themselves out, their parachutes quickly deploying."

Abayon paused, and this time Fatima was able to get some words in.

"How do you know all this?" she asked.

"Afterward I met one of the members of that plane's crew," Abayon said. "They managed to make it to China, but ran out of fuel and had to bail out. They suffered the misfortune of being captured by the Japanese. I had suffered the same misfortune almost two months before and was shipped to China en route to Unit 731 in Manchuria."

Fatima frowned. "But I don't understand why this is important. Three men parachuted out of one of those planes. And . . . ? Do you know who they were? What they were going to do? It sounds as if the crew of the plane certainly didn't."

"No, the crew had no clue who the men were or why they were parachuting into Japan," Abayon said. "But I discovered more."

"How?"

He held up a hand. "First, let me tell you a little more about what happened after the Doolittle raid so you get a sense of perspective. History, particularly American history, paints the raid as a great success and a turning point in the war. The Americans, as is their way, made a movie about it in 1944, even before the war was over. The commander, Doolittle, was given their Medal of Honor.

"Militarily, the raid accomplished very little. Each plane—other than number sixteen—carried only four five-hundred-pound bombs because of weight restrictions. The damage done was negligible. And all sixteen planes were lost when they crash-landed after running out of fuel.

"The Japanese, as they did here in the Philippines against the guerrillas, responded to this gnat's strike with fury. Since the planes all went on to China, and most of the crews were saved by Chinese partisans, the Japanese vented their rage on the Chinese people. First, they conducted more than six hundred air raids of their own on Chinese villages and towns. Any village where an American airman passed through was burned to the ground and the people murdered. No one knows the exact number, but the American moral victory cost almost 100,000 Chinese their lives."

"And the Americans did not care." Fatima said it as a statement.

Abayon nodded. "Most Americans care nothing for people killed as long as it is not their own people. A hundred thousand Chinese dead so that there can be exciting headlines in their newspapers and newsreel was fine for them.

"Some Americans did suffer. The Japanese captured eight of the men who were on the planes, including the crew of the *Bat Out of Hell* that the three mystery men had jumped out of. The eight were first taken to Tokyo by the Kempetai, where they were interrogated."

"But you said you talked to one of these men in China," Fatima noted.

"Yes," Abayon said. "That was later. The Americans were kept in Tokyo for about two months, where they were tortured until they agreed to sign documents admitting they were war criminals. Then they were shipped back to China. I ran into them there in a prison camp. Surprisingly, though, the crew of the sixteenth plane was never interrogated about the three men, even though, under torture, they told of the jump."

Fatima was now intrigued with this story of events over sixty years ago. "You're saying the crew told the Kempetai that three Americans parachuted into Japan during the raid, but the Kempetai never pursued that line of questioning?"

"Yes. Strange, isn't it? And the secret should have died with them. The Japanese held a trial of the crew. It took them all of twenty minutes. The Americans couldn't understand anything, since it was all done in Japanese. There was no defense counsel, and it wasn't until after they were taken out of the courtroom that they discovered they had been condemned to death.

"The sentence was to be carried out several weeks later, but it wasn't until the day before they were to be killed that the Americans were informed of their sentence. They wrote letters to their families—which were never sent. Then, the next day, the Japanese took them into a cemetery. There were three small wooden crosses stuck in the ground, and the men were made to kneel with their backs against the crosses. Their hands were tied to the cross pieces. White cloth was wrapped around their faces—not as blindfolds, but with a large X marked on it just above the nose as a target point. It only took one volley from the firing squad."

Abayon paused. Fatima had seen death in her work

for the Abu Sayef, but the horrors of World War II were on a scale that her generation could not visualize.

She waited a few moments, then asked, "But what does any of that have to do with the Golden Lily? And what is in this complex?"

Abayon ran his hands along the worn arms of his wheelchair. It had been years since he'd been able to walk. Years since he'd left the complex. He knew his present condition was a direct result of what had been done to him by the Japanese so many years ago. He was lucky to have survived when so many others had not, but revisiting that place, even in conversation, was painful. Still, Fatima had to know what he knew and what he suspected.

"The men who jumped out of that bomber into Japan are the connection," he finally said. "After we were captured, my wife and I were taken from the Philippines to China for a while and then eventually to Manchuria, to a place called Pingfan, about twenty-five kilometers southeast of Harbin.

"At first we thought it was just a concentration camp. But the collection of prisoners was strange. There were Chinese, of course, but there were two dozen Filipinos; some Europeans who had been captured; a handful of Australians; many nationalities were represented, in small numbers for some reason. And there was one American."

"One of the jumpers," Fatima said.

Abayon smiled despite the terrible memories bubbling in his mind. She was indeed the right one. "Yes. One of the jumpers. I talked to him. His name was Martin. Kevin Martin. At first he said nothing of his past or how he had been captured or even who he was. But when I told him of the American aircrew from

Doolittle's raid and that I had seen that they were prisoners of the Japanese, it was the key to opening him up. Martin wanted to know what had happened to the men. He was quite upset when I told him they were executed, even though we were in a place where it was obvious we would not live long either."

Abayon paused, gnarled hands moving back and forth on the arms of his wheelchair in agitation. "What do you know of Unit 731?"

"What you have told me," Fatima said. "It was the biological warfare experimental laboratory for the Japanese."

"I have studied the unit and its history as much as any person since the end of the war," he said. "The Japanese made no secret of their interest in developing biological and chemical weapons. Early on, they knew they were at a technical disadvantage to the West, but in this field they felt they might be able to gain the upper hand.

"In 1925 the Japanese made this clear when they refused to sign the Geneva Convention ban on biological weapons. In fact, I believe, given information I have examined over the years, that in a perverse way the fact that there was a ban on these weapons is what made the Japanese actually more interested in them. High-ranking Japanese officers figured that if something was so terrible it was outlawed, then it must be an effective weapon.

"They weren't stupid, though. They knew better than to build facilities in their own country. When they invaded Manchuria in 1932, accompanying the troops was an army officer who was also a physician, Dr. Ishii. He began the preliminary work that would lead four years later to Unit 731 being established. Besides the remoteness of the site, it also allowed them access to numerous test subjects: namely, Chinese soldiers and citizens, whom they considered less than human.

"It was a large compound," Abayon said, remembering. "Around 150 buildings covering several square kilometers. The Japanese used bubonic plague, cholera, anthrax, and other diseases in controlled tests on humans. They decided they also needed to make sure that the diseases worked the same on different races, so they began importing prisoners from other theaters of the war. That is how I ended up there.

"They did more than experiment—they also used the weapons. In their war against China, the Japanese used poison gas over one thousand times. They dropped bacteria from planes numerous times, starting plagues among not only enemy troops, but the civilian population. The estimates of how many died run into the hundreds of thousands."

"But . . ."

Abayon paused. "Yes?"

"Biological warfare has never been considered particularly effective for the battlefield. That is why it has so rarely been used."

Abayon nodded. "True. And it wasn't particularly effective then either. Even though they killed many, the Japanese couldn't control what they had unleashed. Japanese troops also died. But still, the experiments at 731 went on."

Abayon fell silent, and Fatima did not disturb him as his mind wandered down the dark alleys of his past. Finally he stirred. "My wife. They took her before they took me. They called us *meruta*—logs. That's what they thought of us."

"Why logs?" Fatima asked.

"Because that's what we looked like when they stacked the bodies," Abayon said. "Seventeen days after we arrived at Unit 731—shipped there packed in trains like cattle—they took my love along with several dozen others. Out to the testing range. They tied them to stakes. A plane flew by overhead, spraying whatever latest germ the scientists had come up with.

"The lucky ones died quickly and on the stake. My wife wasn't one of the lucky ones. The Japanese doctors wanted to see how quickly the disease progressed and what it did to the victim. So at a certain schedule, soldiers garbed in protective gear would go out to the field of death and take a harvest. They would bring several living prisoners back to the doctors. Then . . ."

Abayon fell silent.

"Your wife was one of these chosen?" Fatima asked.

"Yes. I was in my barracks. Locked in. I could look through a split in the wood. I saw them drive the truck in, the bodies in the back, sealed in a protective tent. Still alive. The doctors wanted them alive. So they could cut them open and see what their diseases were doing to a living person.

"I heard my wife's screams. They went on and on. I had seen the bodies of others who had been taken into the operating lab before, so I had a good idea—too good—of what they were doing to her. Vivisection. Cutting her open without anesthesia. The screams became so bad, they couldn't even be recognized as coming from a human being anymore. It was like an animal that had been trapped and was being tormented."

Abayon spit. "*Doctor* Ishii. Whatever oaths he had sworn in medical school were long forgotten. One hears so much about the Nazis and their death camps, but no one talks about 731. Everyone acts like it didn't exist. The Japanese premier and emperor both denied ever hearing of it at the end of the war. But Tojo personally gave Ishii a medal for his work there.

"And it was the Americans who would have paid the price if the Japanese had managed to make their weapons program effective. They planned to use balloon bombs to carry diseases to America. In 1945 they made a plan to use kamikaze pilots to dump plague-infected fleas on San Diego. There was another plan to send cattle plague in grain smut to affect the American economy. As the war wound down, Ishii came up with his most daring plan, which he named 'Cherry Blossoms at Night': use kamikaze pilots to hit the entire coast of California with plague. A sort of reverse of the Doolittle raid.

"Submarines were to take pilots and planes off the western coast of the United States. The submarines would surface and the planes would be launched. The date scheduled for this attack was September twenty-second, 1945. Fortunately for the Americans, the Japanese high command interceded and the submarines were diverted to be used against a closer threat: the American fleet at Ulith. All the Japanese managed to do was launch nine thousand incendiary bombs attached to balloons in the hopes that the jet stream would carry them across the ocean to America. They hoped to cause forest fires and terror. Several bombs made it, and one unfortunate woman was killed, but that was it."

"So 731 was a failure," Fatima said.

"For the Japanese," Abayon said.

"What do you mean?"

Abayon sighed. "Let me finish my story and you judge for yourself. The war was coming to a close, but still Ishii ran his experiments. Then came my day. I was taken out to the field. Tied to a stake. To my right was the American, Martin. We waited, and then the plane came flying by, releasing something from the tanks under its wings. We knew we were dead men. Finally Martin told me his story.

"He had been recruited into the OSS—Office of Strategic Services—the American precursor to the CIA. He had been briefed that his team's mission was to parachute into Japan and make their way to a university where Japan's only cyclotron was located. It's a device that is needed to develop atomic weapons."

"But that wasn't their real mission," Fatima said, once more jumping a step ahead of the story.

Abayon nodded. "Correct, it wasn't, as Martin found out, to his shock. They were picked up by the Kempetai on the drop zone, as if the Japanese were waiting for them and knew exactly when and where they would be jumping." Abayon paused, then gestured. "Could you get me some water?"

"That will take a while," Fatima said, knowing how far away the nearest room where she could fulfill his request was.

"We have time," Abayon said. "Talking has made me parched. And I need a little time to collect my thoughts before I continue."

When Fatima left the observation point, Abayon checked his watch. It would begin soon. Very soon.

Over the Philippines

"Six minutes," the crew chief warned Vaughn.

Vaughn repeated the warning to Tai. They were standing next to the oxygen console. Vaughn made a twisting motion as he gave the next command. "Go on personal oxygen."

They both unscrewed their oxygen hoses from the console and connected them to the small tanks strapped to their chests. Vaughn took a few breaths to make sure the tank was feeding properly. Everything was working perfectly so far.

"Depressurizing begun," the crew chief announced.

Both Vaughn and Tai swallowed as air began to leak out of the cargo bay so they could equalize with thin air outside at 25,000 feet.

Hong Kong

The room was on the top floor of one of the tallest buildings in Hong Kong. To be allowed access, the half-dozen occupants had to suffer through a tedious two-hour security check. And these were not people who submitted easily to such checks. But the lure that had been dangled in front of them about what was to occur in this room at this late hour was more than enough to convince them to put aside their pride.

The half dozen were seated in comfortable chairs arranged in a semicircle facing a small stage with a podium on the right side. A curtain hid whatever was on the stage.

Ruiz stepped from behind the curtain and walked to the podium with a black three-ring binder in his hands. He set the binder down, then checked his watch.

"Gentlemen, and lady," he added, acknowledging the jewel-bedecked older woman seated in one of the chairs, "the first item will be up for bid in five minutes."

Australia

"The recon team is just about on target for drop."

The man who announced this wore black combat fatigues, unmarked by any rank, insignia, or patch. He sported a pistol in a quick draw holster on his right hip. A fighting knife hung in a sheath on his left hip. He was addressing three other men, all dressed in black fatigues, all armed in one form or another. He had a satellite phone pressed to one ear.

"A fucking chick on a bloody mission," one of the men said with disgust.

The man who had made the announcement turned to the board near his right rear. Pictures of all six members of Section 8 were tacked there. He reached out with his free hand and ran his fingers over Tai's image, almost a caress. "She's supposed to be a badass," he noted. "That's what her file says."

"File," the second man snorted. "I'll show her a fucking file."

The team leader gave a cold smile. "I don't think she's going to be around for our reckoning with these fellows." He was a tall man, head shaved completely bald. A jagged scar ran across his forehead. On top of the scar a barbed-wire tattoo had been laid, making it seem part of the artwork. His accent indicated he was from South Africa, with the trace of Afrikaaner showing through.

The other man who had spoken had an Australian accent. The third man, Sicilian, had a swarthy complexion, and was tumbling a throwing knife through the fingers of his right hand seemingly without paying attention. The fourth man was black and huge, his chest as wide as a barrel, his head also shaved, and gleaming under the fluorescent lights in the operations room they occupied.

The black man stirred uncomfortably. "You have a link into their commo?" he asked.

The team leader nodded. "We get copied on everything that goes on inside the team and that comes out of the isolation."

The black man frowned. "Ever occur to you that *they* could be doing that to us also?"

"Who the fuck knows who *they* are," the Australian noted.

"What the hell are you talking about?" the team leader demanded.

"Well," the black man noted, "if we're spying on them, how do we know there's not a team spying on us?"

"A little paranoid, aren't you?" the team leader asked.

"Occupational hazard," the black man said.

The team leader stared at him. "Just focus on your job, all right? Don't get to be thinking beyond what you're capable of."

The muscles on the black man's face tightened, but he said nothing.

Everyone was startled when, with a solid thud, the throwing knife slammed into the wall, dead center on Tai's face. The man who had been playing with it slowly got up, walked to the wall, and pulled it out.

Over the Philippines

The pressure equalized. With a hiss, the back ramp began to open, revealing a sliver of night sky. Vaughn focused on his breathing, making sure it was slow and steady. He had never liked being on oxygen. It made him very aware how hostile the environment around him was. A chill was already settling into his bones from the freezing air swirling into the cargo bay, easily overwhelming the plane's heaters.

"Goggles," Vaughn said over the FM radio.

Both he and Tai slid the night vision goggles mounted on their helmets down and switched them on. The cargo bay was lit only by a few small red nightlights, but with the goggles, everything appeared as if brightly lit. Vaughn looked out over the ramp and could see hundreds of bright stars. It was beautiful.

Hong Kong

Ruiz lifted a single finger ever so slightly on his right hand, and the curtain behind him slowly began to open. "Gentlemen and lady, it is time."

Over the Philippines

Vaughn could feel the weight of the parachute, reserve, rucksack, weapon, and combat vest all weighing him down. Over a hundred pounds, all focused on the top of his shoulders, pressing down on him. He remembered jumps where his rucksack had weighed over twice as much and his only thought after standing at the six-minute warning had been to pray for the green light to go on so he could get the hell out of the plane and get this weight off his shoulders.

He glanced to his left at Tai. She stood ramrod straight, as if denying the weight on her shoulders.

Over the Mid-Pacific

The plane was descending. Even without access to the cockpit, David could tell that. Looking out one of the windows, he saw the ocean slowly approaching. He estimated that he had already passed through 10,000 feet, and the descent seemed to be picking up speed.

His attempts to get into the armored pilot's compartment had all failed. Whoever prepared this plane had done a good job. Naturally, there were no convenient parachutes lying around. His attempts to wake up the other passengers had also failed. Whatever had been in that gas was very powerful. David figured he had a couple of minutes left. He stared at the unconscious occupants of the passenger compartment and almost envied them. They would simply pass out of this life without the terror of seeing their end coming. For people in this profession, it was almost a mercy.

He went back to his seat, took out his PDA and satphone. The message he had begun earlier was still there.

He began typing.

Hong Kong

There was a collective gasp in the room as the object behind the curtain was revealed. This from people who had more money than many small nations and were not known to gasp at anything.

A slight smile curled at the sides of Ruiz's mouth. It was as he'd hoped. He had picked this particular item to be first for shock value. A jewel-festooned golden box over two feet long by one foot wide and high, it was a unique piece, dating back over six hundred years to the height of craftsmen at the Chinese Imperial Court. It was well-known among collectors—known for its extreme value and beauty, and known to have been lost during World War II, disappearing during the Rape of Nanking.

Ruiz left the podium, went to the box and carefully lifted the lid. The box had just been a precursor. Out of its interior he lifted a jade sculpture. The half-dozen in the audience, stunned already by the box, could only sit there with jaws agape at this even rarer, and greater, treasure.

"The bidding will commence on this," he announced, bringing the object forward and showing it to the six people.

The first of the six to collect his wits immediately shouted out a number. An insanely large number to begin the bidding with. The smile grew larger on Ruiz's face as a second person topped that number by over a million U.S. dollars, the currency of all world business.

In his other hand, Ruiz held a stopwatch, which he now showed to the bidders. "As agreed, the bidding will be over in sixty seconds."

The amount escalated at a pace the person taking in the numbers could barely keep up with as the buyers scrambled under the dual pressure of little time and even greater greed.

Over the Philippines

"One minute," the crew chief announced, holding up a single finger.

Vaughn and Tai edged closer to the ramp, side by side. Glancing down, he could see that they were over open ocean. The plan was to offset from Jolo over ten miles. That would keep anyone on the island from being aware a plane was anywhere nearby. They would fly their parachutes to the island.

Australia

"One minute," the team leader announced to the others. He lowered the satphone for a second. "This is going to be very interesting."

Over the Mid-Pacific

David glanced out the window. He could see the horizon now, which meant the plane was very low. There was so much more he wanted to write, but there was no more time.

He hit the send button on the satphone.

The SENDING message flickered on the small screen.

"Come on, come on," David whispered. He glanced around. Should he assume the crash position that was always briefed? He smiled bitterly to himself. With the engines still at full thrust, there wasn't going to be much left of this thing after it hit the water.

He looked at the screen. SENDING was still flashing.

Over the Philippines

Vaughn still couldn't see land below. He had to trust the plane's navigator that they were going out where they'd planned. He looked up into the tail of the plane at the red light that glowed there. In a flash it went out and the green light above it flickered on.

"Go," he yelled.

Hong Kong

Ruiz held up his hand, but still had to shout to stop the frenzied bidding. "Time."

He turned to the shaken woman who had been taking in the bids. "Who and how much?"

The woman swallowed. "Sixty million. Bidder number four."

There was silence in the room as the number sank in. It was as if, during the actual bidding, the reality had been lost in the lust for a one-of-a-kind piece of history.

Over the Mid-Pacific

David's complete focus was on the message flashing on his screen. He didn't want to see how close the water—and his death—were.

The letters SENDING began to dissolve and were replaced.

He cursed.

BLOCKED

They'd thought of everything, and cut him out of the Milstar loop.

The nose of the plane hit.

Over the Philippines

Vaughn and Tai went off the ramp in step and fell into the darkness.

Hong Kong

The room exploded in excitement. Money wasn't the issue. Questions were hurled at Ruiz. Where had these artifacts come from? Who was behind this?

He did not answer nor did he give them time to collect themselves. "We will now bid on the box. And . . ."

He paused for effect. ". . . after that, there will be sixteen more articles just as rare and exquisite."

Pacific Ocean

A piece of seat cushion and a rapidly dissipating fuel slick marked the grave of all those who had been on the plane.

Over Jolo Island

As soon as he was clear of the plane, Vaughn assumed a stable position, back arched, arms and legs spread wide. Then he quickly reached down and pulled the rip cord for his main parachute.

The opening shock jerked him upright. He looked up and checked his canopy. It was fully deployed and appeared intact. His hands snaked up and grabbed the toggles controlling the chute. Then he looked about for Tai. She was low jumper, according to the plan, the primary navigator to the drop zone on the island.

Even though they had radio communication, they would not use it unless absolutely necessary, for fear that the Abu Sayef would pick up the transmission. Vaughn spotted her chute below him and to the right. He pulled on his right toggle and turned to follow her.

Australia

"They're in the air," the team leader announced. "Let's see how well the bitch can do."

The black man abruptly stood up and headed for the door.

"Were the hell you think you're going?" the Australian demanded.

"I'm going to get some sleep." The black man paused and stared at the Australian. "You got a problem with that?"

"Oh, fuck off," the Australian muttered.

Over Jolo Island

Tai had a navigation board strapped on top of her reserve parachute, just in front of her oxygen cylinder. Built into the board was a compass, a GPS unit, an altimeter, and a small scale copy of the map of their target area. Through her night vision goggles she could see all them, although not at the greatest resolution. Enough to get the job done, though.

She never looked up. She had to trust that Vaughn was tracking her. Her entire focus was on the nav board. Every once in a while she would glance beyond to try to see the island far below them, a reflex that was impossible to resist. Ahead, far ahead, she could spot a dark mass: Jolo Island. They were on track for it, visually confirming what her instruments were telling her.

According to the altimeter, she was passing through 20,000 feet. The chutes were like large wings that they could fly, and were practically undetectable to radar. The C-130 was long gone, traveling along on the same track it had been on, as if nothing unusual had occurred.

She wasn't so focused that she didn't register the slight hitch in her gear, a tug on the right side. She looked up, tracing her riser up to where it connected to nylon cords that spread out to the chute itself. One of the cords had broken. As she was watching, another one popped. She'd never seen anything like that happen. Another let loose. Then another. The right side of her canopy began to flap loosely.

Above Tai, Vaughn could see that something was wrong, since she was now making a slow turn to the right. Even without the nav board, he could see Jolo Island, and she was turning away from it. Vaughn pulled in on both toggles, dumping air so he could get closer to her.

The rest of the nylon cords on the right side of Tai's parachute let go all at once, and the parachute went from a flying wing to a streamer of material wrapped into itself. Her descent practically unchecked, she plummeted toward the earth.

Vaughn cursed as he saw the chute collapse. He dumped as much air as he safely could without causing his own parachute to collapse and chased after her, losing ground.

"Cut away," Vaughn urged, not using the radio yet. He knew she had to know what to do next.

Tai was already in the process of doing that. She couldn't deploy her reserve with the main still attached because the reserve would get caught up in the main, so she had to get rid of the malfunctioning canopy before she could deploy the reserve. She flipped open the metal covers on her shoulder that protected the cutaways, the loops of metal cable attached to pins that locked the attaching point for the canopy to her harness. She put her thumbs through the metal loops and pulled both at the same time.

She was rewarded with two metal cable loops dangling over her thumbs but no released main. It was still firmly attached to the rig. Shocked at this second and most unexpected event, Tai lost her concentration and began to tumble, held partly upright by the streamer.

She was a good two hundred feet below Vaughn and moving farther away with each second. He couldn't understand why she hadn't cut away yet. The only possibility was that she was unconscious. But he could see her arms moving purposefully, pulling at her shoulders.

Tai was trying to dig into the cutaway, to pull the small pins out with the tip of her fingers, but she couldn't get leverage on them. She did a quick check at the nav board. The altimeter read 10,000 feet and indicated she was descending at almost terminal velocity.

Realizing there was no more time to mess around, she stopped trying to pull the pins and reached for the *shoto* tucked under her vest. She slid the blade out. With a quick slash, she cut through her right riser, the razor-sharp edge easily slicing through the nylon. Then the left. The main parachute fluttered away and she tumbled into full free fall. She slid the *shoto* back into its sheath, then arched her back, spreading her arms and legs to get stable before she pulled the reserve. If she pulled it while tumbling, there was a good chance it would just wrap around her body.

Vaughn flew past Tai's fluttering cutaway main canopy, his eyes focused on her. He watched her stop her tumbling and get stable, all the while mentally urging her to pull her reserve. They were getting low and running out of altitude.

Tai reached for the handle for her reserve and pulled it, tensing her body for the rapid opening shock that would follow its explosive opening.

Nothing.

Three malfunctions in a row. There was no training for this. She had run through all the emergency procedures correctly and was still plummeting toward earth at almost terminal velocity. The only thing slowing her down now was her own body spread as wide as she could make it.

Above her, Vaughn decided it was time to ignore security. "What are you doing? Over." He transmitted over the short-range FM.

Tai was struggling to maintain a stable position, her training pushing her to do it even as her mind realized it was worthless. She was going to die. At this speed, hitting the water would be like hitting concrete. She faintly heard Vaughn's voice in her earpiece.

"Reserve malfunction!" she screamed.

Reserves weren't supposed to malfunction, Vaughn thought as he glanced at his altimeter. Five thousand feet. She was at least four hundred feet below him, and the gap was growing wider.

There was only one option. It was stupid, it was insane, but he didn't hesitate.

He reached up, grabbed the metal covers over his cutaways, flipped them open, put his thumbs in the loops and pulled. The pins popped and his main separated from his harness. He was now in free fall.

Vaughn briefly went into the free-fall stable position, then tucked his head down, moved his arms back tight against his sides, legs together, and became an arrow, shooting down toward Tai.

"I'm coming for you," he yelled, the mike picking it up and transmitting. "Stay stable."

"What?" Tai was confused. How could he be coming for her? Then she realized what he had to have done. She wanted to yell at him, to curse him out for being so foolish, but she also knew it was too late. Still, there was a spark of hope in her chest. She didn't know what he planned to do, but whatever it was, it was her only chance at living.

Four thousand feet.

Vaughn looked past the black spread-eagle form that was Tai. Jolo Island was off in the distance, at least a mile or two offset from them. They were over open water and there was no way they would make landfall. That was the least of their problems right now. Vaughn could tell he was closing on Tai, but he wasn't sure if it would be enough.

Three thousand feet.

Tai was only fifty feet below him now, and he was inching closer. It was going to be close, very close.

Two thousand feet.

She was ten feet below him . . . five feet. Vaughn moved out of the dive position to stable as he came alongside her. He knew that grabbing her and pulling his reserve wouldn't work—the opening shock would be stronger than his ability to hold onto her. He had to make sure there was a secure connection. With one hand, he reached out and grabbed her harness.

"Stay stable," he ordered over the radio. She was staring at him, the night vision goggles making her seem more like a flying machine than a flesh and blood human being.

One thousand feet.

With the other hand, Vaughn reached underneath his reserve, fingers ripping at the nylon casing around the eighteen-foot lowering line attached to his rucksack. A nail ripped away, but he ignored the pain and managed to hook his finger around a piece of the nylon strap. With all his strength, he pulled, extracting a length about two feet long.

Five hundred feet.

Tai was having a hard time keeping them stable and oriented. Their bodies were beginning to tumble, but Vaughn knew there was nothing to be done about that as he took the length of nylon strap and pressed it against the snap link on the front of Tai's combat vest, trying to press it through the gate. Tai realized what he was doing and grabbed his hand with both of hers. The nylon popped through the snap link.

Vaughn's other hand grabbed his reserve handle. Out of the corner of his eye he could see the ocean surface. Close, way too close. He pulled the rip-cord grip on the reserve and the chute spewed out. Vaughn was jerked upright, then cried out in pain as the lowering line ripped out of its casing, burning down the inside of his right thigh, and then abruptly stopped at its full length, and he was jerked again as Tai came to a halt at the end of it.

She hit the water barely two seconds later, then Vaughn splashed down hard next to her.

CHAPTER 12

Abayon was staring out to sea, looking at the moon reflecting off the water. He felt bone-tired. Telling the story to Fatima had exhausted him, and there was more still to tell. He sighed as he heard the door behind him open and then quietly swing shut. Fatima walked up to him with a bottle. He took several deep drafts before putting it down.

"Where was I?" he asked, although he knew quite well where he'd left off.

"The Americans who parachuted into Japan," Fatima said.

"Ah, yes. One of the Americans was killed right there on the drop zone. Beheaded by a Kempetai officer. The officer turned to behead Martin, forced him to his knees, but another officer stopped him, saying there was a need for living Americans. Martin and the other survivor were taken into custody, thrown in the back of a truck, surrounded by guards, and driven to a Kempetai base. There, to Martin's surprise, his partner was greeted as if he'd been expected—by a well-dressed Japanese man, obviously someone with great power, given the way even the Kempetai officers were treating him."

"Who was this other man?" Fatima asked.

"David Lansale was his name. Here's the interesting thing, and what made Martin wonder what was going on: Lansale turned to Martin and said he was sorry, then left in the company of the mysterious Japanese man. Martin was then taken away, eventually transported to Manchuria and 731. He never saw or heard of Lansale again. He knew he'd been betrayed, but he had no clue why."

"And you do?"

"I do now, to an extent." Abayon fell silent, and Fatima patiently waited. "I was in that field, tied to the stake for five days," he finally said. "Martin died quickly. On the second day. I heard the others crying out. That was bad. But the worst was the smell. Whatever they used on us made us vomit and unable to control our bowels."

Abayon stayed quiet for a few seconds, recalling that horrible field of death. "I was the last one alive. I could sense it on the morning of the fifth day. They had taken about half of the prisoners away to do with them as they had done to my wife. Others, who died on the stake, they left to rot. They were timing the deaths. In the middle of the fifth day, the soldiers came once more. They wore their protective suits. Gas masks. Many, I could tell, were not happy with their task. It was just as easy for them to be infected.

"A few went up and down the rows of stakes, confirming that all were dead. I knew this was my only chance. I slumped forward against the ropes holding me. I had vomit all over my chest and down my legs. Excrement and urine soiling my pants. I held my breath so the soldier coming along my line would not see my chest move. They didn't want to touch the bodies to check pulses. They were confirming death just by looking for breathing.

"The soldier was in a rush. He looked at me for no more than ten seconds, then moved on the next one. He made it to the end of the line, then joined his comrades. They drove away in their truck. Several hours later, just before nightfall, a truck came back. This one contained the prisoners whose job it was to clear the field. Take in the harvest, so to speak.

"The Japanese used Korean laborers for this. The Japanese did not care if the Koreans became infected. Once more I pretended to be dead. I nearly was, so it was not difficult. I was very sick. I was running a fever. I was dehydrated. Almost delirious. A man cut me loose from the stake and dragged me to the cart behind the truck, which was full of bodies. He threw me in. I weighed perhaps eighty pounds after months of captivity and because of whatever they had infected me with.

"They threw bodies on top of me. *Meruta.* Logs. And that is how we were tossed in that cart. I lay there, buried among the dead. I almost wished I was."

Again Abayon fell silent.

"How did you survive?" Fatima asked.

"Hate," he said. "And love."

"I don't understand."

"Even though my wife was dead, I still loved her,"

Abayon said. "That kept me going. And because I loved, I hated those who had killed her. That gave me strength. All I thought of while I was in that cart was revenge. They drove to a ditch and dumped us in. I lay there until they were long gone, then clawed my way out. Through all the bodies. I crawled all night. Just to put distance between myself and that place of death."

He turned from the ocean and stared at his god-daughter. "After that, you can well imagine that I wanted to know everything there was about Unit 731. And about that American."

"I don't understand the connection," Fatima said.

"Neither did I at the time," he replied. "When I escaped from 731, the war was winding down. The Japanese in the camp released all their plague-infected animals. Over thirty thousand people died in the Harbin area in the next couple of years because of that.

"But here is where it gets interesting and lines begin to cross," Abayon continued. "The good Dr. Ishii was captured by the Americans. And did they put him on trial for the war criminal that he was?" Abayon did not wait for an answer. "Of course not. He—and the information he had—was too valuable. In exchange for immunity from prosecution, he gave the Americans the results of the so-called field tests—the tests my wife and I and hundreds of thousands of others had been part of. Valuable data on biological warfare that the Americans wanted.

"Thirty members of 731—none of the important ones—were put on trial as part of a big show. They were brought before the Allied War Crimes Tribunal in Yokohama on the eleventh of March, 1948. Charges ranged from vivisection to murder to wrongful removal of body parts." Abayon shook his head.

"Wrongful removal of body parts—can you believe there was ever a need for such a charge?

"Twenty-three were found guilty. Five were sentenced to death. None of those were ever executed, though. By 1958 every single one of those convicted was free. The Russians weren't so nice. Those members of 731 they captured, they executed. I suppose it was because the Americans got Ishii and all the good data.

"There is even a shrine in Japan dedicated to the members of Unit 731. Can you believe that? No collective sense of guilt for what they did. It is only in the last few years that the Japanese even acknowledged what they did in Nanking.

"But back to Lansale. He was supposedly an operative of the OSS—Office of Strategic Service. But that was just his cover. And the mission of the other two men who accompanied him was obviously a sham also. It took me many years to find out who Lansale met with and why. He was an envoy from a secret organization sent to negotiate with the Japanese. Even though the two countries were at war, there were those on both sides who were looking past the war and to the future."

"What was this secret organization?" Fatima asked.

"Why do you use the past tense?" Abayon asked, but did not wait for a reply. "I've only heard rumors of it. And never a name."

Fatima frowned. "How can something not have a name?"

Abayon shrugged. "Surround yourself with enough layers of protection and cutouts and you can do anything. This group is very secretive. Which makes me wonder if they are really part of any government, because governments—especially democracies—are sieves when it comes to keeping secrets. But let me continue my story.

"Lansale was taken from the Kempetai headquarters to a meeting with Hirohito's brother, Prince Chichibu, to coordinate the Golden Lily project. Also present at the meeting was Admiral Yamamoto, who carried out the Pearl Harbor attack. You see, this organization knew what the Japanese were doing, the systematic looting of all the lands they conquered."

"How did they know this?" Fatima asked.

"That is a good question," Abayon said. "And I don't know the answer. But I talked to a senior Japanese officer who was Yamamoto's adjutant. He was on trial in the Philippines for war crimes. He'd been sentenced to death, and perhaps that made his lips a little looser. He told me that at this meeting a verbal agreement was made: the Americans would allow the Japanese to continue the Golden Lily. But none of it was to be shipped back to Japan. It was to be hidden in the Philippines."

"Why?"

"As every Filipino is taught in school, Douglas MacArthur had vowed to return to the islands. Essentially, the Americans were allowing the Japanese to do their dirty work for them."

"But why would the Japanese agree to this?"

"Because Lansale pointed out something that most smart Japanese knew, even back in those dark early days of World War Two when they seemed unstoppable: that the end of the war, with Japan losing, was inevitable. Yamamoto was particularly aware of this, having spent considerable time in the United States prior to the start of the war. Even though he planned the Pearl Harbor attack, up to the last moment he had argued vehemently against implementing it.

"Do you think the amazing recovery Japan made after the war was a coincidence? Plain good luck? From this meeting forward, elements in both the United States and Japan were already planning the economic recovery of the defeated nation."

"But . . ." Fatima drew the word out. "I still don't see why the Japanese would agree to this. What did they get in return—beyond this plan for economic recovery?"

"The emperor was assured that he—and his family—would not be tried for war crimes. Not only that, but that he would be allowed to keep his position after the end of the war. Think about it: why was the leader of a nation that had blatantly and so dishonestly ordered a surprise attack on the United States not only pardoned, but allowed to remain in power?

"Of course, there were some other angles to the whole deal," Abayon continued. "Chichibu had to give Lansale assurances that the Japanese would not try to develop atomic weapons. So in a way, the cover story for the OSS mission was true, just not in the way the other two unfortunate souls who accompanied Lansale anticipated."

"So Chichibu and Yamamoto sold out their own country," Fatima said.

"Is that the way you see it?" Abayon asked, staring at her hard.

She'd seen that look before, and turned over what she had just learned in her mind, examining the various angles as Abayon had taught her. "They knew they could not win the war so they looked to the future and the higher good."

"That is what they believed."

"Do you agree with what they did?" Fatima asked.

Abayon smiled grimly. She had thrown the gauntlet back at him. "It was an interesting moral dilemma: betraying your own country in the present to serve its future prosperity. Most would not agree with betrayal."

"And you?" she pressed.

"No. I do not agree with betrayal. I think they admitted defeat before they were defeated. But . . ."

"But what?"

"Who is to say whose allegiance Chichibu's lay with? What if this secret organization is something more than just an American group? What if it is international? And Chichibu had a higher allegiance?"

"But Yamamoto—" Fatima protested. "He was a soldier. A man, supposedly of great honor. He—"

"Ah," Abayon said, cutting her off, "there is more to this. Remember, the Americans killed Yamamoto. The story written in history books is that they broke the Japanese code and knew where he would be flying. So they sent long-range fighters to shoot him down over Bougainville on the eighteenth of April in 1943. But what if the Americans were meant to get that message? It was a mightily convenient intelligence coup otherwise."

"Plots within plots," Fatima said. "So if Chichibu was part of this secret organization, then Yamamoto might not have been, and they arranged for him to be killed."

"Yes."

Fatima mulled this over. "So you believe there is a secret organization that crosses—indeed supersedes—national interests and manipulates events?"

"Yes."

"To what end?"

"To further their own end," Abayon said simply. "I

don't know exactly what that is, but from what I've gathered it seems to be the accumulation of wealth for the very few who are members of this group. And the controlling of economies, governments, the military—people, essentially—to maintain their status quo."

"The auction. And my father's mission—which he told me nothing of, of course. Those are designed to draw this group out."

Once more she made it a statement, not a question. "Yes. Remember, this organization wants what we have in these tunnels. They've wanted it for sixty years."

"That is why you've never used any of it before," Fatima said.

Abayon nodded. "Not only do they want it, but I think they put it here, if the meeting between Lansale and Chichibu is true. Golden Lily was designed from the very beginning by this group. They used the cover of the war to gather their riches."

Fatima mulled that over. "But . . ."

"Go ahead," Abayon prompted.

"Why now?"

"Two reasons. One is that I will not be here much longer."

"You look fine—" Fatima began to protest, but Abayon held up a hand, silencing her.

"You have been very observant and wise up until now. Please do not change. I have less than a year to live. So, perhaps it is selfish of me, but I want to find out who I've been shadow-boxing with all these years."

"And the second reason?"

"It's time," Abayon said simply. "Since 9/11 the gloves have come off. We are entering an age of a new type of conflict, and this group is probably quite aware of that. The Americans came after us the other night and many people died. We can sit and let them come to us or we can go after them. I prefer action over reaction."

Fatima nodded. "All right. What happened to this Lansale?"

"He managed to make his way back to the United States via diplomatic channels. He then became a career spook, as near as I have been able to find out. Strangely, though, he was photographed in Dallas on the twenty-second of November, 1963, but he always claimed he was never there."

"What is so important about that?"

"Something very significant happened that day."

"What?"

"President Kennedy was assassinated."

CHAPTER 13

Jolo Island

Vaughn lay on his back staring up at the stars, savoring the cool night breeze blowing across his soaked clothes and the feel of sand beneath him. They were on the shore of a small, deserted cove on the north side of Jolo Island. As soon as they made landfall, they conducted a quick box reconnaissance of the immediate area, and both were confident they were on an isolated part of the island.

"That was fucked," Tai said.

Vaughn turned his head and looked at her in the moonlight. She was lying next to him, still breathing hard from the long swim to shore. In her hand she had the GPS, which she'd just pulled out of a waterproof bag in her rucksack.

"We're alive," Vaughn noted.

Tai looked up from the GPS screen at the sky. "It will be dawn soon. We're over ten kilometers from where we're supposed to be." She pointed. "Hono Mountain is there."

Vaughn could see a large dark mass in the moonlight towering up into the sky.

"We're way behind schedule," Tai added.

"Is that what bothers you?" Vaughn asked.

"Hell, no," she said angrily. "Three malfunctions in a row. Bullshit. Bullshit. Bullshit."

They'd hit the water hard, then had to scramble out from underneath the reserve canopy that draped over them. Unspoken between them was the fact that they hadn't worn life vests. They'd been so confident they could make the flight to the island, it was never brought up. For Vaughn, that mistake brought echoes of the designator battery. What saved them was that they followed standing operating procedure and water-proofed the contents of their rucksacks before the jump, which served as flotation devices in the pinch. They'd cut away from the reserve, Vaughn got rid of the harness, and then they tied themselves together using a short length of rope, put their elbows on their floating rucks, and started swimming toward the silhouette of Jolo island. It took them almost an hour to make it.

Tai had explained all the failures to him. Vaughn had to agree with her succinct assessment of what happened to her, but he wanted to wait and let her lay out the obvious.

"Someone was trying to kill me," she finally said.

"You think?"

That earned him a slight smile that momentarily wiped away the tension and anger on Tai's face.

Vaughn checked his watch. "We're overdue on the initial entry report." He sat up, grabbed his rucksack, and began to open it to get to the satellite radio inside.

Tai put out a hand and stopped him.

"What?" Vaughn asked.

"Someone was trying to kill me," she repeated.

"I know, and—" Vaughn stopped and slowly nodded. "I see." He let go of the ruck. "Why? And who?"

"I don't know."

"The Abu Sayef?"

"I think getting to my chute and disabling it would have been a little hard for them to do."

"Someone tried to kill you," Vaughn said.

"I already said that twice," Tai responded.

"Yes. So, you're dead."

Tai stared at him. Their eyes locked in the moonlight, and she slowly nodded and smiled. "Very good." Her smile was not of the pleasant variety.

Hawaii

General Slocum was none too pleased, and he was letting his staff know it. The initial entry report from the recon team was overdue. This raised a lot of questions, none of which anyone knew the answer to. Had the team been compromised, which meant that the entire mission was compromised? Was it equipment failure? Had both jumpers died on infiltration? Or were they too severely injured to make commo?

From behind the one-way glass in the observation room, Royce watched the general lash questions at his staff, none of which could be answered by any of them. It was a fruitless exercise, but one Royce had seen far too many times in his dealings with the military. Von Clausewitz, the great Prussian general, who many military men liked to quote, had once said, *"In war, everything is simple, but even the simple is difficult."* Royce always remembered that saying when he dealt with the military.

There was another element that began to enter into the discourse in the operations room: someone dared ask the question whether this was simply a twist thrown into the simulation to see how they reacted. That earned the speaker an even fiercer tongue-lashing by Slocum, who got them back on track by pretending this was a real exercise.

For Royce, there was another issue bothering him. One that had nothing to do with the recon team or even the mission. He'd used one of his connections to the National Security Agency to check on the progress of the jet David was on. The NSA was wired into Space Command out in Cheyenne Mountain, which controlled a ring of satellites that tracked every single object that flew.

The reports had been fine up until a little while ago. Then the jet disappeared.

At first Royce had assumed that it landed on some island. But when he checked the last confirmed satellite spotting, projected out speed and time, and drew a circle, all he was left with was ocean. There was no place it could have landed.

It had vanished.

Royce did not believe in the Bermuda Triangle, or the Devil's Sea, the Pacific's version of that famed locale. Planes didn't vanish. They crashed, they blew up, or they landed somewhere. Instinctively, he knew that David—and everyone else on board that plane—was dead. The Organization had retired them. Permanently.

He shook his head. It wasn't his instincts, it was reality. He'd sensed David's fatalism the last time they met. And he had to assume that David had not made the decision to retire, despite what he'd told him. He'd been forced out.

Royce held his emotions at bay and considered that. True, David was old. But he was still an effective agent. A man with loads of experience. So why "retire" him?

There was only one reason Royce could come up with: David had fucked up.

And David had been working this op.

Royce's jaw clenched. Tai. The bitch. She— His thought abruptly ended as a red light flickered in the operations center. An incoming message. It began to scroll across the screen in front of the room. The over-due initial entry report:

> ON JOLO. WATER LANDING. TAI DEAD. MAL-
> FUNCTION. BODY GONE. WILL CONTINUE WITH
> MISSION. VAUGHN

The muscle on the side of Royce's face relaxed. Payback was a motherfucker.

Australia

"One down, five to go," the team leader announced.

"But that only leaves five to do the job," the black man noted. "They are supposed to do the job, aren't they?"

"Oh fuck off."

Johnston Atoll

It was a worthless piece of ground if taken by itself. But as realtors always say: location, location, and location. In this case the key to the location was isolation. Many believed Johnston Atoll was the most isolated reef in the world. It is eight hundred kilometers southwest of Hawaii—the nearest island—and fifteen hundred kilometers north and east of North Line Island and Phoenix Island, respectively.

The United States and the Kingdom of Hawaii annexed Johnston Atoll in 1858. The United States mined the guano deposits until the late 1880s. When they ran out, it was designated a wildlife refuge, in 1926. Then the Navy saw the strategic position of the place and took over in 1934.

The atoll consists of four coral islands: Johnston Island, Sand Island, North Island, and East Island. The largest of the four, at 625 acres, is Johnston Island, and the only one that could support an air strip. It was the place where the Navy settled in, and the island has continued to be the center of what little human community there is. At present, there were 960 civilian and 250 military personnel stationed on the island. They were not there on vacation.

The United States government designated the atoll a national wildlife refuge jointly administered by the U.S. Fish and Wildlife Service and the Department of Defense: two distinct, incompatible organizations. As with any jointly administered operation in the U.S. government, when DOD was on one end, things tended to slide down the table to it.

The major facility on the atoll was operated and maintained by the Field Command, Defense Special Weapons Agency, Kirtland Air Force Base, New Mexico. Its mission made perfect sense for the remote location, and as usual for the military, was given an acronym: JACADS: Johnston Atoll Chemical Agent Disposal System.

The Department of Defense claimed that JACADS had fulfilled its mission, which begged the question as to why so many people were still stationed there and what exactly they were doing. If the U.S. military wasn't developing any more chemical weapons and JACADS had fulfilled its mission of destroying the stockpile, there seemed no point for the large contingent of personnel, all of whom had top secret security clearances.

Six kilometers south of Johnston Atoll, a submarine periscope pierced the surface, cutting a slow, smooth wake as the craft ran parallel to the atoll. Standing in the cramped control room, Moreno could see the lights on the island reflected and magnified through the scope's mirrors.

Satisfied, he ordered the scope down and the sub to come to a halt and submerge—to sit on the bottom in one hundred feet of water. They were here, but it wasn't time yet. Tomorrow would be another day.

Hong Kong

Ruiz slumped down on the podium. The room was empty. He looked at the piece of paper the woman who took the bids had left him. He knew Abayon's goal with the auction was not about the money, but about the attention it would bring. But still, the figure was staggering.

His cell phone had already rung four times with inquiries from major news agencies wanting to know the source of the auction items. His reply had been to sink the hook in deeper and invite the reporters to another auction, where he promised even more rare pieces would be put up for sale.

And he dropped a hint, asking the reporters in return if they had ever heard of the Golden Lily project.

Okinawa

"Vaughn is on the island, ten klicks from where he was supposed to land," Orson announced.

"Vaughn?" Sinclair repeated. "What about Tai?"

"Dead."

That brought silence to the four people in the isolation area.

"How?" Hayes finally asked.

"Apparently some sort of parachute malfunction," Orson said. "The initial entry report wasn't specific." He shrugged. "Nothing changes. Vaughn can do the recon. The mission is still a go."

"Lot of fucking empathy there," Sinclair muttered.

Orson glared at him. "You want empathy, you should have joined the Peace Corps. There's nothing any of us can do about Tai. Let's get back to work, people."

Hawaii

Royce frowned as he began to read the latest message on the laptop from David's—now, his—boss. A job needed to be done in Hong Kong. Hong Kong? he wondered. What the hell did Hong Kong have to do with the current mission? There was no explanation, just instructions.

There was no point in pondering the reasons, and from experience, Royce knew he wouldn't get any explanation if he asked. The problem was, he would have to divert assets that were allocated to the Abu Sayef mission. There was time, but not much.

He brought up a blank message and typed in the address. Then he quickly typed out the orders and transmitted the command.

Then Royce sat very still for several minutes, thinking hard, trying to come to a decision he didn't want to face. Some said ignorance was bliss. But ignorance could also be dangerous.

Australia

"Grab your gear and let's get moving," the team leader announced. He was ahead of his own order, as he had his rucksack slung over one shoulder and his weapon in his hand.

The three other members of the team looked up from what they were doing. The Sicilian slid his knife into its scabbard and without a word, began gathering his equipment. The black mercenary considered the order for a few seconds, then complied. The Australian began gathering his gear, but had to ask: "What's the rush? The main team hasn't even gone in yet."

"We're going to the Philippines," the team leader said, "but just to cross-load."

"Where to then?" the Australian wanted to know. "What's the op?"

"We're staging out of Manila," the team leader said. "Civilian flight from there."

The Australian was getting exasperated by the slow flow of information. "You bloody well gonna tell us where we're going and what we're gonna be doing or you going to wait till we get there?"

The team leader walked up to the Australian. The blood was pulsing in the scar on his head, backlighting the barbed-wire tattoo. "You want to run this team?"

"I want to know what I'm going to be doing."

"You'll know when you need to know," the team leader growled.

The black man stepped between the two, dwarfing both. "There's no reason for you not to tell us where we're going and what we're going to do." He put a hand on the team leader's chest, forestalling whatever he was about to say, and looked at the Australian. "But you know what, *mate,* what the fuck difference does it make?" He spread his massive arms, pushing the two back. "It's the job we signed up for, and it isn't like we can quit. So let's shut the fuck up and get going."

Jolo Island

Vaughn and Tai didn't need the GPS to make their way to the mountain. From the beach, they shot an azimuth to the crown of Hono Mountain and then moved out into the jungle, staying on that track. Tai was on point, Vaughn right behind, close enough to reach out and touch her. All he could see were the two reflective cat eyes sewn into the back of her patrol cap. He knew all she was focused on was the glowing needle of her compass. Her concentration was verified by the occasional grunt of pain as she walked into a tree or log.

It was hard going, breaking their way through the tangled vegetation. Vaughn kept a pace count, and after two hours he reached out and tapped her on the shoulder, signaling a halt. They did rucksack flops on the jungle floor, each half sitting, half lying on their packs, weapons across their laps, facing each other but offset, so they had clear fields of fire.

Not that they were likely to bump into anyone around here. They had yet to see any sign of civilization, not even a trail. Vaughn remembered from isolation that the north side of the island was almost completely unpopulated, which was a blessing, given the screw-up this mission had been so far.

"I need to call in a situation report," he whispered.

"I know. Wait until we stop for daylight," Tai advised.

"No. I want to call it in from a location where we won't be staying."

Tai digested that. "You're that worried?"

"You're the one that had three malfunctions on one jump. I've done over two hundred jumps and never had one malfunction. I'd say that constitutes reason for worry. I'd prefer that the only one who can pinpoint our location be us."

"All right."

By feel, Vaughn got the satellite radio out. He typed a message into the keyboard, telling the rest of the team that he would not be on the mountain until the following night and would send in a report as soon as he discovered something. He signed off and put the radio back in his rucksack.

"We should be pretty close to the hot spot," he said to Tai.

She already had her GPS unit out. She turned it on and waited while it acquired the nearest positioning satellites, then put a poncho liner over her head and turned on the back light on the unit.

"How close?" Vaughn asked as he kept watch on the surrounding darkness. Even if they had their night vision goggles, he doubted they would see much in the pitch-black underneath the jungle canopy.

"Eleven hundred and twelve meters. Two hundred and four degree azimuth."

Vaughn remembered blundering around in the dark

years ago at Fort Benning on night land navigation courses. Technology had certainly changed things, although the loss of the night vision goggles during their water landing and the disaster of the laser targeting during the earlier raid he'd led made clear that one could not totally count on the equipment. He clicked in the correct azimuth on his compass, an older but more reliable technology.

"Let's move," he told Tai. "Do you want me to take point?"

"For a little while." She turned off the backlight.

Vaughn got to his feet and shouldered his rucksack. He felt Tai's hand on his shoulder as he led the way through the dark jungle. He had his MP-5 slung over his shoulder. In one hand he had the compass, while he held the other out in front of his face to prevent losing an eyeball on the vegetation they were moving through.

The ground was sloping up, which didn't aid movement. Checking the altimeter on his watch, Vaughn saw that they were up over a thousand feet in altitude. He was taking short, careful steps, but that didn't help him as he tried to plant his left foot and it touched nothing but air. He tried to pull back, but his momentum was too strong and he tumbled forward.

Behind him, Tai was surprised to see the two little reflective cat eyes on the back of Vaughn's cap disappear and his shoulder vanish from her hand. She froze, knowing right away he'd fallen. The question was, how far? She could hear his body breaking through brush and a muffled curse.

Kneeling down, she felt forward with her free hand, found the dropoff and leaned over it. "Vaughn?"

"Yeah." He didn't sound too far away, but his voice had a strange echo. "I think we found the heat source."

CHAPTER 14

Hong Kong

Ruiz watched the computer screen and the large numbers go from the single account on the left to the fourteen accounts on the right. Those fourteen represented various groups around the world, most of which were on the United States watch list for terrorist activities.

A large sum from the previous night's auction still remained, and he shifted that to an account representing the government of China. At least that's what the Chinese liaison had told him, but Ruiz had his doubts since the routing number indicated it was a Swiss bank. Corruption was nothing new to China, or any other government for that matter. Still, that large sum had not only paid for the platform to hold last night's auction and the one to be conducted this evening, but would be forwarded through cutouts to other organizations that the Abu Sayef supported in the war against the West.

Ruiz was no fool. And Abayon had not tried to fool him. The old man had been blunt. While the money was a great benefit to the worldwide cause, the real purpose of the auction was to draw out the hidden enemy. Abayon had told him of the secret pact between the Americans and Japanese regarding the Golden Lily. The visit by the Yakuza representative indicated the matter was far from forgotten.

Ruiz was located on the top floor of a sixty-four-story skyscraper in the heart of Hong Kong. The top two floors were his, with the floor below packed with security guards, the best money could hire in the city. The room where the auction had been held was on the same floor as his, as well as the rooms holding the rest of the items to go on stage tonight.

Business done, Ruiz sat back in the deeply uphol-stered chair and gazed about the suite. He knew Abayon would not approve of the luxury. The old man had been in his cave and tunnel complex too long. Ruiz remembered the first time he'd seen the stacks of gold bullion. He had not been able to equate the sparse con-ditions surrounding it with such wealth.

The hidden enemy. Ruiz shook his head. The old man had been out of touch with the real world for too many decades. The Yakuza came because the old men in Japan who had been part of Golden Lily sent them. The Yakuza worked for the highest bidder. As far as the World War II conspiracy, Ruiz had nodded politely when the old man told his story, but found it hard to believe that it happened the way it was described, and even if it had, that such an organization still existed.

The phone rang and Ruiz picked it up. The head of the

security detail on the floor below informed him that his expected visitor had shown up. Ruiz walked to the door and waited. When there was a tap, he swung it open.

A Japanese woman stood there. She bowed, ever so slightly. Ruiz did the same. "I am appreciative that you could come," he said.

"After last night's performance, the argument was most persuasive," the woman said.

Ruiz led her into the suite and they sat across from each other. She was still, waiting. For the first time, Ruiz felt a sense of discomfort.

"About your representative. It was a rash act by—"

The woman dismissed the issue with a brief wave of her hand. "He was nothing. A messenger. And the message he brought was understood. I just am not sure what your message is."

"Tonight's auction."

The woman waited.

"I will preempt it and deliver all I have to you for fifty million dollars."

"You would sell us what was ours?"

" 'Was' is the key word," Ruiz said.

"And the rest?"

" 'The rest'?"

"The rest of the Golden Lily? What you have here is but a fraction of the whole."

"I cannot speak for the rest," Ruiz said. "I have what was shipped here."

The Japanese woman looked around the suite, as if contemplating the offer. "I assume you will not be returning to Jolo?"

"I cannot—if we make this deal."

"And if we do not?"

"Then I do as planned and hold the auction tonight."

Ruiz shifted in his plush seat uncomfortably. "The items sold separately at auction—based on last night—will cost well over one hundred million. I am making you a very good proposition."

The woman abruptly stood. "You will have my answer one hour prior to the auction."

"I'd prefer—"

"I do not care what you prefer. To be able to transfer that large a sum takes a little bit of time. You will have my answer."

With that she strode to the door and was gone.

Jolo Island

Tai waited until it became light enough to see before climbing down to join Vaughn. He was at the bottom of a twelve-foot shaft cut into the side of the mountain. The sides were overrun with growth and the opening was almost completely blocked. If Vaughn hadn't fallen in, Tai wasn't sure they'd have found it. When she finished climbing down, she found Vaughn sitting cross-legged, staring straight ahead at a two-foot-wide black hole at the side of the shaft.

"What do you think?" she asked.

Vaughn glanced at her. "That's the way in. The question is, do we want to go in?"

Tai glanced at him. "What do you mean? Abayon is in there."

"I think there's more than Abayon in there."

Tai sat down next to Vaughn at the bottom of the shaft. She could feel the warm air blowing out of it on her face. The hot spot. "There probably is."

"Such as?" Vaughn asked.

She sighed. "What do you think of the team?"

"What?"

"Our illustrious team. Orson. Sinclair. Kasen. Hayes. You. Me. The team."

Vaughn shrugged, still staring into the dark hole. "Special Ops people. The kind you'd want for something like this."

"Fuck-ups," Tai said.

Vaughn turned to her. "What did you say?"

"I was relieved of command in Iraq because I complained of prisoner abuse. My career was over. Kasen—I checked on him. He was up for manslaughter for killing an Afghani not under rules of engagement. Couldn't get much more than that, but his time in the green machine was over."

"He's also an addict," Vaughn added.

Tai didn't seem surprised. "Lots of drugs in Afghanistan. He's not only an addict, but he has AIDS. And it's not responding well to treatment. Then there's Sinclair. Came here from Leavenworth."

"What was he in there for?"

Tai looked at him. "Running weapons out of Thailand."

Vaughn had heard about the scandal in the First Special Group. "Orson? Hayes?"

"Hayes is dying."

"He's what?" Vaughn remembered Hayes's late night trip to the latrine and the coughing.

"Cancer. Very aggressive. He was diagnosed three weeks ago. From what I could find out, he's got one to two months left to live."

"Fuck."

"Right on that."

"And Orson?"

"On him, nothing recent that I could find. He was in the SEALs. SEAL Team Six, as that spook said. But he left the team four years ago and simply vanished as far as a paper trail, even a classified paper trail."

"How did you get access to the information you got?"

"I was Military Intelligence," Tai said. "I still have contacts."

Vaughn wondered about that. How could she communicate with her contacts about the other members of the team if she only met them once they went into isolation? The facts didn't add up. But he wasn't about to point that out to the one person who was supposed to cover his back here on an island full of terrorists.

Vaughn shifted back to what she had told him about the other members of the team. "So one guy who is going to die shortly, one who has a potentially fatal infection, and three people who fucked their careers up. And one mystery."

"A bunch of losers."

"Speak for yourself."

Tai smiled. Her short dark hair was plastered to the side of her face. Her skin was splattered with mud. Her gear was still wet from the ocean. All in all, quite the mess. She had her MP-5 across her knees and had gone back to staring at the dark hole that beckoned to them.

"I don't think we should go in until night," she said.

"What difference will it make in there?" Tai asked, nodding toward the opening.

"Because most people still work on a normal biological clock," Tai said. "I guarantee there will be less people about at night."

"You guarantee?"

Once more she gave a slight smile. "All right. But come on—"

Vaughn nodded. "I agree. I'm in no rush anyway. And I don't see why Orson is either."

He shifted his rucksack into a more comfortable position. "Do you buy that killing this Abayon guy will destroy the Abu Sayef?"

"No."

Vaughn waited for amplification but none was forthcoming. Finally he was forced to ask: "Why not?"

He could just barely see the dark form of Tai's head moving in the growing dawn as she turned toward him. "Come on. You've been in Special Operations. All we've been doing the last several years is fighting terrorism. You know better."

This time Vaughn remained silent. She was right, but he wanted to hear her thoughts, because the more she spoke, the more he would learn about her. And he needed to know more about her because it was the two of them alone on this island, and tonight they were going in that dark hole that beckoned in front of them.

Tai finally continued. "Capturing Saddam didn't stop the insurgency in Iraq. The Israelis have killed many Palestinian leaders and the movement continues. These are people who haven't dedicated themselves to their leaders, but to their causes. And the only way to defeat a terrorist movement is to defeat the cause."

Vaughn had spent two rotations in Iraq and one in Afghanistan while he was in Special Forces before going to Delta Force, and he knew she was right. The U.S. military was waging the wrong type of war in both places—as it had done before in Vietnam.

"So then why are we doing this?" he asked.

"I've been thinking about that," Tai said.

Vaughn could now see that she was also lying back on her ruck, the infamous rucksack flop. Her eyes were closed.

"There's something else going," Tai said. "Something that Royce and Orson aren't telling us."

"There's always something else going on," Vaughn said. "And it's usually about money."

A slight smile graced Tai's thin lips. " 'Ours is but to do and die.' "

Vaughn was startled. "Tennyson?"

It was Tai's turn to be surprised. "Every soldier should know Tennyson. The Abu Sayef have never been high on the United States terrorism target list for a simple reason—there's no oil here."

"Cynical," Vaughn said.

"Skeptical," Tai countered.

"So what's changed?"

"That's the big question, isn't it? But I bet it has something to do with wealth in some form or another. Now, you want first watch?"

Johnston Atoll

Moreno looked through the periscope at the small island, focusing on the cluster of buildings. His position was a couple of hours ahead of Jolo Island, so the morning sun was well up already. He could see little activity on the island. An occasional vehicle moving on the few miles of paved road. There had been no activity at the airfield so far.

Moreno had the military flight schedule for the atoll. He'd downloaded it from the Internet, and he thought it was very nice of the American military to publish it on the Web. One Air Force plane was scheduled to land just after noon on its way across the Pacific on a regular run.

Moreno had an entire binder of information on Johnston Atoll, all gained from simply surfing the

Web. He even knew the exact number of guards on the island. Not U.S. military, but rather, civilian contractors. And probably not the best that could be recruited, since they were serving in places where the pay was much better, such as Iraq.

Thirty-two rent-a-cops guarded the facility, probably in three shifts of eight, if they were working at full strength. But that implied they were all working seven days a week, which Moreno doubted, since one had to add in days off. He guessed a guard shift was at most six, possibly four. There were several hundred U.S. military personnel on the island, but they were scientists and supply officers and clerks—not infantrymen. He had to assume those people had access to weapons, but he hoped to be on the island before an alert could be issued.

And then it would be too late.

Oahu

Royce sat in the clearing on top of David's truck, staring aimlessly to the north. He had no doubt the Organization had killed David and all the others on the plane. Not being a fool, Royce also could extrapolate that eventually he would suffer the same fate, probably under a different guise and at a different time.

Knowledge was power. And for the first time in his career with the Organization, Royce was thinking about how little he knew about it. He had contact points laterally. Orders from above via secure encryption on a computer from an unknown source. And below him, those he recruited. He was a piece of a machine that he had little idea of the true nature or extent of, and like any piece, he was sure he was replaceable.

He had a strong suspicion that David had been re-placed because of some aspect of the current mission. It had been David's mission, and to pull him off it and "retire" him before it was completed was a sure sign of that. So there was more going on with this mission than appeared. The Tai angle wasn't good, but he didn't think that had been enough to cause David's death.

Royce blinked, bringing his attention back to his im-mediate surroundings. Action. When in doubt, take ac-tion. But very, very careful action. Because the wrong action could bring the wrong attention.

First, he needed to know more about David's death, and in the process, more about the Organization.

Second, he needed to know more about this mission against Abayon of the Abu Sayef. What was the real goal? Because the Hong Kong angle meant this was much bigger than just a terrorist leader on Jolo Island of the Philippines. He doubted very much that the Or-ganization would launch this mission simply in retali-ation for the botched rescue mission. The Organization, in his experience, did not react to such things. The Organization acted.

And thus, he had to act. But very carefully.

Hong Kong

The Japanese woman met the team from Australia planeside, standing next to a stretch limousine with heavily tinted windows. The Learjet in which they had flown from Okinawa to Hong Kong was unmarked and parked far from the main terminal. There were no cus-toms officials in the area, and she silently directed the team into the limousine.

No words were exchanged as the long car drove away from the airport. The woman pointed at a pile of gear stacked in the middle of the passenger compartment. The team leader pulled off the blanket covering it. Weapons, body armor, explosives—all that had been requested was there.

"When do we go?" the team leader asked, speaking first as they approached the city.

"When I tell you to, if I tell you to," the woman replied.

Jolo Island

Abayon was in pain. There was nothing unusual about that. His life had been full of pain ever since his encounter with Unit 731. But today he felt it more deeply than usual. And he knew it was not a spike, but the heralding of even more pain to come. The doctors had given him six months. But that was only a guess.

He leaned back in his wheelchair, taking a deep breath and letting it out slowly, trying to expel the agony with the air. It did not work. He closed his eyes for several moments, then opened them and reached for the piece of paper that had been brought to him several minutes earlier. It detailed the money made and disbursed the previous evening in Hong Kong. The numbers lessened the pain. If tonight's auction did the same, his group would have gone a long way toward funding the war against the rich for many years to come.

There was, of course, no word from Moreno. Security dictated that. The only way to know if he was successful would be to watch CNN and wait for the news.

CHAPTER 15

Oahu

"I have a job for you." Royce stared at Foster and waited.

The scientist in charge of the Sim-Center avoided his eyes. "I'm doing the job I was given."

"Multitask," Royce said simply.

Foster glanced into the control room where the military people were changing from day shift to evening shift. "Did that person really die in the parachute drop?" He nodded his head toward the control room. "They think it's part of an obstacle in their exercise, losing half the recon element. But you and I know better, don't we? I didn't program it in. That was a real message from real people."

Royce folded his hands in his lap. "You think you know better? Than what? You don't have a clue." And neither do I, he thought.

"You're doing all this for deniability," Foster said. "You're using me as a cutout—don't think I don't realize that I take the fall if the shit hits the fan on this."

Royce had read Foster's file. The man was not stupid, that was certain, although he had been rather indiscreet years ago. Royce briefly wondered how many people worked for the Organization simply going around and gathering blackmail material on people the Organization might eventually use someday. And not for the first time he wondered what the Organization had on him.

"You know what happens to you if the shit hits the fan?" Royce asked.

"What?"

"You die."

Foster blinked, then ran his tongue over his lips. "Who are you? That other guy said he was NSA. But you're not NSA, are you?"

"No." Royce said nothing more.

Foster fidgeted in his seat for several moments. "All right," he finally said. "What do you want me to do?"

"I want you to hack into Space Command's tracking records." He gave Foster the time period and estimated location in which David's plane had gone down. "I want whatever they have on it. I want to know exactly when and where it went down. I know they track every goddamn thing moving in the sky now with their satellites." Ever since 9/11, keeping an eye on the skies had become a much higher priority.

"Who was on this plane and why do you think it crashed?"

"That's not something you need to know," Royce said.

Foster was confused. "But why don't you send a request—"

"I want you to do this without anyone knowing you're doing it. Between me and you. Are you capable of that?"

Foster slowly nodded. "I should be able to get in there. I have access to the government's secure system, so that helps a lot. The hard part will be leaving no trace of my visit."

"I recommend you don't," Royce said. "Or else you'll get visitors who won't be as nice as me."

Johnston Atoll

Moreno knew he should stay on the submarine. He'd even promised Abayon that he would, though at the time they both knew it was a promise that would not be kept. Since their first days together as teenagers fighting the Japanese, they had always held the belief that a leader led from the front. Moreno knew that a major reason why the Abu Sayef had not been as active as it might have been was Abayon's confinement to the wheelchair. While it had been a politically prudent move for the group to lay low for many years, it was also partly because it took Moreno a long time to convince his old friend that even though he could not personally lead his men, he could—and had to—issue orders for others to go out and kill and die.

Moreno, though, was not confined to a wheelchair, and the spry old man slid down the side of the submarine into the waiting rubber boat crowded with his men. There were two other similar boats, each holding sixteen men. That left a skeleton crew of five on board the submarine, enough to hold it in place until they returned.

Moreno sniffed the air as they cast off in the dark. The wind was shoreborne, as he had planned. There was no moon yet, leaving only the scant illumination of the stars. He didn't need a compass to find Johnston Atoll, though. The complex was well-lit, glittering like a beacon three kilometers away.

Using small electric engines, the three Zodiacs glided silently through the water toward the lights. Moreno sat in the bow of the lead boat, his silenced submachine gun across his knees. A kilometer from shore he directed the small fleet to the left, to the landing spot he had picked, out of the glare of the lights. The three boats ran up on the beach and the crews jumped overboard, dragging them above the tide mark.

There was no need for Moreno to issue any orders now, since they had rehearsed what they were about to do at least a hundred times on a mock-up of the facility on Jolo Island. The forty-eight men moved toward a fenced compound set about three hundred meters away from the main complex. Inside the eight-foot-high fence topped with razor wire, there was a bunker shaped like a pyramid with the top half cut off. According to the intelligence Moreno had been able to gather, it was built according to U.S. government specifications. He had been able to find the exact same type of bunker in Subic Bay at the abandoned American base there. It was used to hold precision munitions when the American fleet operated out of Subic—at least, that's what the Americans had publicly claimed. The persistent rumor was that the bunker had held the fleet's nuclear weapons.

Moreno grimaced as he pushed through a spiny bush. The Americans lied. They lied, and then they said no one else could do what they did. They bombed and invaded at will, yet acted like they were protecting the world.

Moreno paused in the cover of the bushes as four pairs of men crawled up to the fence and began snipping the links with bolt cutters. He looked left and right and was satisfied that his flank security sections were doing exactly as they had been trained. There was no sign of any guard, which he found surprising and a bit disconcerting. He could not believe the Americans would leave what was supposed to be in the bunker unguarded. Had the intelligence they'd bought at such great price been wrong?

They made four holes in the fence. The lead scouts crawled through. Moreno forced himself to hold back and let the scouts do their job. A minute passed. Another. Then a dark figure reappeared near the fence, gesturing. Moreno led the rest of the force out of the bushes and through the fence. The force deployed around the bunker as he and four men went to the large steel doors.

It was as the source had said. A lock was bolted in place on a thick hasp. One of the men shrugged off a backpack and removed a bottle of powerful acid. The others stepped back as the man donned a breathing mask, then opened the bottle and began to drip the acid on the lock. They had timed this on the same grade and amount of steel, and it would take fifteen minutes. But it was quiet, as opposed to the quick work an explosive charge would make of the lock.

As one poured the acid, other men checked the outside of the doors, searching for any alarm systems. There were none. The arrogance of the lack of security systems only played into what Moreno already believed about the Americans.

He could feel the tension mounting among his men as each minute passed. They had expected to meet at least one guard. If there were none posted, then there was a good chance there would be a roving patrol. The last thing they needed was gunfire or any sort of alarm to be given. Everything relied on stealth. Moreno's men were all armed with silenced weapons, but the guards would certainly not be. One shot and the plan would unravel. There were contingencies, but Moreno preferred not to have to use them.

With a startling clank the lock fell off.

Moreno and the others stepped forward and slid open the hasp, then grabbed the handles for the heavy doors. With a slight squeak of protest, the doors swung wide open. The interior of the bunker was pitch-black. Half of the group edged in, the other half staying outside. The doors swung shut and flashlights were turned on.

Moreno let out a slight sigh, not enough to be noticed by others, but enough to release the tension that had been building ever since he noted there was no guard on the bunker. The target was there, the only object in the large cavernous space. Set on a cart were four large, stainless steel canisters, each five feet high and two feet in diameter. Prominently displayed on the side of each was the warning triangle for a deadly chemical agent.

The U.S. government had long claimed it had destroyed all toxic agents in its inventory at the plant here on Johnston Atoll. As with many other things, Moreno knew for certain now that it was a lie. In those four canisters was a classified nerve agent, a variation of the extremely dangerous VX, which had been designated ZX.

He directed his special handling teams forward. Four men to each canister. They removed the four canisters and placed them on stretchers. They then strapped the canisters down and gathered near the large doors. The flashlights were turned off, the doors opened, and the group exited.

They carefully made their way through the holes in the fence and back to the Zodiacs. The rubber boats were shoved off and they headed back toward the submarine. There was still no sign of any alarm being raised.

Moreno sat in the bow of the lead boat staring at the steel canister that rested in the center of it. Not only was information about ZX a highly held secret, the fact that it had been developed *before* its sister agent, VX, was something very few people were privy to. According to most sources, VX was developed in 1952 by the British. In fact, ZX was developed in early 1945 by the Japanese at Unit 731. The formula for it was appropriated by the Americans when they gathered several of the lead scientists from 731 under the auspices of Operation Paper Clip. The information was shared by the Americans with the British, who developed a less lethal version they designated VX.

All this information had been gained by the Abu Sayef at great expense and effort. Bribery, torture, and murder had blazed a trail to these truths. While VX was considered by many to be the most lethal chemical agent in the world, it had half the lethality of ZX. Anyone exposed to just five milligrams of ZX died. Each of these canisters contained the potential for two million lethal doses. What made ZX very different and much more dangerous than VX—besides the higher lethality—was while the latter was in liquid form and difficult to make into a gas, ZX was already in a compressed gas state inside the tubes.

They arrived at the submarine, and looking toward shore, saw no sign of any alert or activity. With great care they hauled the canisters on deck. They slid three of them through the deck hatch into the sub, securing them in the forward torpedo room in place of the longer weapons. Moreno remained on deck with the fourth. Where a three-inch gun had once been bolted, there was now a device that resembled a gun with an oversized barrel that flared out to a four-foot-wide nozzle.

The fourth canister was slid into a rack at the base of the erstwhile gun placement and tied down. Moreno then ordered everyone else off the deck except one man. He was their chemical expert and wore a protective suit and mask. The man glanced at Moreno, waiting for him to leave also. The elder man shook his head. He wanted to set an example and make sure everything was done exactly right. He gestured for the expert to continue.

The man shrugged, then connected a hose to the back of the tube. As he was doing this, Moreno climbed up the outside of the conning tower and took his position on the small space on top. He held onto the railing with one hand as he picked up the mike with the other. He issued orders for the submarine to get under way, setting a course that would bring it closer to the atoll.

Moreno glanced down at the deck. The expert gave him the thumbs-up.

When Moreno nodded, the man walked to the bottom of the tower and stripped off the protective suit, then joined him on the bridge. Johnston Atoll was now less than two kilometers away.

Moreno and the expert went into the sub. "Seal all hatches," Moreno ordered.

When the board showed all green, Moreno turned to the expert. "Do it."

The man held a small remote. He pressed the red button.

It was anticlimactic, Moreno thought, as he went to the periscope. The sub was still on the surface. "Turn to course one eight zero, maintain slow," Moreno ordered.

He shifted the periscope as the sub turned and ran parallel to the atoll. Moreno could see no sign of the agent being sprayed, so he had to trust that the job had been done right. He glanced at the expert, who was watching a stopwatch.

His attention back on the periscope, Moreno saw they were now even with the island. He watched as it slowly slid by. He turned the periscope and glanced at the expert. The man clicked the watch and gave a thumbs-up. Moreno looked one more time at Johnston Atoll. Still no sign of anything unusual. He snapped up the handles.

"Dive," he ordered. "Course one-one-four degrees, full speed." He looked at the digital clock in the control room. "We must make the rendezvous in three hours and six minutes exactly."

On Johnston Atoll death came on the air, unseen and odorless. Some of the buildings in the main complex had been designed to handle Level IV contaminants, but these building with their complex filtering systems were designed to keep biological and chemical agents *inside,* not prevent outside agents from entering.

The first to be affected was the lone guard on duty at the airstrip control tower. The ZX was borne in from the ocean by the wind, carried across the runway. He had been reading a novel while the raid was conducted a kilometer and a half away. He was still reading as the first molecules of ZX arrived. He blinked as he felt unexpected tears form in his eyes. Two seconds later his throat constricted and he gasped for breath. His mind was desperately trying to figure out what was happening as it passed from consciousness to unconsciousness.

Which was fortunate for him. Every muscle in his body began to convulse as the agent spread, the ZX binding to the acetylcholinesterase enzymes at the end of each synaptic membrane. This made the AChE inactive, which then made it impossible for the nerve endings to stop firing, thus the uncontrolled muscle activity. Which quickly led to paralysis and death as the lungs stopped working.

All of this happened within thirty seconds.

The gas floated into the main complex, sucked in by the air-conditioning units in all the buildings and spewed out into the rooms inside. The results were the same. Most of those on the island were contaminated while they slept, and went from sleep to unconsciousness to death in half a minute without any awareness. The few others who were awake had those few moments of awareness that something was wrong. Then they too died.

Nine hundred sixty civilians and 250 military personnel were dead within five minutes.

The generators, amply fueled, continued to run, and the lights on the island continued to glow in the darkness.

Jolo Island

Vaughn looked up and could see the first stars. He tried to count the days back to the failed raid. He had to assume his brother-in-law's body was back in the

States by now. Most likely even in the ground. A military funeral. And he hadn't been there for his sister or to pay his respects. He looked up at the shaft still blowing hot air out. The one who was responsible was in there.

"You all right?" Tai asked.

Vaughn was startled. He'd forgotten all about his partner. "I wish we hadn't lost our NVGs on the jump. They'd be real helpful in there."

Tai's dark eyes regarded him for several moments. "What were you really thinking about?"

"A military funeral."

"I don't think we'll get one with this outfit."

That brought a slight smile to Vaughn's lips. "Not for us. I plan on us getting out of this in one piece."

"That's a good plan," Tai said. "Let's hope everyone else is on the same sheet of music."

"What do you mean?"

Tai grabbed her ruck and slid the shoulder straps on. "Nothing."

"Ladies first," Vaughn said.

"Don't go bullshit on me now," Tai snapped.

In reply, Vaughn grabbed the edge of the tunnel and pulled himself up and in. It was about five feet wide, which meant they couldn't stand upright but wouldn't have to crawl. It was made of corrugated metal and sloped upward at about a twenty-degree angle.

Vaughn pulled his red lens flashlight off his combat vest and clicked it on. The light penetrated ahead as far as he could see, about twenty meters. And the tunnel showed no end at that distance. He felt Tai's presence behind him. She put her free hand on his shoulder and he began to move forward, crouching slightly.

He held the MP-5 in one hand and the flashlight in

the other. Had he known he'd be without night vision goggles, he would have made sure to bolt a light to the side of the gun. He was glad that he had the red lens flashlight, or else they would literally be in the dark.

Vaughn tried to keep a pace count as they went up the tunnel but knew it had to be off because of the awkward way he was walking. He estimated they had gone over one hundred meters when the pipe changed angles and went level. The blow of warm air continued unabated as they moved onto the level part and faced their first decision. The large pipe split into two smaller ones, each about four feet in diameter.

"This keeps up, we're gonna be on our bellies," Tai whispered as Vaughn shined the light up each passage. Both went level and straight as far as he could see.

"Any preference?" he asked.

Instead of answering, Tai stuck her head in the left tube and cocked her head, listening as she sniffed. Then did the right tube.

"The air is warmer in this one," she said, pointing to the right.

"And?"

Tai smiled and shrugged. "I don't know what it means. I was just mentioning it."

"That's a lot of help," Vaughn muttered. "All right. This way." He led the way into the warmer tube. The only sound was their boots scraping along the metal and their breathing as they went farther into the mountain. After another fifty meters Vaughn paused. Tai bumped up against him and then also became still.

There was the slightest of sounds. Rhythmic.

"Air pump," Tai finally said.

Vaughn thought about the information he'd researched on underground bunkers. Where were the intake for the air handlers usually located? Above. That was good, he thought. It was always best to approach an objective with the higher terrain advantage, even if, as in this case, the terrain was inside a mountain. He continued forward, Tai close behind.

The sound of the air pump grew louder and the blow of air seemed stronger, though Vaughn figured that was just his imagination working overtime. He froze when he saw a metal grate at the far reach of the red light, immediately switching the light off.

He and Tai waited in the darkness, and gradually they began to see a faint light on the other side of the grate. Vaughn got down on his belly and crawled forward, careful not to make any sound. Tai was right behind him, her face scant inches from his boots.

The light grew stronger as he got closer to the grate. He arrived at it and peered through. All he could see was a gray plastic tube that curved down. Warm air blew on his face, pumped up into the tube. The light was dimly coming through the plastic. The sound of the air pump was loud now, right ahead of and below them.

Vaughn scooted as far to one side as he could, and Tai crawled up next to him. Their bodies were pressed together as they considered their situation. Vaughn looked at the grate. The metal strips were only about a quarter inch thick, spaced every three inches or so. He was sure it was designed more to keep animals from coming in than to prevent human entry. He reached out and tugged on it, and the entire thing gave about half an inch. He looked over at Tai and raised his eyebrows in question.

She nodded and grabbed her side of the grate. Together they pushed inward until the metal gave and then popped loose. Twisting, they slid it over their heads and farther down the tunnel.

"Hey," Tai hissed, pointing to the left. Engraved in the metal were Japanese characters and a series of numbers. "So this was built during the war by the Japanese."

"Looks like," Vaughn agreed. He pointed forward. "Take a look. I'll hold you."

Tai scooted forward as Vaughn moved back, wrapping his arms around her thighs. She moved farther into the plastic tube, and he had to exert more effort to keep her from tumbling forward. Finally he felt her pull back and helped her, bringing her back into the steel tube.

"There's a damn big fan at the bottom of that thing, about eight feet down from the curve," Tai reported. "We do *not* want to go into that."

Vaughn slid his knife out of its sheath. She nodded. He moved to the edge and put the tip of the knife against the plastic. Bearing down on it, he broke through the thin material and then began to cut. On the other side, Tai did the same. They met in the middle on the bottom, having severed the lower half of the plastic tube. Securing his knife back in the sheath, Vaughn grabbed the plastic and pushed it open. A dirty tile floor was about twelve feet below their position in a narrow space between the large machine holding the fan and the rock wall. The space was about two feet wide.

Vaughn moved forward but Tai grabbed his arm. "How do we get back in here?"

"If we need to leave this way," he said, "we crab up between the wall and the machine."

Tai nodded, and Vaughn edged out, swinging his

feet down. His toes scrambled for purchase, one foot on the wall, one on the machine. He flexed his legs, pressing outward, then began his descent. Within seconds he was on the floor. He quickly scooted to the edge of the machine and looked, half expecting to see some sort of custodian or engineer. But the ten-by-twenty-meter cavern was empty. At the far end was a steel door.

Tai was right behind Vaughn, weapon at the ready. He nodded toward the door and they moved forward.

Okinawa

Sinclair walked into the latrine and heard the sound of vomiting from one of the stalls. He walked over and, given that Kasen and Orson were still in the planning room, knew that it was Hayes occupying the stall.

"You all right?" Sinclair asked.

The noise had stopped and now there was a strange silence.

"Hey?" Sinclair tapped on the door. "Hayes. You okay, man?"

There was no reply. Cursing, Sinclair pulled his knife out and slid it between the door and the jamb, releasing the latch. The door swung open, revealing Hayes passed out next to the toilet, bloody vomit everywhere.

"Goddamn," Sinclair muttered. He reached down and grabbed the man. He pulled him out of the stall and then into the operations room. "Hey, guys. We need a medic."

Orson and Kasen ran over as Sinclair put Hayes on one of the planning tables. Sinclair slapped his face a few times and Hayes's eyes flickered, then opened.

"What happened?" he muttered.

"Clean him up," Orson snapped.

Sinclair grabbed some paper towels and dabbed off the blood and vomit on Hayes's face while Kasen offered his canteen. Hayes weakly took the canteen as he sat up, his upper body wobbly. He took a swig, washed it around in his mouth, then spit to the side. Then he took a deep drink.

Orson was standing still, watching, hands on hips.

"We need a medic," Sinclair repeated.

Orson slowly nodded. "All right. I'll take care of it." He went over to the phone linking them to the ASTs and quietly spoke into it. "An ambulance is on the way," he said afterward.

Then he went to his laptop, typed in a message and transmitted it.

Hong Kong

Ruiz wiped the sheen of sweat off his forehead as he stood in the warehouse. Behind him were three large wooden crates resting on pallets. They contained the rest of the Golden Lily treasure from the cave that was supposed to be auctioned this evening. He checked his watch once more. It was time, but where was—

He looked up as the small door set into the large sliding door for the warehouse opened. The Japanese woman walked in. She was dressed all in black: slacks, shirt, and leather coat. She was carrying a metal briefcase. She walked up to the small table set in front of Ruiz and put the case on it without a word. Then she gestured with one hand, indicating for him to open it.

Ruiz hesitated as he considered the possibility the case was rigged. But his greed overcame his fear and he flipped the two latches and swung the lid up. Stacks of cash along with a plane ticket were lying on top, and a Japanese passport.

"As promised," the woman said. "Only half the money. The other half will be given to you at the airfield after we ensure you have given us what we paid for and to make certain that you truly are gone. We don't want you having second thoughts."

A second thought was the last thing on Ruiz's mind as he checked the plane ticket and saw his picture in the passport along with a new name. "Is this real?" he asked, holding up the passport.

"Yes."

He stared at the cash. "Everything remaining is in the crates."

"I'm sure it is," the woman said. She was looking at him strangely, and he wondered what she was thinking.

His focus shifted back to the case and the money.

"Abayon," she said.

Ruiz was startled. "What?"

"Abayon. Why did he put these pieces out for auction? He's been sitting on them for over half a century."

Ruiz shrugged. "He wants to help fund other groups. He has so much there . . ." He paused, not sure how much he should say.

"He has the Golden Lily, of which this is only a taste," the woman said.

"You knew that," Ruiz said. "Or else you would not have sent the envoy."

"Who you killed."

Ruiz licked his lips. "Abayon did that. I wasn't even there."

"What else does Abayon have planned?"

"Nothing."

"You lie."

Ruiz took a step back from the table. "No. I have no idea. This was my job . . ." He indicated the crates. "Abayon is very good at keeping things compartmentalized. I only know what I needed to know to do this."

"That is too bad," the woman said. Her hands were on her hips, the long leather coat pulled back. For the first time Ruiz noted a sword hanging at her side. A samurai sword.

"We have a deal," Ruiz said, his throat tight.

"Yes, we do." The woman indicated the case. "Take it."

Ruiz tentatively stepped forward, snapped the case shut and picked it up. He held it at his side.

"Our deal is complete now, yes?" the woman asked.

Ruiz frowned. "Yes."

"Very good. I am a person of honor. I would never allow it to be said I do not fulfill my word."

"Well, that's good," Ruiz said. He glanced over his shoulder toward the back door. He froze as he saw a large black man with a wicked looking gun in his hand standing there. "What the hell?"

"The deal is done," the woman said.

The door behind her opened and another man walked in, short and muscular, with a submachine gun in his hands.

"Hey." Ruiz held up the briefcase. "I—"

"Made a deal," the woman said. She flipped aside the right side of her long leather coat and smoothly drew the sword. "Both of us kept our word. But now the deal is over."

"Wait!" Ruiz begged.

"For . . . ?" The woman cocked her head.

"Abayon is up to something else," Ruiz said.

"We know that," the woman said. "That statement is of no help."

"A submarine. It involves a submarine."

The woman lowered the sword. "If everything is so compartmentalized, how do you know this?"

"I talked to one of the men who was to be part of her crew. They kept the submarine hidden, probably in one of the coves on Jolo, but they had to get men to operate her."

"What does Abayon plan to do with the submarine?"

"The man didn't know," Ruiz said. "He said it was an old submarine."

"That is not very specific."

"He was very drunk," Ruiz said. "He said it was a one-way mission. They were all volunteers who had agreed to give their lives."

"That is all?"

Ruiz nodded, a sheen of sweat on his forehead again.

"Good, then you will not mind giving your life either."

She gestured at the black man, and he drew a similar sword from a scabbard on his back.

"Take it," the woman said as the man came forward and laid it on the table.

Ruiz shook his head. "No. This is not—"

"Take it or they will shoot you," she said. "An honorable death is to be preferred over being shot down like a dog."

"But we made a deal," Ruiz whined. "And I told you all I know."

"And we completed the deal. And you told me all you know, so you are of no more use to me. Now you must go through me to get out of here."

"But why?" Ruiz was frozen.

"Pick it up." She tapped the table with the tip of her sword. "There really is no choice."

Ruiz's shoulders slumped. There was now a third armed man in the warehouse. With a trembling hand, Ruiz picked up the sword. He awkwardly held it in front of him, blade vertical, trying to protect his upper body.

The Japanese woman smiled coldly. She stepped around the table, her sword gripped in both hands, blade held low. Ruiz did the unexpected, charging forward, the blade swinging in a wide arc at the woman's head. Unexpected to the members of the team gathered around, but apparently not to the woman. She ducked under the swing and jabbed her sword into Ruiz's stomach, piercing right through and coming out his back. Just as quickly, she withdrew the blade and, as the first gasp of pain left his lips, gracefully spun, blade level and extended, and severed his head from his body.

Ruiz's lips were still open in the gasp as the head bounced off the concrete floor.

The woman pulled out a lace kerchief and wiped the blade clean, then slid it back in its scabbard.

Jolo Island

The corridor was six feet wide by eight high. The walls were roughly hewn rock, and Vaughn assumed that an existing tunnel had been expanded to make this passageway. He doubted that the technology existed during World War II to completely carve this out of solid rock. His assumption was confirmed as he noted occasional natural openings on either side as they moved farther into the mountain.

Their progress was stopped after about a hundred meters by an iron door that appeared to be bolted on the other side, since it did not budge when both he and Tai put their weight on it.

"What now?" Tai asked as she considered the door.

They had a limited amount of explosives, but using them was the last thing Vaughn wanted to do. "The room we just left," he said.

"What about it?"

"It's moving air out of the complex, right?" He didn't wait for an answer. "So there have to be air shafts coming into it from below. Beneath that big fan."

Tai nodded and turned back the way they had come. They retraced their steps and entered the room. Vaughn looked at the large air handler. There was a service panel on one side, so he pulled out his multipurpose tool and unscrewed it.

"Shit," Tai said as the opening revealed the large, six-foot-diameter fan, spinning, the blades thumping through the air, pushing it up. There was an open shaft below it. "How do we—"

Vaughn answered by pointing at a bundle of wires. "We cut those, we stop it."

"Won't someone notice?"

"Probably."

"Then we need a better plan."

Vaughn waved his hand, indicating she could do whatever she wished. He stepped back as Tai stuck her head in the opening, looking about. "The tips of the fan don't make it to the sides," she noted. "There's about eighteen inches of room."

Vaughn was already shaking his head. "We hit those fans and it'll cut us in two."

"There's room," Tai insisted.

Vaughn looked. She was right. But it would be damn close. He shined his flashlight down and saw. The shaft below the fan curved, so he couldn't see how far it dropped.

"I don't like it," he finally said.

"We don't have much choice," she replied.

She was right about that. But he didn't see how they were going to get out of there once they went in. He took a deep breath. This was representative of what he'd been feeling ever since becoming part of Section 8. They were on a one-way trip.

"Ladies first," Vaughn said, and the tone of his voice indicated it wasn't a choice.

Tai responded by edging over into the opening. She gripped the side with her hands and slowly lowered herself. Vaughn anxiously watched as her legs reached the level of the fan. The metal whipped by, less than six inches from her flesh. She continued to lower herself until her arms were fully extended. The fan was at chest level, barely missing her. She looked up at Vaughn, gave him a wan smile, then let go. She slid down the tube and out of sight.

Cursing to himself, Vaughn climbed into the machine and duplicated her actions. As he lowered himself, he could feel the power of the fan so close. As he extended his arms, the edge of one of the blades hit the back of his combat vest, cutting through it and the shirt underneath but barely missing his skin. Abandoning caution for speed, Vaughn let go and slid down, safe from the fan now but uncertain where and when his fall would be arrested.

The tube curved, but only slightly, and he gained speed as he went down. He tried slowing his progress with his hands but there was nothing to grip. The tube was steel, too new to be from the original World War II structure. Vaughn gasped as he suddenly went airborne into a black void. He braced himself for impact, hoping the fall would be brief.

It was. He slammed onto a steel platform with a solid thud.

"That you?" Tai asked.

"No," Vaughn grunted as he inwardly reviewed his body for injuries.

A red light came on, and he could see Tai now, about four feet away. He slowly got to his feet. They were in an open space, and as Tai slowly shifted her light, he saw that it was about ten meters square with a steel floor. He looked up and saw the opening he had fallen out of about eight feet above his head. Not good, he thought, as he considered how the hell they were going to get out of there.

Tai directed her light toward a couple of openings in the floor. She walked over to the closest one, and Vaughn joined her. There was a two-foot depression, then a metal grate in the three-foot-wide hole. Air was being drawn up through the opening. They both knelt next to the opening and she shined her flashlight down. The red light penetrated the darkness for a few feet but they couldn't see anything.

"I assume no one's in there since it's dark," Tai said.

"Unless it's a barracks room," Vaughn said, "and there's a bunch of guys with guns sleeping."

"Always the optimist."

Tai turned off her flashlight, leaving them in darkness. Vaughn could hear her unscrewing the cover. She turned the light back on, flooding the room with white light. She pointed it down at the grate.

Both of them gasped as a golden glow was reflected back at them. Directly below the grate was a five-foot-high stack of gold bullion.

CHAPTER 16

Oahu

"Space Command did track the plane," Foster said.

It didn't surprise Royce, because Space Command had tracked everything flying since 9/11. He waited out Foster. There was little activity in the operations center. Everyone was still waiting for the report from the surviving recon team member on the ground—if he lived long enough to make a report.

Foster slid a piece of paper across his desk, and Royce recognized the location it displayed: the middle of the Pacific Ocean, west of Midway Island. A thin red line went from Oahu to a point about four hundred miles away from Midway, where it ended.

"That's where it disappeared," Foster said. He cleared his throat nervously. "There was no report of a plane missing in that area or anywhere close to it. But there was also no flight plan for a plane flying in that area at the time. No one has reported a plane missing either."

"Of course not," Royce said as he stared at the end of the red line. A watery grave. At least David's brother had gotten the honor of being buried in the Punchbowl here on the island. There would be no markers to commemorate David's service. It was as if he'd never existed.

Royce folded the piece of paper and slid it into his pocket.

"Also—" Foster hesitated.

"Yes?"

"We just got a report that one of the team members, Hayes, is very ill."

Royce stood up. "Inform me as soon as the recon element reports in."

He went out to David's Defender and drove into the hills. Once in the clearing, he opened his laptop and typed out two messages. The first one was to the isolation area on Okinawa. The second went to the backup team that should now have been departing Hong Kong to converge on the primary mission.

Okinawa

The Humvee ambulance slowed to a halt outside the door to the isolation area. The medic/driver hopped out and went to the rear, pulling out a folding stretcher. Orson was waiting for him, arms folded. "This way."

He led the medic to where Sinclair had Hayes lying on a couch, a cold compress on his forehead. The medic checked Hayes's pulse while he looked at the other members of the team. "Any idea what's wrong with him?"

"Pancreatic cancer," Orson said succinctly, which

earned a surprised look from Sinclair and a not so surprised look from Kasen.

"Jesus," the medic muttered. "What the hell is he
doing here?"

"His job," Orson said.

The medic shook his head. "He needs to be in a hospital ASAP."

Orson frowned and glanced at the other members of
the team. "I'll go with him. You two continue mission
preparation. Contact me ASAP if you hear from the
recon element."

Orson and the medic put Hayes on the stretcher and
carried him to the Humvee. They slid the stretcher in
and Orson climbed up next to Hayes. The black man
was sweating profusely, his gaze vacant. The medic
slammed the back door shut and got in the driver's
seat. The Humvee ambulance slowly wound its way
through the tunnel toward the outside world.

Orson glanced at the front—the medic was focused
on the road. Orson leaned over and placed his forearm
across Hayes's throat, applying pressure. Hayes's eyes
went wide and he reached up and weakly grabbed
Orson's arm, trying to push it away, but he was too
sick. Orson kept the pressure up as he watched the
front of the Humvee.

The panic in Hayes's eyes disappeared as the life
drained from them.

When the Humvee cleared the tunnel, Orson rapped
on the back of the driver's seat. "Let me out."

The medic stopped the Humvee and turned, confused. "What?"

Orson indicated Hayes's body. "He's gone. I've got
to get back to isolation."

" 'He's gone'?" The medic hopped out and came

into the back. He checked Hayes's vitals, confirming that the man was indeed dead. "I don't get it," he muttered as he pulled a blanket over Hayes's face. "He was sick, but—"

Orson stepped out of the Humvee. "We really needed him to last a while longer." He shrugged. "Some things you just can't control." With that he disappeared into the black gaping mouth of the tunnel entrance.

Johnston Atoll

The Navy F-14 Tomcat came in low and fast. It had made the flight from Hawaii in less than two hours, dispatched after the tower on Johnston Atoll failed to respond to repeated radio queries. That, combined with a complete electronic blackout from the atoll—no e-mails, faxes, phone calls—absolutely nothing, had caused the jet to be scrambled.

It roared across the island one hundred feet up, the pilot peering out of the cockpit. He saw nothing out of the ordinary except that he saw nothing happening on the island. No movement. No people. He did a wide loop then came back, flying slower, just above stall speed, while transmitting, trying to contact the tower. There was only the sound of low static in reply.

The pilot knew that the sound of his engines could clearly be heard, even by people inside the buildings. Yet no one came running out to look up. Absolute stillness.

Then he noticed something else. There were no birds.

Pacific Ocean

"Target bearing zero-six-seven degrees, range four hundred meters."

Moreno nodded at the sonar man's report. Exactly where it should be. "Periscope depth," he ordered. It wasn't necessary to make a visual confirmation, but Moreno believed in double-checking.

He grabbed the handles for the periscope as it ascended, flipping them down, and pressed his head against the eyepiece, turning in the direction the sonar had indicated the target. Moreno blinked as he saw the massive ship. He'd seen pictures, but that had not prepared him for the real thing.

It was one of the largest oil tankers in the world—the *Jahre Viking*. It wasn't moving through the ocean so much as plowing through the water, ignoring the four-foot swell that pounded against its steel hull, heading almost due east, toward San Francisco. The tanker was over a quarter mile long and seventy meters wide.

"Down periscope," Moreno ordered. "Descend to fifty meters."

According to the intelligence he had, the tanker drew almost twenty-five meters when fully loaded. Moreno went forward to the sonar man. "Range?"

"Three hundred meters," the man announced.

Moreno waited. He cocked his head as a noise began to reverberate through the hull. The sonar man turned down the volume on his set and looked up at Moreno. "The screws."

They were hearing the sound the *Jahre Viking*'s propellers slicing through the water. It grew in intensity as they got closer.

"Two hundred meters."

"Slow to one half," Moreno ordered. The *Viking* was big, but it was slow, making no more than ten knots.

The entire submarine had begun to vibrate, and when the ship rolled almost ten degrees before righting itself, Moreno knew they were passing through the massive tanker's bow wake.

"One hundred meters!" The sonar man had to yell to be heard over the vibrating sound echoing through the steel tube.

"Slow to one-quarter," Moreno announced. "Are we past the propellers?" he asked, leaning close to the sonar man.

The man nodded, his eyes closed, focusing on the sound. "Fifty meters," he announced.

Moreno felt a bead of sweat dribble down his temple onto his cheek. He did not raise his hand to wipe it off, knowing the action could be more easily seen than the perspiration.

"We're under!" the sonar man yelled.

"Up, slow, very slow," Moreno ordered. "Maintain one quarter speed." He licked his lips, as this part was guesswork. It they were over and didn't make contact squarely or hit the propellers—he didn't allow himself to project those lines of thought further.

"Forty-five meters," the dive master announced. "Slow and steady. Forty meters."

Moreno slowly walked back into the center of the crowded control room. Every eye was on him, except those of the dive master, who was watching his gauges, hands resting lightly on his controls. "Thirty-five meters."

The submarine was rocking even more violently now, turbulence from the proximity to the massive ship right above them.

"Thirty meters."

"All stop. Brace for impact!" Moreno yelled, and the order was relayed through the submarine. "Turn on the magnets."

His executive officer threw a red switch, and power ran to the two horseshoe-shaped brackets fore and aft. The energized magnets caught the nearest attraction—the steel behemoth above the submarine. The invisible lines of force reached out and pulled the much smaller submarine toward the vessel above it.

Moreno's knees buckled as the magnets made contact with the oil tanker with a solid thud.

"Contact!" the executive officer yelled unnecessarily.

Moreno stood still for several moments, the only sound that of the tanker's screws behind them and the turbulent water rushing by.

"Maintaining contact," the executive officer said.

Finally Moreno allowed himself to smile. They had their ride to San Francisco.

"Power down to minimum," Moreno ordered. "Silent running." Not that anyone was going to hear anything from the sub, given the sound of the tanker's massive screws churning just a couple of hundred meters behind them, but it never hurt to be careful.

Jolo Island

"The Golden Lily," Vaughn said.

"Literally," Tai confirmed. They both sat back on their rucksacks, listening to the air being pulled by them. "At least part of it."

"But our target isn't the gold," Vaughn noted. "We still have to find Abayon."

"And when we find him?" Tai asked. They were

seated on their rucksacks, the only light the dim red glow of Tai's flashlight.

Vaughn pulled out a canteen and took a deep drink. "Then we get out of here, call it in. The rest of the team comes in. We kill him. We leave."

"Hell of a plan, since we still haven't pinpointed his location."

"That, we do next."

"And go where, after the mission is done?"

"That's too far ahead," Vaughn said.

"All right," Tai allowed. "Say we find him. The rest of the team comes in. We kill him. Then what?"

Vaughn shrugged. "Then he's dead and the Abu Sayef are fucked."

"And the gold?"

Vaughn stared at her in the glow from the red lens flashlight. "Not my business."

"Whose business do you think it is?"

Vaughn closed his eyes and rubbed the lids, trying to momentarily drive away the irritation he felt there. He'd been up now for over thirty-six straight hours and it was beginning to wear on him. "Who are you?"

When there was no answer, he opened his eyes and looked at Tai. She was staring at him, and he knew she was trying to figure out if she should trust him, which he didn't give a shit about, because he had no clue whether he could trust her.

"Remember back in isolation where I mentioned the Black Eagle Trust?" she finally said.

"Yes."

"It came out of the Golden Lily," Tai said. "After the war, we recovered a good portion of the treasure that the Japanese and Germans looted. Some of it was given back to the rightful owners, mostly pieces of art in Europe where the scrutiny level was higher. But gold—like that below—a lot of it was untraceable, or could be melted down into bars that were untraceable."

"And that became?"

"The Black Eagle Trust," Tai said. "At the end of the war some far-thinking people saw the threat that communism posed for the West. And they realized that they would need money—a lot of it—to wage the fight."

"I thought that was called taxes," Vaughn noted.

"The Black Eagle fund was a slush fund," Tai said. "Used to bribe people, influence elections, pay for black ops with complete deniability."

The last thing she'd mentioned caught Vaughn's attention.

"There was an OSS operative by the name of Lansale," Tai continued. "He went into the Philippines before MacArthur invaded and linked up with the guerrilla forces—not to mobilize the guerrillas, but with the explicit order to find as much of the Golden Lily as he could. Which wasn't as easy as it sounds, since the Japanese were brutal about trying to hide places like this. They thought nothing of executing all the slave labor they used to build them—and even killing their own engineers who worked on them—in order to keep the locations secret."

"How did this Lansale know about the Golden Lily?" Vaughn asked.

Tai shrugged. "That's an interesting question. After the war, General Yamashita, the Japanese commander in the Philippines, was captured. He never talked before his execution, but his driver, a Major Kojima, was secretly tortured, and it was rumored he gave up the location of several of the caches, including some that Marcos recovered directly for his own fortune."

"But you said Lansale went in *before* the war was over," Vaughn noted.

Tai nodded. "I don't know what Lansale knew or how he knew it, but however he found out about it, he realized its significance right away. He went to three of Roosevelt's top advisors—the Secretary of War and the two men who would shortly become the Secretary of Defense and the head of the World Bank. They told Roosevelt that they needed to gain control of as much of the Golden Lily as possible—and when Roosevelt died, we have to assume they went to Truman with the same cause. The treasure they recovered was spread out around the world, to a lot of banks. They used that to create gold bearer certificates that could be used in any country in the world. The war against communism was, in a way, fought in a most capitalistic way.

"There was more to it than just fighting communism, though," Tai continued. "If so much gold flooded the market, it would have destabilized all the currencies that were based on a gold standard."

"So this Black Eagle Trust was a good thing," Vaughn said.

She shrugged. "It was illegal."

He gave a short laugh. "You think what we're doing here is legal?"

"No, it isn't," Tai allowed.

"So what the fuck is your point?" Vaughn snapped, tired of being strung along.

"My point is that there's a lot more going on in the covert world than we know—or maybe than anyone except a select handful know."

"So?"

"So, I think we better be damn careful and watch our backs."

Vaughn let out his anger with a deep breath. "I agree to that." He stood, shouldering his ruck. "Let's go find Abayon."

"How do you propose to do that?" Tai asked.

Vaughn pointed at the various openings that lined the walls. "Pick one."

She walked to the wall and went to each opening, shining her light into them. Vaughn waited in the middle of the room, listening to the thump of the air circulator.

"This one," she finally said.

"Why that one?"

"It goes up. Bosses always like being above it all. Plus the air intakes should be up there—and we're going to need another way in and out of this place."

It made as much sense as anything else. Without waiting, Tai climbed into the tube. Vaughn followed.

The pipe went upward at about a twenty-degree angle and was about two and a half feet wide. It was uncomfortable moving through it, and Vaughn was forced to tie his rucksack to his boot and drag it behind him. Every so often they came to a grate and paused to check out what was on the other side. So far the grates had opened onto dark rooms, and Vaughn was reluctant to shine a light into them for fear one might be a barracks room with sleeping guards.

Finally they came upon a grate with light shining through it. Tai peered through, then moved up, gesturing to Vaughn. He crawled to the grate and looked inside at a room with a half-dozen long tables. From the odor wafting in, he assumed it was some sort of mess hall. There was no one in sight.

Tai was already moving, and he followed her.

Another grate. A single lightbulb glowed in what

was obviously a storage room. Tai kept moving. Vaughn estimated they had gone up at least two hundred feet in altitude, but it was hard to tell.

They came to another grate where light shone through. Tai spent several moments looking, gesturing for Vaughn to be very quiet, then slid up, giving him access.

He slid up to the grate, peered through and saw a medical dispensary. A woman in a white uniform was working on some sort of machine, checking it. It seemed they were getting closer, since the dispensary would be close to where the people were.

As they continued to ascend, Vaughn began to wonder how much farther they could possibly go. He also worried about a way out. Reversing course meant they would have to find a way to get back up into the tube they had slid down, which he didn't think would be possible. He hoped his information about air intakes was correct.

Tai stopped at another grate, and Vaughn waited as she peered through for over a minute. Finally she moved up the tube and signaled. He crawled up and peered through.

An old man sat in a wheelchair behind a desk in a room portioned by what appeared to be a blast-proof clear wall. Even though the photo they had was out of date, Vaughn had no doubt the man was Rogelio Abayon. His hand slid down to his holster, but he paused as Tai's boot tapped him on the head. He looked up.

She shook her head, then pointed up. She clicked on her red lens flashlight briefly, showing that the tube ended at what appeared to be a hatch. Without waiting, she began crawling upward.

Vaughn took one last look at Abayon, then followed.

CHAPTER 17

Oahu

Royce was driving toward Fort Shafter when his pager went off. He glanced at the number, then pushed down on the accelerator. He made it to the tunnel entrance, flashed his identification card to the guard, and entered. Foster was waiting for him in the control room. From the bustle of activity in the operations room, Royce had a good idea about what had happened.

Foster confirmed it immediately. "The recon element has pinpointed Abayon's location and found a way into the complex."

"Has the rest of the team been alerted?" Royce asked as he scanned the short message.

Foster nodded. "The message was forwarded to the AST." He glanced at the clock. "Wheels up for the infiltration aircraft in four hours."

"How are they going in?" Royce asked.

"Low level Combat Talon. They're parachuting at three hundred feet right on top of the mountain. Rough terrain suits. The recon element found a tube that goes right in."

Royce pondered that. There was a very good chance the Talon flying low over the mountain would alert the guerrillas. On the other hand, it was fast. "How are they getting out?"

Foster frowned. "They've requested Fulton Recovery right off the top of the mountain by the same plane that puts them in. The general isn't too happy about it. He wants them to walk away from the mountain to an open field five kilometers away."

Generals always wanted people to walk, Royce thought. "Approve the Fulton Recovery. Send me the contact information with the Talon and the code words for recovery."

"I'm going to have to lay on an in-flight refuel to allow the Talon to stay on station that long and—"

Royce stared at Foster and he fell silent.

Okinawa

Orson looked at the prisoner, then issued an order to the two military police who had brought him. "Uncuff him. Then leave."

The two MPs glanced at each other, but they had their orders. They removed the cuffs, then departed the isolation area. The prisoner looked around the room, noting the maps and satellite imagery, then returned his gaze to Orson. He was dressed in an orange jumpsuit that had seen better days. His head was shaved and his skin pale and sallow from little time spent outdoors. But he appeared to be in shape and he had the right background, which was all that mattered.

Orson briefly read the paperwork the MPs had brought with the man, then looked at him. "Clarret, Gregory, former staff sergeant in the First Special Forces Group. Convicted of arms trafficking and sentenced to twenty years awaiting transportation back to the States and a long stay in the big house at Fort Leavenworth."

Kasen and Sinclair were silently watching the exchange.

Clarret didn't say a word.

Orson tossed the file in the burn barrel. "You're coming with us on this mission. When you get back, it will be as if none of this happened. You can't go back in the Army, but you'll have your freedom. Roger that?"

Clarret nodded. "Roger that."

Orson pointed toward what had been Hayes's locker. "Uniform and equipment are in there. Get out of that. We're wheels up in a little over three hours."

"How are we going in?" Sinclair asked.

"LALO." Low altitude, low opening. He looked at Clarret. "According to your records you are certified LALO, right?"

The former sergeant nodded. "But it's been a—"

"Don't worry about not being current. Gravity will take care of things. Be happy. That certification got you out of prison."

Sinclair was still looking at Orson. "How are we getting out?"

"Fulton Recovery system."

Sinclair blinked. "But we don't have the rigs or the balloon."

"Don't worry," Orson said. "They'll be on the plane."

Johnston Atoll

The C-141 cargo plane did three passes over the runway before touching down on the fourth. It rolled to a stop and the back ramp slowly descended until it touched the ground. A half dozen men dressed in bright yellow contaminant protection suits awkwardly waddled down the ramp.

They went directly to the tower. They entered and saw the body immediately. While two of the men began deploying sensors, another went to the body and checked it out. Within two minutes the sensors confirmed their worst fears: there were traces of ZX in the air.

Checking the blueprints they'd brought with them, part of the reconnaissance element pinpointed the bunker where the ZX had been stored and made a beeline for it. Another element headed toward the main compound to confirm what was already becoming apparent: that there was no one left alive on the island.

When they arrived at the bunker, the holes in the fence, the doors open, and the lack of the containers that the manifest said were supposed to be inside confirmed this was not an accident. The team leader grabbed the satcom radio and called in his report.

Jolo Island

Rogelio Abayon stared at the IV in his arm for several seconds, then looked up as the door to his office opened. Fatima came in, her lips tightly pressed together, and Abayon knew she brought bad news. But that was part of the plan.

"Ruiz is dead," she said without preamble.

Abayon nodded. "I expected that."

"You expected him to be killed?"

"I expected him to betray us and in the process get killed."

Fatima tried to digest that. "You had him—"

"No," Abayon stopped her. "He got himself killed. He contacted our enemies and tried to broker a deal for half of what he took with him to Hong Kong. They took the deal, then they killed him, because they do not make deals."

Fatima sat down. "What is going on?"

"A plan many years in the making is being implemented," Abayon said. "Ruiz was one part. He accomplished what was needed, by bringing the Golden Lily back into the public spotlight. It is in the news, which is good for us and bad for our enemy."

"And my father?"

"He goes to strike a blow for us. A powerful blow."

"And us?"

Once more she was thinking some steps ahead. "You are to take our organization and move it as we discussed to our alternate location."

"The emergency plan? But—"

"The emergency is here," Abayon said. "Issue the orders and get everyone moving."

"I'll get the nurse—"

Abayon shook his head. "I am staying here." He reached into a drawer and pulled out a thick folder. "This is all the information I have on our enemy. It is yours now." He slid it across the desk, but Fatima did not pick it up right away.

"And you?"

Abayon reached down and slid the intravenous needle out of his arm, dotting the small drop of blood with a piece of gauze. "I am staying here." He held up a hand as Fatima started to say something. "I am old. I am tired. I do not want to do this again," he said, indicating the dialysis machine. "It is your time now."

Fatima reluctantly turned toward the door.

"There is one more thing," Abayon said, causing her to turn back, tears in her eyes.

She waited.

"We might not be alone."

Fatima frowned in confusion.

"This battle against our unknown enemy—I think there might be others out there also opposed to them."

"Al Qaeda and—" Fatima began, but Abayon raised a hand, silencing her.

"Not other groups like us. I think there might be a group, or groups, as secret as our enemy in the world who fight against it."

"Why do you think this?"

Abayon shrugged, tired beyond belief. "I should not have mentioned it. But there have been times over the years when I received information or heard things that made me think there was a force in place opposing the enemy and trying to manipulate me in this battle. I mentioned it because if there is, you must be careful."

"The enemy of my enemy is my friend," Fatima quoted.

"Not necessarily," Abayon said.

Vaughn checked his weapons one more time, while Tai slumbered uneasily next to him. Waiting was always the hardest. And most of his time in the Army had been spent waiting, in one form or another. They even had a saying for it: "Hurry up and wait."

They were on the very top of the mountain, a

rounded cone with a flat open space in the center, which dropped off precipitously on all sides, giving them about a sixty-meter circle to work in. Very little space to drop the remaining members of the team on. He glanced at the short message that had come back in response to his report on finding Abayon. The team was coming in low and fast. And the exfiltration was to be by Fulton Recovery via Combat Talon. Not the best of plans, not the worst.

A Fulton Recovery with six people was dicey at best. The basic concept was sending up a cable attached to a small balloon. The six people would all link together their harnesses to the cable. The Combat Talon would come flying in low, below the float, and "whiskers" on the nose of the plane would catch the cable and draw it to the center, where it would be snatched and held.

The six people would then be jerked up into the air, their momentum causing the cable to swing underneath the plane, where it would be caught by a small crane on the back ramp. The crane would then winch the people into the cargo bay. Vaughn had done one Fulton Recovery, as a single, two years ago, and it had been quite an experience. With six, he envisioned some bumps and bruises—that is, if all six of them survived to make it to exfiltration.

He turned as Tai stirred. She sat up, blinking sleep out of her eyes, and he saw that moment of confusion as her conscious brain tried to figure out where she was. He'd experienced that himself many times in the past.

Her eyes focused on him. "Everything all right?"

"As all right as things can be sitting on top of a mountain full of terrorists," he said. "I've been hearing a lot of trucks moving over there." He nodded to the

southern side of the mountain. "Headlights going back
and forth. Something's happening."

Tai checked her watch. "Not much longer."

"What are you going to do?" he asked her.

"What do you mean?"

"You're supposed to be dead."

Tai nodded. "Yeah. I figure I'd best find a hide spot
up here. Cover the infiltration and then the exfiltration.
The guys coming in will have a plan to take down
Abayon without my participation. I'll cover your back
when you come back up for the exfil."

"You think there's a double-cross?" Vaughn asked.

"I don't think we can trust Royce or Orson," Tai
said. "And I think I had too many malfunctions coming in."

"Why did they try to take you out and not me?"
Vaughn asked. The question had been on his mind the
past hour.

Tai sighed and leaned back on her rucksack. "Because I'm Military Intelligence."

"Yeah, Orson said you came from—"

"I didn't just come from," Tai said. "I still am."

Vaughn lay the MP-5 across his knees and stared at
her. "I'm a simple guy. Why don't you lay it out for
me?"

"Some people very high in the military intelligence
community have become concerned about . . ." She
seemed to be searching for the right words. ". . . certain operations occurring around the world."

"Such as this one?"

"Yes."

"Because?"

"Because we're not sure who is sanctioning these
operations."

"Ah, shit," Vaughn muttered.

"The orders are not coming down the military chain," Tai said. "Our requests to the alphabet soups—most particularly the CIA and NSA—have been met with blanket denials."

"It could just be highly classified and compartmentalized," Vaughn said.

"That's what Royce says," Tai acknowledged. "And the goal of this mission seems in line with national security interests. As were a couple of others we got wind of."

"But . . . ?"

"But there are some people in the military who are very concerned that there might be something else going on."

"Such as?"

Tai shrugged. "We don't know. That's why I'm here."

"And that's why someone tried to take you out on the jump," Vaughn said.

She reluctantly nodded. "They doctored my records to make it look like instead of reporting prisoner abuse in Iraq, I instigated it and was going to be charged. Just the type of person Section Eight comes looking for."

"This is fucked," Vaughn said. "If that's the case, they're not going to let you on that cable for exfiltration."

"What makes you think they're going to let you on? What makes you even think the plane is going to come by to do the snatch?"

Vaughn stared at her. "That bad?"

"Could be. I had three malfunctions coming in."

"Fuck."

"Got that right."

Oahu

"What's going on?" Royce demanded when he saw that the simulation operations center was empty. "Where is everyone?"

Foster held out a folder with a red top secret band across the cover. "They all were called back to the real operations center for a real emergency."

"What happened?" Royce asked as he opened the folder.

"Someone took out Johnston Atoll and escaped with four canisters of ZX nerve agent."

Royce scanned the message traffic. Over a thousand estimated dead. The Pacific Fleet was on alert, beginning to scour the sea and sky for whoever had done it. He closed the folder.

"No one has any idea who did this?"

"So far nobody has claimed responsibility. But the amount of ZX they have is enough to wipe out a major city."

"And our operation?"

"The simulation was shut down thirty minutes ago."

"And our operation?" Royce pressed.

Foster nodded. "I've kept the message traffic up as if the operations center and the mission are still running."

"Good."

"The team is taking off from Okinawa as we speak."

"Very good." Royce waited until Foster went back to his bank of computers and message traffic before opening his laptop. He scanned his own traffic, and there was nothing from his contact about the Johnston Atoll issue. The second team was en route from Hong Kong to Manila and would be arriving shortly.

Hong Kong had gone smoothly, except word about the Golden Lily was already in the media. That was unfortunate. Royce had been tracking Abayon for many years and he respected the old man. They'd short-circuited him in Hong Kong, but Royce was wary—he knew Abayon would not move without having carefully considered the situation.

His satphone buzzed and he checked the screen. A message from the Organization. He hooked the phone to his computer and downloaded the message, allowing the computer to decipher the text.

ABU SAYEF SUSPECTED BEHIND JOHNSTON ATOLL RAID AND ZX THEFT. HIGH LIKELIHOOD THEY ARE ON BOARD AN OLD DIESEL SUBMARINE. DESTINATION UNKNOWN. CHECK FOR LOCATION. PREPARE A TEAM FOR ACTION. ABAYON'S INTENTIONS UNCERTAIN. HANDLE WITH DISCRETION AND EXTREME PREJUDICE.

Royce cursed when he finished reading the message. It was a bit late to be getting this now. There was no way he could prepare a new team quickly. Which meant he had to use a team he already had. He glanced at the board for the location of the second Talon. Less than an hour from drop. He'd have to use them after they took care of their current mission.

Royce sighed. Check for location? He had no doubt the entire Pacific Fleet was doing that. And if the Abu Sayef were using a submarine, they had to have a line on it. Royce had worked the Pacific theater long enough to know that.

He hooked his computer to the Sim-Center computer and then accessed the Pacific Fleet's mainframe using his passwords. He quickly found the program he was looking for: SOSUS—the Navy's Sound Surveillance System, which blanketed the entire Pacific Ocean.

Developed at the height of the cold war, SOSUS consisted of groups of hydrophones inside large tanks, each almost as big as a large oil storage tank. They were sunk to the bottom of the ocean and connected by cables, which were buried to prevent the Soviets from trailing cable cutters off their trawlers and severing the lines.

The series of underwater hydrophones were so sensitive that since the cold war, the Navy occasionally let marine biologists have access to the system to track whale migration. The entire system was coordinated using FLTSATCOM—the Fleet Satellite Communication System—which Royce currently was accessed into.

He brought up all submarine activity and their corresponding tags: their identifiers. The Navy had belatedly realized after hooking the SOSUS system together that while it could pinpoint a submarine's location, it wasn't able to tell friendly subs from unfriendly. And since the U.S. Navy didn't know exactly where half its own subs were—the boomers, nuclear missile launchers patrolling wide areas of ocean entirely at their commanders' discretion—they had to come up with a way when SOSUS pinpointed a sub to know whether it was friendly or enemy. Thus, every U.S. and NATO sub had an ID code painted in special laser reflective paint on the upper deck.

SOSUS pinpointed a sub's location, then one of the FLTSATCOM satellites fired off a high intensity blue-green laser. It penetrated the ocean to submarine depth, was reflected by the paint, and the satellite picked it up and read it. If there was no reflection, it was assumed to be an unfriendly sub.

Since the *Kursk* disaster, the Russian fleet had stopped sending its boomers out to sea, and most of them were rusting away in port. That meant that other than the Chinese, few countries would be sending submarines out to sea. Looking at the display, Royce immediately noted that the time-delayed tracking for the past twenty-four hours had only one unidentified submarine—located between mainland China and Taiwan—and it didn't take a rocket scientist to figure out who owned that one.

Where the hell was the Abu Sayef submarine if it had taken part in the raid on Johnston Atoll? Royce pondered this while staring at the display of the Pacific Ocean. The only thing he could come up with was that the submarine was sitting on the bottom somewhere, waiting.

He shook his head. That didn't sound like Rogelio Abayon.

Royce looked forward to closing out this mission, but beyond that he was uncertain. He'd been moved up a notch in the Organization, but toward what end? The same end that David had just met?

On the other hand, he knew there was no way out. He couldn't just tender a resignation because that was the same as "retirement," and he'd seen how that went. He was bound to the Organization by invisible chains that he had to be careful not to even tug on or else bring unwanted attention.

It would be helpful to know who exactly the "Organization" was, but that was a chain he knew he would have to be very careful about tugging. Or get someone else to tug.

CHAPTER 18

Jolo Island

Abayon kissed Fatima's hand. Then he reached up and wiped away the tears on each of her cheeks. "You will do well."

"I will miss you," she said.

The last of the trucks carrying the treasure rumbled down the narrow jungle trail toward the dock where an old freighter waited for them. They had rehearsed abandoning the Hono Mountain facility many times, and the execution had gone off flawlessly. Abayon was in his chair, between the two large doors that had sealed this cave off so many years ago. A jeep waited for Fatima, the last to leave. When she was gone, he would be alone.

"It is all for the people," Abayon said.

Fatima nodded, at a loss for words.

"Go now," Abayon said, wheeling his chair back. She hesitated, then turned and headed to the jeep. Abayon hit the control that shut the doors. Protesting on rusty hinges, they slowly swung shut with a resounding clang.

Abayon slowly turned his chair and began heading farther into the complex. He could feel the presence of ghosts all around. Japanese and Filipino. And others. This mountain had been the hub of much death and destruction. He knew the recent raid had been the signal he'd been both dreading and looking forward to.

Abayon wound his way through the complex until he reached the stone balcony from which he had watched the raid. He rolled out onto it and looked to the west, where the sun was setting. This night would bring much change. He looked down at the red button on the handle of the wheelchair and sighed.

Pacific Ocean

The *Jahre Viking* was cruising smoothly less than forty miles southwest of Oahu. It was en route to Long Beach where it would off-load its cargo of oil. The captain of the large tanker was surprised when a United States Navy destroyer appeared off his starboard bow, bearing down at almost maximum speed.

The radio crackled with an order from the captain of the destroyer to prepare to be boarded. Since they were in international waters, the captain of the *Jahre Viking* did not have to comply with the request. But the tone of the American officer's command left little doubt about the extreme seriousness of the demand.

Having nothing to hide, the *Viking*'s captain acceded, and within minutes a helicopter from the destroyer landed on the huge tanker's helipad. A squad of armed Marines jumped off. The chopper immediately lifted and went back to the destroyer, staying long enough to fill up with troops before returning. And then again and again, until the captain estimated he had half the destroyer's crew on his ship, searching.

One of those who came over was the Navy captain, and he was escorted to the bridge. The American apologized but said the search was over an issue of grave concern to all human beings regarding a recent event at an island in the middle of the Pacific. He also admitted that American satellites had tracked the *Jahre Viking* ever since leaving Indonesia and knew it had stayed on course, but orders were orders and they were taking no chances.

The search took an hour, and then the Americans left, the destroyer leaving at flank speed to find another ship to search.

Moreno's sonar man had heard the American destroyer approach and then listened to it run alongside for over an hour. Then he heard it move away. Moreno watched both the clock and his chart, waiting until the American would be out of range.

Finally, he could wait no longer. "One quarter ahead." For the first time since they'd mated with the tanker, the submarine's engines began to turn the ship's screws. Satisfied he had power, Moreno issued the next order. "Cut power to the magnets."

The instant the power was cut, Moreno ordered the sub to dive, to get clear of the *Jahre Viking*'s screws. The submarine descended as the tanker passed by overhead. When it hit the wake caused by the massive screws, the submarine vibrated violently for half a minute, then slowly settled.

"Course five-five degrees," Moreno ordered. "Half ahead. Bring us up to just below the surface."

The nose of the old submarine turned to the north-west, directly toward Oahu and Honolulu.

Jolo Island

Vaughn checked out the small redoubt Tai had built for herself next to the open spot on the top of Hono Mountain. She had two logs stacked, facing the clear area, with enough space between them for her to get a clear field of fire. She'd covered the logs with vegetation so that unless someone walked right on top of her location, she wouldn't be spotted.

He checked his watch. "They should be five minutes out."

Tai nodded in the dark. "Time to get ready." She checked her FM radio, hitting the transmit button. "You set?"

Vaughn heard her in his left ear. He nodded and transmitted himself. "Roger. You got me."

"Roger."

Vaughn tapped the radio. "This isn't going to do me much good once I'm inside the mountain."

"It will give us a couple of seconds to react once you're back up top." She paused before she climbed behind the logs and stuck her hand out. "Good luck."

Vaughn shook her hand. "You too." He wasn't sure what else to say because he still wasn't sure if he trusted her. He walked into the center of the open area and pulled out his infrared strobe. He wasn't sure he trusted any of those who would be parachuting in either. It was a hell of a situation. He had always been able to count on his teammates in combat situations, and now he was getting ready to conduct a mission where he wasn't sure of anything.

He checked his watch once more. Two minutes.

He turned the strobe on.

The Combat Talon was coming just above the wave tops. The back ramp was already down, and the four members of the team were clustered just near the edge in a line, the two outermost with a solid grip on the hydraulic arm holding the ramp in place.

That grip tightened as the nose of the Talon abruptly went up and the pilots headed straight for the top of Hono Mountain.

The four jumpers also had night vision goggles on and static line parachutes strapped to their backs. They didn't have reserve parachutes because at the altitude they were jumping, if their main didn't open, there would be no time to deploy a reserve.

"One minute!" the crew chief yelled to the team, holding up a single finger.

Vaughn had to assume the IR strobe was working, because without his own night vision goggles, he couldn't see anything. He cocked his head as he heard the familiar sound of turboprop engines. He almost ducked as the Talon roared by low overhead, barely one hundred feet above the top of the mountain.

He stared up and saw four parachutes pop open, halfway between him and where the plane had gone by. The jumpers hit the ground scant seconds later, three of them in the clearing, the fourth in the trees along the edge, not far from where Tai was hidden.

"I've got four jumpers," he transmitted to Tai. "Over."

"Roger. I see them. Out."

Vaughn ran over to the closest jumper, who was trying to get to his feet.

"Goddamn," Sinclair cursed. "That was low."

Vaughn helped him shrug off his harness. "Good to see you guys."

"Not sure I can say the same," Sinclair said as one of the other jumpers came up.

"Let's go," Orson growled. "No time for bullshitting."

The three gathered up the next jumper. Vaughn peered at the man in the dark but didn't recognize him. Orson wasn't making introductions. "Where's the rest of the stick? Hayes? Kasen?"

"Hayes didn't accompany us."

Vaughn pointed. "Someone went just off the edge into the trees." He took the lead to make sure they didn't walk right across Tai's position. They scrambled to the edge of the mountain and immediately saw a parachute in a tree about thirty feet down. While Orson and the fresh face remained topside anchoring a rope, Sinclair and Vaughn carefully made their way down to the jumper dangling at the bottom of the risers.

Vaughn immediately knew something was wrong, because the body dangled motionless. He reached out and grabbed a handful of risers, pulling the jumper closer to them. Sinclair cut the body free and they grabbed hold, keeping it from sliding down the mountain.

Vaughn could tell by the way the man's head rolled that his neck was broken. He pulled the night vision goggles off the body and recognized Kasen.

"Fuck," Sinclair hissed, checking for pulse and finding none. They jammed the body against a tree growing out of the side of the mountain and Sinclair headed back up, using the rope to climb. Vaughn slid Kasen's goggles on and followed, glad he now had night vision capability.

Orson took the news of Kasen's demise exactly as Vaughn had expected—with no reaction. Orson turned to him. "Where's the way in?"

Vaughn led the way to the air shaft, the other three following. They tied the rope off and threw it down into the shaft as insurance.

"You lead," Orson ordered Vaughn. He turned to Sinclair. "You stay up here and get the Fulton gear ready. We might be coming out hot, so make sure you have the Talon on the horn to pick us up within two minutes."

Vaughn climbed into the tube and began heading down toward where he'd last seen Abayon.

Over the Pacific

The second team was spread out in the rear of another Combat Talon. It was following the same track as the one the first team had used, except at a much higher altitude, over 30,000 feet.

From Hong Kong to Okinawa to cross-loading onto this plane, the team had had little time for rest, so they used this opportunity to rack out. That is, until the loadmaster woke the team leader and told him they were one hour out from drop.

It was time to rig.

Oahu

Foster was catching a nap on a cot in his office, and Royce had the entire Sim-Center to himself. He had the locations of both Talons on the display board. The first one was in a holding pattern twenty miles off of Jolo. The second was on a beeline for the island.

So far, so good.

Royce shifted the data flowing to the display, bringing up the SOSUS information once more. Once more all the submarines in the Pacific were displayed. And all were tagged except the one between Taiwan and mainland China.

Royce blinked as a dot suddenly appeared southwest of Oahu. It was green but not tagged. It flashed for several seconds and then disappeared from the screen.

Perplexed, he picked up his satphone and dialed his contact at fleet headquarters. He wasted no time on preamble, knowing that his contact would know his voice.

"What's the story with that brief contact that was displayed on SOSUS southwest of Oahu?"

There was a short pause. "Wait one." Another pause. "The hydrophones picked up what was thought to be a submarine, but on checking was determined to most likely be a fishing trawler."

"I don't understand."

"Well, the contact just appeared out of nothing, which is weird, so it appears to be a glitch in the system. Also the sound is at very shallow depth. And the sound is a diesel engine and nobody uses those anymore in subs. We figure it's a fishing trawler that took on a heavy load and settled much lower in the water to trigger SOSUS. Why? Is there something I should know? We're focused on Johnston. We figure someone flew in and out of there, but Space Command has nothing for us."

"Nothing," Royce lied. "I just was wondering. I'm

checking on another operation. Out." He shut the phone off.

That son of a bitch Abayon. Royce saw the pieces falling in place. He was going to try to re-create Pearl Harbor with the ZX. From the deck of the submarine, which he had probably bought from the dead boatyard in some third world country and rebuilt.

The only positive news was that from the brief location he'd had, Royce figured it would take six or seven hours for the sub to get close enough to Oahu to be able to disperse the nerve agent, which he assumed they would do from a sprayer on the deck of the sub. Probably park the damn thing right off of Diamond Head and let loose on Honolulu. That would get Abayon plenty of attention.

Royce reached for the satphone to call fleet headquarters to warn them, then remembered the message from the Organization. This was to be kept in house. And it was his responsibility.

Instead of dialing fleet headquarters, Royce turned to the laptop and typed in orders to be transmitted to the Combat Talon that would recover his Australian team off of Jolo Island.

Jolo Island

Vaughn looked in the grate where they had seen Abayon and silently cursed when he saw the room was dark and empty. Still, he had to assume that wherever Abayon was bedded down for the night had to be close to his office. He used the crowbar he'd radioed the team to bring in to pry open the grate. Then he dropped into the office, MP-5 at the ready, infrared light on, revealing a clear desktop. Vaughn heard the others come in behind him and felt someone press against his side.

"Where is he?" Orson whispered hoarsely.

Vaughn pointed with the muzzle of his weapon toward the door. "Somewhere through there."

Orson grunted, whether in disgust or for some other reason, Vaughn wasn't sure. He edged forward toward the door, sensing the rest of the team behind him. He grabbed the handle and pulled the door open.

Sinclair opened the canister containing the Fulton equipment. In-out. He liked it. That's what this mission was shaping up to. He opened the top of a long tube as he turned the valve on a helium canister. A blimp-shaped balloon slowly slithered out of the tube. As it inflated, the blimp became eight feet long and four feet in diameter, connected at the bottom to the climbers' 12mm rope, which he clipped to a snap link on the blimp. Holding on to keep it from rising, he turned on the small infrared strobe attached to the top of the blimp, making sure through his night vision goggles that it was working, then let go.

As the helium rushed in, the blimp rose into the night sky. Sinclair paid out the rope through his hand so there were no snags. It finally came to a stop with the blimp over three hundred feet above his head.

He tied that rope off to another snap link on the waistband of his harness, then reached into his vest and pulled out an FM radio headset, settling it on his head. It was already set to the right frequency.

Sinclair spoke into the voice-activated mouthpiece. "Condor, this is Charlie One-two. Over."

The reply was instantaneous. "Charlie One-two, this is Condor. Over."

"The balloon is up," Sinclair said. "I will inform you when to begin your run. Over."

"Roger that. We'll be there. Over."

On board the second Combat Talon en route to Jolo Island, the Australian team leader heard the radio traffic and nodded. Everything was going smoothly. He cinched down the straps on his parachute harness one last time, then checked his submachine gun to make sure there was a round in the chamber.

He signaled to the loadmaster that they were ready. Each team member switched over to his personal oxygen, and the cargo bay began to depressurize.

Vaughn moved down the tunnel, the stock of the weapon tight to his shoulder. He felt as if he were walking into the belly of the beast, but so far they had yet to encounter any opposition. He had opened three doors off the tunnel, and all the rooms were empty.

He reached a fourth and paused as the other members of the team deployed around him. He still had no idea who the new member of the team was, or where Hayes had gone, but they had all been trained the same way so they were functioning well tactically.

The others covered him as he pushed open the door. Another tunnel beckoned. And at the end of it Vaughn could see the glow of moonlight and something else. A bright red dot. He realized it was someone smoking. Not a cigarette, but something larger. A cigar, he could tell by the odor wafting in.

Vaughn moved forward, the others behind him. He exited the far end of the tunnel onto a level area cut into the side of the mountain. And there was Rogelio Abayon, seated in a wheelchair, smoking a cigar. Now that he was outdoors, Vaughn pressed the transmit button, but didn't say anything.

"I've been waiting for you," Abayon said as the three team members circled him, weapons at the ready.

Orson stepped past Vaughn and placed the muzzle of his submachine gun on the old man's chest. "I hope the wait was worth it. Where is everyone else?"

"Long gone," Abayon said. "I would like to know something before you kill me."

Vaughn looked from the old man to his team leader. The contrast was striking. Abayon was a frail figure in a wheelchair, peering up in the darkness at the forms around him, a cigar held in one hand that was shaking ever so slightly. Orson was in black, his face covered by the night vision goggles, the weapon in his hand not shaking at all.

Vaughn released the transmit button, knowing Tai would hear the break in static. He was rewarded a second later by her voice in his ear.

"I copied all that. I assume you're on the outside. Probably where the video was shot from. The Fulton rig is ready on top of the mountain. Let me hear what's going on." There was the burst of static as she let go of the transmit.

Vaughn pulled up his goggles, turning them off, trying to control his shock at what Tai had just told him. He pulled the flashlight off his web gear and turned it on, causing Orson to curse and the other team members to quickly rip off their goggles.

"What the hell are you doing?" Orson demanded, the muzzle still on Abayon but his dark eyes on Vaughn.

"Let's get this over with," Vaughn said. "He has something he wants to say. Let him say it, then let's get out of here."

"I have a question," Abayon said. "Not a speech to make. There is no one else here, so you do not need to be afraid we'll be interrupted."

"Where did everyone go?" Vaughn asked.

Abayon smiled. "That is a foolish question."

Orson poked the old man with the barrel of his weapon. "The Golden Lily? Is it still here?"

"No."

"That was a mistake," Orson snapped.

Vaughn felt the energy drain out of him. The adrenaline high that had kept him going was depleted, and Orson's question confirmed Tai's suspicions.

"Where did you move it to?" Orson demanded.

"That is another foolish question."

"I can make you talk," Orson threatened.

"No, you cannot." Abayon raised his right hand from the arm of his wheelchair, revealing a red button. "If my hand falls on this, numerous explosives will detonate throughout the complex. We will all die."

Tai watched Sinclair check his watch from her hide position. Then she watched him die as a burst of red tracers came out of the sky and hit him. Sinclair tumbled to the ground, his dead weight still holding the Fulton blimp in place.

A parachutist holding a submachine gun landed less than ten feet from the body, quickly followed by three others. Tai took a deep breath, her finger on the trigger, but she didn't fire. She could hear the conversation taking place below her on the side of the mountain and knew this had yet to run its course.

She noted the group discard their parachutes and then take up positions watching the vent. She had no doubt what they were waiting for. She cocked her head to listen to what was happening with Vaughn and waited for her chance to transmit to him what had just happened.

"Who do you work for?" Abayon asked.

"The U.S. government," Orson said.

"That is not true," Abayon said. "That might have been what you were told, but someone else is pulling the strings."

"Listen you—" Orson began, but Abayon's hand wavered over the button, silencing him.

"You do not even know," Abayon said, almost to himself. "That is not surprising. I have spent over six decades fighting whoever it is you work for, and I don't know who they are either."

Vaughn could see a vein bulging on the side of Orson's face. He remained still and let go of the transmit button, and Tai's voice immediately crackled in his ear. "Take them out. All of them. We've been betrayed. Sinclair is dead. There are four men who just parachuted in, waiting in ambush at the top of the vent." There was the brief burst of static.

Vaughn felt numb. He was back on Jolo Island and things were going as wrong as they possibly could once more. That thought shocked him out of his stupor because for the first time it occurred to him that his Delta Force team might have been betrayed. Had this all been one long, elaborate setup?

He shifted the muzzle of the MP-5 and pulled the trigger twice in rapid succession. The rounds hit Orson right where the vein was pulsing, taking most of his head off as they plowed through. Vaughn shifted and fired twice at the new man, again double-tapping him in the head.

Then he shifted his attention to Abayon, whose hand

still hovered over the red button but whose face showed surprise. "Who are *you*?" Abayon asked.

"The raid to free the hostages," Vaughn said. "You filmed it from here?"

Abayon nodded.

"And you knew it was coming?"

Abayon nodded once more.

"How?"

"One of my men received a tip from someone we knew to be a CIA informant."

"I led that raid," Vaughn said.

Comprehension flooded Abayon's face. "So you were betrayed also."

Vaughn didn't lower the muzzle of his MP-5. "There's a team waiting up top to ambush me when I try to leave."

Abayon sighed. "So I assume you do not know who is the puppet master either."

"I thought I was working for the U.S. government—as he said." Vaughn indicated Orson's body. "Do you have any idea who is behind all this?"

"Something bigger than the U.S. government. And while you were probably told the goal of your mission was to kill me, the real goal was to reacquire the Golden Lily."

Vaughn let go of the transmit, and Tai's voice immediately was in his ear. "You need to get out of there. These guys up here aren't going to wait forever. Abayon knows as much as we know, which means he knows nothing."

Vaughn stared at Abayon. "My brother-in-law died in that raid."

Abayon stared back without reaction. "It is a war. You were pawns being played by unseen hands."

"Why are you going to kill yourself?" Vaughn asked.

"After what will happen shortly on my orders, it is better that I be dead."

"What do you have planned?"

"It need not concern you."

"If I promise to try to find those hands that have been playing us, will you let me leave before you destroy this place?"

Abayon was very still for a long moment. Then he nodded, ever so slightly. "You have five minutes."

Vaughn didn't hesitate. He took off running, retracing his steps.

One of the four men walked over to a spot in the woods less than ten feet from Tai's position in order to urinate. He slung his weapon over his shoulder and reached to unzip his pants when Tai shot him through the head, the suppressor on the end of the MP-5 letting off a sound like a low cough. She swung the gun back toward the other three waiting at the vent.

She could see two of the men aiming their weapons down the tube. It was going to be close. She fired three times. The third man had half a second of realization that something was wrong before he died.

She jumped and ran forward, keying the radio on the Talon frequency at the same time.

"Charlie One-two, this is Condor. Begin your run. Over."

"This Charlie One-two. Roger that. I'll be there in two minutes exactly. Over."

Vaughn had the MP-5 at the ready as he approached the top of the tube. He cautiously led with the muzzle as he popped his head up to take a look. He saw Tai silhouetted against the night sky less than five feet away, next to a rope that rose into the clouds. She was surrounded by three bodies.

"Damn," Vaughn said as he climbed out of the vent. "Where's the fourth?"

Tai gestured toward the treeline. "Dead."

"Abayon gave me five minutes. That was over two minutes ago."

"The Talon is inbound. Two minutes."

Vaughn wondered if that minute in between was going to be enough. And if Abayon was going to keep his word. He walked over next to Tai, slinging his MP-5 and then clipping his harness into the same loop of rope she was attached to. They linked arms and waited.

The pilot of the Talon saw the flashing infrared strobe clearly in his night vision goggles and lined the nose of the aircraft up with it and for a point slightly below it. He throttled back to just above stall speed.

Vaughn could hear the inbound aircraft although he couldn't see it. "Come on," he whispered.

"Shit," Tai exclaimed as the ground shook beneath them. Then it shook again, closer.

"Linked charges, firing in sequence," Vaughn said.

Another explosion, even closer, rumbled up from below. Then another, and this time a spout of flame came out of the vent. Next one is it, Vaughn thought, and at that moment the rope above them suddenly gave a jerk.

A second later both were lifted straight up off the ground as it exploded beneath them.

*   *   *

The rope was caught by the whiskers on the nose of the Talon. It slid to the exact center, where the sky anchor automatically clamped tight on it. Right after that, a blade above the anchor cut the blimp free.

"Jeez," the crew chief yelled over the intercom. He was looking out the back ramp. "The top of the mountain just blew."

"Do we have them?"

"Roger that."

The pilot of the C-130 pulled back on the controls, putting the aircraft into a steep climb. This brought the rope along the belly of the plane. The loadmaster lowered a hook attached to a small crane bolted to the rear platform. Fishing, he managed to snag the rope on his second attempt. Then the crane began to reel the rope in.

The Talon continued to gain altitude, and the rope was reeled in until the two bodies reached the ramp. The crew chief, secured in the plane by a tether, reached over and helped them both to their feet.

"Where are the others?" the crew chief asked.

Vaughn began unbuckling his harness. "Dead."

"There's a message waiting," the crew chief said. He held out a sheet of paper as the ramp began to shut.

Vaughn took it in the swirling wind and read it.

Team en route for further assignment. Contact as soon as able. Royce.

Vaughn handed it to Tai. "Where are we headed?" he asked the crew chief.

"Hawaii."

CHAPTER 19

Pacific Ocean

Moreno knew it was just a question of hours now, as he sat at the captain's small fold-down desk in his wardroom. Then the greatest blow against the first world by the third would be struck; 9/11 would dwindle to insignificance. Attention would have to be paid to the gap between the two worlds, and the message that those who had been oppressed would not tolerate it anymore.

Of course, Moreno also knew that everyone on board this submarine would be dead within twenty-four hours. Not all of them knew that. They had been told it was most likely a one-way mission but that anything could happen. What only he knew was that he had a remote control in his pocket that would detonate charges preplanted in the submarine, breaching the hull in four points.

Moreno bowed his head and placed it on the cool metal. He knew Abayon was probably gone by now. Six decades of comradeship. Moreno also knew his daughter was now in charge. He silently prayed that she would stay on a true and steady course for the movement.

Over the Pacific

"What's going on?" Tai asked as they sat down on the red cargo web seats along the side of the cargo bay. The throb of the engines was so loud, they almost had to shout to be able to talk to each other.

"You heard Abayon. He has—had—something big planned. Based on this—" Vaughn held the message— "I think it has something to do with Hawaii."

"But Royce is the one who betrayed us," Tai pointed out. "He sent in that second team. You know that."

Vaughn leaned back and rested his head against the web. "I know. But . . ."

Tai waited and when he didn't continue, demanded, "But what?"

"Abayon was a bad man," Vaughn said. "I'm glad he's dead. He was a terrorist. I don't know who Royce works for, and neither did Abayon. He was punching at shadows."

"Real shadows," Tai said.

"And Royce is a shadow among shadows. What makes you think he's any more aware than we are?"

"He tried to have us killed," Tai said.

"He was closing out a mission," Vaughn said. "Our team was to do the mission, and the perfect deniability and secrecy was to have a second team, who only knew about us, come in and wipe us out. It's a hard world out there. With bad people in it. I'm not concerned with

Royce, I'm concerned with who he works for and what their goals are. That's the issue."

Tai fell silent for several minutes as they winged east, toward Hawaii. "Do you want to contact Royce?" she finally asked. "He thinks we're dead, and he's talking to the team that was supposed to take us out."

Vaughn sighed. "Yes. Because this is bigger than us." He got up and went forward into the front half of the cargo bay, to the rows of computer consoles the flight crew used. One of the crew members nodded at him and pointed to an empty chair. Vaughn took it and stared at the screen. A blinking cursor awaited.

He pondered it for a while. Who was Royce expecting to talk to? Orson? Or the commander of the team that had jumped in to ambush them? Or both? Wheels within wheels.

Vaughn sensed someone at his shoulder and looked up. Tai stood there. "What should I write?" he asked.

Tai shrugged. "I have no idea."

Vaughn's finger hit the keyboard: *Team here. Two casualties. Mission accomplished. En route to Hawaii as ordered.*

Seconds passed. *Abu Sayef has obtained ZX nerve agent from Johnston Atoll. Killed over one thousand to do so. ZX on submarine en route to Honolulu. Interdict and destroy. Last known location in attachment. Will update shortly.*

"Shit," Tai muttered. "ZX. Pearl Harbor Two."

"What the hell is that?" Vaughn asked. "I've heard of VX, but—"

"Many times more deadly. Abayon is going to take out Honolulu."

"How do we stop a submarine? Why doesn't he call in the Navy? The Air Force? The Marines?"

"To keep the secrets," Tai said.

"What secrets?"

"The Golden Lily. Abayon. This mission. To stay in the shadows."

"That's worth losing Pearl Harbor again?"

"Some think the first Pearl Harbor attack was worth what happened afterward. It got us into World War II when we'd just been sitting on the sidelines. And then we lost the World Trade Center."

"You don't think—" Vaughn didn't finish the thought.

"I don't know what to think anymore."

"This is screwed."

"That seemed to have been Abayon's opinion," Tai noted.

"But what he's doing is wrong."

"Yes, it is."

Vaughn pressed his fists against his throbbing temples. "Who the hell are these people?"

"We're going to have to put that one on the back burner for now," Tai said. "We've got to stop that submarine."

Vaughn swiveled in the chair and stared at her. "How the hell are you and I going to do that?"

"The sub is going to have to surface to release the agent, most likely using some sort of sprayer on deck into an onshore breeze. We take out the sprayer, we stop it."

"Great plan."

"That's not a plan," Tai said. "That's a concept. We need to work on the plan. Let's check what gear we have in back and then we come up with a plan. There's a palletful of stuff back there."

Oahu

Royce called his contact at Pacific Fleet headquarters once more. This time he didn't ask questions, he issued orders. He wanted the diesel engine contact back on the SOSUS board. He wanted two Marine F-16s with live ordnance in the air with direct contact to him and under his orders. He had the proper code words authorizing these actions.

When he disconnected, Royce realized that for the first time he had gone beyond his Organization orders. The F-16s were not authorized. But he was damned if he was going to let Honolulu get wiped out just so the Organization could stay hidden. That thought made him sit bolt upright.

September 11, 2001.

Had someone in the Organization known and dropped the ball? Or had the ball been ordered to be dropped?

Over the Pacific

"Someone was prepared," Vaughn said as they stared at the gear laid out on the cargo bay floor. Parachutes, weapons, explosives, night vision equipment—it was a Special Operator's dream pallet.

"We could always ram this plane into the sub," Tai said.

"That's what the bad guys do," Vaughn said. He was connecting what he saw in front of him with what needed to be done. "Okay, here's the plan . . ."

Pacific Ocean

Moreno had his eyes pressed against the periscope. He strained to see as far as the scope would let him. There was the slightest smudge directly ahead on the horizon. Land.

Diamond Head.

Oahu

Royce was looking at the display when Foster came walking into the control center. "What's going on?" Foster asked.

Royce turned in his seat and drew a pistol from a shoulder holster.

"What the hell are you—"

Royce fired once, the round going through Foster's heart. The Sim-Center director fell to the floor. Royce stared at the body for a few seconds, then checked David's computer, searching for someone who could come sweep the body. He made the call, then turned his attention back to the board.

A green flashing dot was now there, not far off Diamond Head. Royce noted the coordinates, typed them into the computer and hit the send button. Then he unhooked the computer and slid it in the carrying case.

Satphone in hand, he left the Sim-Center and went out to the Defender. He got in and drove toward Pearl Harbor. On the way, he called ahead, and using the proper authorization codes, lined up a search and rescue Blackhawk helicopter to be ready to take off as soon as he arrived.

Over the Pacific

"This isn't much of a plan," Tai noted. She had a parachute on her back, a rucksack rigged in front, and her MP-5 tied on top of the rucksack.

"You got a better one?" Vaughn asked.

"Just because I don't have a better one doesn't make this a good one."

"Point taken," Vaughn said as the crew chief held up five fingers. "But five minutes out, it's all we got."

They had received the location of the submarine from Royce, and the plane was on a direct line toward it at 10,000 feet of altitude. The back ramp slowly opened, revealing sunlight and a glittering blue ocean far below. Vaughn and Tai edged forward, one on each side. They poked their heads into the slipstream and peered out. Off to the left and ahead was Oahu, with Diamond Head the most prominent and recognizable feature.

There was no sign of the submarine, but at the speed the airplane was flying, Vaughn didn't expect to see it yet. He pulled his head back in and glanced over at Tai. She shook her head.

The crew chief held up four fingers.

Royce could see the track of the Talon and the location of the submarine on the screen of his laptop, automatically forwarded to him via satellite from the Sim-Center. He was in the back of the Blackhawk, the engines powering up in preparation for takeoff.

The plane was on a direct intercept course. He also could see the red dot representing the two F-16s circling. He looked out of the helicopter and couldn't spot any of them, but knew they would be in visual range shortly, as the helicopter raced past Waikiki. Royce noted the people lying on the beach, enjoying themselves, not knowing death was approaching.

He keyed the radio. "Dragon Leader, this is Control. Over."

"This is Dragon Leader. Over."

"You will attack only on my order. Is that understood? Over."

"Roger that. Over."

"Out."

Moreno could clearly see Diamond Head now. He had studied the data and knew the prevailing winds. That, combined with the effectiveness of the sprayer and the time the ZX would stay airborne—all the factors had been considered to come up with the spot where they would surface and release death.

It would not be long now.

He blinked as something flashed across his field of vision. He adjusted the focus and realized it was a sailboat. Probably a thousand meters in front of his position. He could see the people on board. Two couples. Rich Americans, indulging themselves. The women were dressed indecently—in fact, one of the women wore no top.

Whores. They deserved what was coming.

But he could not turn the periscope away. He tracked the boat cutting across his path. He saw the topless woman go up to the man at the helm and give him a kiss. A tender one. Not like a whore would. *Young lovers.* The thought flashed across his mind.

Moreno twisted the scope away and took readings off the landmarks.

They were very close now.

"Prepare for surface operations," he ordered.

The man in the containment suit was already prepared. Dressed and with a container of ZX resting on the decking, held in place with both hands.

The crew chief held up one finger. Vaughn nodded at Tai, and once more they leaned out of the plane, peering ahead.

Vaughn saw a sailboat cutting through the waves ahead.

That was it.

The seconds ticked by. The green light high up in the tail section flashed on, indicating they were over the submarine's location, but Vaughn saw nothing. He glanced over his shoulder and met Tai's gaze. She shook her head. Nothing.

Vaughn looked at the crew chief and twirled a finger, indicating they needed to circle around.

"Surface," Moreno ordered. He looked at the man in the containment suit. "Are you ready?"

The head inside the hood bobbed in the affirmative, and the man made his way to the metal ladder leading to the conning tower hatch. Moreno moved to him and placed a hand on the rung at eye level. "I will lead."

From periscope depth to surface took only a few seconds, and a klaxon sounded, indicating they were up. Moreno bolted up the ladder.

The Talon was banking in a wide circle, turning right, away from Oahu. Vaughn looked out and saw Diamond Head with Honolulu off to the left. He returned his attention to the ocean and cursed. The long cigar shape of a submarine heading straight toward the island was now apparent. And they were still banking in their turn at 10,000 feet.

Vaughn jumped to his feet. He looked up at the lights in the tail section. Red. He mentally willed the plane to turn faster.

Moreno brought the binoculars to his eyes as the man in the containment suit carefully climbed down to the sprayer with the canisters, then began to screw one of them into the hose.

Satisfied they were in the right spot, Moreno licked a finger and held it up to the wind. Even given the forward movement of the submarine, the wind was strong from the aft, which would blow the agent from the sprayer on the forward deck toward Honolulu.

Perfect conditions.

Vaughn couldn't control himself. He quickly knelt and peered ahead into the prop blast. He could see a tiny figure on the deck of the submarine next to some device, which he had to assume was the sprayer for the nerve agent. There was another person on top of the conning tower.

Two.

That was good.

Time.

That was bad.

Vaughn looked up at the jump lights.

Red.

Red.

Red.

Green.

He stepped off the ramp, seeing Tai do the same out of the corner of his eye. He spread his arms and legs, getting stable. Then he began to move his arms and legs ever so slightly to direct his descent toward the submarine. He could see the man in the protective suit working on the machine just forward of the conning tower.

Shit.

Vaughn inclined his body forward into an almost direct dive down. He couldn't see Tai but assumed she was right behind him.

"Control, this is Dragon Leader. We have the target on the surface. Two personnel in sight. One in what appears to be a protective suit and working on something that looks like a weapon. Over."

Royce clenched his hands into fists. "Do you have the Talon in sight? Over."

"Roger. And two people just parachuted out. Over."

"Hold your position. Out."

Royce closed the computer—it was of no use now—walked forward and leaned between the pilots, peering ahead. He saw the submarine now, about two kilometers off Diamond Head, nose pointed directly toward Honolulu.

The man in the suit looked up at Moreno and nodded that he was ready. Moreno looked across the blue water at the lush island ahead, the shoreline scarred with high rises and developments. The way the rich always did—destroying the beautiful for their own selfish purposes.

Moreno raised his arm to signal release of the agent.

Vaughn passed through 3,000 feet, and Tai was now alongside him in a very steep dive. "They're going to do it," she yelled into the radio.

And with that she went vertical, head down, terminal velocity, outstripping Vaughn, who was still maintaining a stable position in order to be able to deploy his parachute.

Two thousand feet.

Vaughn went fully stable and reached for his rip cord, his eyes on Tai, who had to be a thousand feet below him and belatedly trying to do the same. He pulled his rip cord and was jerked from horizontal to feet down, head up, controlled descent. He immediately grabbed the toggles and dumped air from the chute.

Below him, Tai pulled her rip cord while still falling at a rate of speed beyond what was safe. The chute deployed, and the opening shock was so great, the straps of her harness ripped into her body. Her left thigh, taking the strong point of impact, dislocated out of the hip joint.

Tai screamed in pain. Worse than her pain, though, was the fact that the chute had not been designed to take such an opening. With a ripping sound, several seams split open in the canopy. She was less than two hundred feet above the submarine and falling fast.

Moreno heard the scream of pain—coming from above. Startled, he looked up and saw the two parachutists, one of whom was coming down very fast. Then he heard another sound, which distracted him— helicopter blades. Turning to the east, he saw a Blackhawk helicopter coming toward them low and fast.

"Do it now!" Moreno yelled.

The suited man put his hand on the knob that would open the flow of nerve agent into the high-powered sprayer.

*   *   *

Through tears of pain, Tai saw the man in the protective suit put his hand on the knob less than a hundred feet below. Ignoring her injuries, she reached up and grabbed the toggles. She aimed herself, then dumped what little air was left.

A hundred feet above her, Vaughn saw what she was doing even as he untied his MP-5 from the rig.

Tai hit him at forty miles an hour, smashing him into the metal deck with a sickening sound of bones breaking in both their bodies. Then the two lay sprawled on the deck, motionless.

Cursing, Moreno jumped to the ladder and slid down to the deck. He ran forward from the conning tower toward the sprayer. As he ran, he pulled out the remote detonator. A burst of bullets ricocheted off the deck in front of him, but he ignored them.

Vaughn had a choice between controlling his landing or firing once more. He chose to fire.

The second burst hit Moreno, stitching a pattern from his right hip up his side, with the last round hitting him in the head, killing him instantly.

Vaughn dropped the gun and grabbed the toggles. He was able to make one adjustment, then hit the side of the submarine hard. The only thing that saved him was the parachute draped across the deck, snagging on some tie-down points, preventing him from sliding down into the water.

Reaching up, he used the risers to pull himself onto the deck. He drew his knife and cut loose from the parachute. Hearing the clang of a hatch opening somewhere farther back, probably in the conning tower, he knew he had little time. He ran toward the sprayer, leaping over Moreno's body, when he saw something that caused him to abruptly halt.

Moreno's lifeless hand held a remote detonator.

A shot rang out. Glancing over his shoulder, he saw someone taking aim with an AK-47 from the conning tower and a second armed man appear. There was no time for any other choice. Vaughn ripped the detonator out of Moreno's hand and pressed the red button.

The submarine shuddered as the first charge, in the engine room, went off.

Vaughn didn't wait for the rest to go off. He dropped the detonator as bullets whistled by his ears, the aim thrown off by the explosion. Grabbing hold of Tai's harness, he rolled with her off the boat, into the water.

A second explosion went off on the submarine.

Vaughn cut Tai loose of her parachute, then swam with all his might, towing her, trying to get as far away as possible from the imploding submarine.

Royce saw the tongue of flame jet out of the conning tower, killing the gunmen. The rear quarter of the submarine was already below the surface, dragging the rest of the craft down. He could see the two swimmers. He knew he should leave them, but the crew of the chopper had also seen them and the pilot was already directing the craft toward them. So he remained quiet.

A safety ring attached to a lift line splashed into the water about ten feet away. Vaughn swam to it and hooked both Tai's and his harnesses up to the line. He gave a thumbs-up and was lifted out of the water.

He looked over at the sub. The bow was lifting out of the water even as another explosion blew open a hole near the torpedo rooms. Within seconds the sub slid back into the water and was gone.

Hands reached out of the chopper, pulling him and Tai inside. Vaughn sprawled on the floor as the medics went to work on her. Looking over, he saw a man sitting on the rear bench, staring at him.

Royce. Whose eyes widened when he recognized them.

CHAPTER 20

Vaughn sat in the stiff plastic chair next to the hospital bed and stared at Tai. She was unrecognizable in the casts and bandages that swathed her body. She had not regained consciousness in the twenty-four hours since they'd been plucked out of the water. The doctor had been by a while ago and told him they would have to take her back into surgery soon. And the prognosis on full recovery was not good. But she would live.

The door to the room on the secure floor of Tripler Army Medical Center swung open and Royce walked in. Since being hustled off the helicopter at the hospital helipad, Vaughn had not seen his recruiter.

Royce grabbed another chair and sat on the opposite side of the bed. The two men stared at each for several minutes without saying a word.

Royce finally broke the silence. "You should be dead."

"I should kill you," Vaughn replied.

"It was nothing personal," Royce said.

"It wouldn't be personal either when I kill you. Just a job."

"And then?"

Vaughn didn't say anything.

Royce leaned forward. "Listen. This whole thing. I got brought in at the last minute. It's dirty work, and—"

"Who gives you your orders?" Vaughn asked, cutting him off, not wanting to hear the bullshit excuses.

"I don't know," Royce said. "That's a question I've begun to ask myself."

"A little late for that perhaps?"

"Better late than never," Royce said, "which is trite, but true in this situation. I thought for many years I was working for Uncle Sam. Just deep, deep cover. But . . ."

"But?"

"Now I'm not sure. This is all so big and so secret. I can go anywhere in the world and make a phone call and get support."

Vaughn gestured at Tai. "She works for Uncle Sam. And she was trying to figure this unit out. Section Eight. What the hell it was."

Royce nodded. "My best friend was killed when the Organization—which is what we called it—found out about her having infiltrated the team." Royce paused. "That's not exactly true. I think it was part of it, but he was retiring. And retiring from this Organization obviously means permanent retirement from life."

Vaughn realized there were two sides to this coin and that everyone was being played—and the playing field was brutal, with no quarter given.

"You have no idea what this Organization is?"

Royce shook his head. "I get everything via text messaging. The only person above me I ever met face-to-face was my boss—and friend—David. And he told me very little."

"Some friend."

"That's the way the Organization operates. Compartmentalized and covert."

"And now?" Vaughn asked. "Since I—and Tai—are supposed to be dead?"

"You are dead," Royce said.

"What do you mean?"

"I've reported everyone from both teams KIA."

"So we're free?"

"No."

Vaughn had known that was going to be the answer. "So what—"

"I want you to work for me."

"I tried that," Vaughn said. "Then you tried to kill me and I barely made it out alive."

"But you saved Honolulu. We saved Honolulu. That was good work."

"We were lucky," Vaughn said.

Royce nodded. "All right. We were lucky. The Organization—while most of the missions I've run for it have been illegal, they've always had a goal that made sense in terms of defending the United States. But . . ." He trailed off into silence.

"But you want me to work for the Organization?"

Royce shook his head. "No. The Organization thinks you're dead. I want you—and her," he added, nodding at the body lying between them, "to work for *me*. To find out who and what the Organization is. It's going to be very hard and very dangerous. And I'll still be working for the Organization while you're doing it.

So things might get confusing at times. But I want you two to be my ace in the hole."

"And if we find out the Organization is really our government, trying to do the right thing, via shady means?"

"Then I'll cut both of you loose and you can start new lives with new identities."

"And if we find out the Organization is bad, doing the wrong thing?"

"Then we take it down."